Claire Marsden

And Jack had never suspected it.

He conjured up an image of a fresh Alpine stream, clear water burbling over mossy rocks. He even resorted to imagining a photograph of his grandmother, the one where she was looking very stern and schoolmarmish. None of it stopped the rest of his body from whooping it up over the sight of Claire wearing only a bra. Suddenly he was thankful for the heat inside the elevator that had necessitated her removing her shirt.

From the soft, even tan across her chest and torso to the gentle rise of her breasts from one of the sexiest bras he'd ever seen, she was a revelation.

She was hot. Damn hot.

His body seemed determined to worship that hotness in its own special way, and no matter what he told himself, he was unable to stop it.

Not since the uncertain years of adolescence had his body been so at odds with his mind. Claire wasn't his type. And they didn't get along. So why was he wondering if she tasted as good as she looked?

Blaze™

Dear Reader,

How fantastic to be writing those two words! I've been reading romance novels since I was twelve, and I'm over the moon to have my first novel published with Harlequin.

The central idea for *Can't Get Enough* came from my experience working on a TV drama in Australia. As a storyliner, I spent most of my time locked in a small room with four other people, bashing around ideas and sharing incredibly incriminating and embarrassing stories from my life. I quickly learned that despite first impressions, it's impossible to hold on to your prejudices when you really get to know someone. It was a great life lesson, and a useful lesson for my characters Claire and Jack, too.

I hope you enjoy reading *Can't Get Enough* as much as I enjoyed writing it. I'd love to hear from you. You can contact me via e-mail at sarahjmayberry@hotmail.com or mail me in care of Harlequin Books, 225 Duncan Mill Road, Don Mills, Ontario M3B 3K9, Canada.

Cheers for now,

Sarah Mayberry

CAN'T GET ENOUGH
Sarah Mayberry

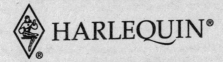

TORONTO • NEW YORK • LONDON
AMSTERDAM • PARIS • SYDNEY • HAMBURG
STOCKHOLM • ATHENS • TOKYO • MILAN • MADRID
PRAGUE • WARSAW • BUDAPEST • AUCKLAND

Many thanks to the gang at Neighbours, and to my friends
and family for always believing. Special thanks to La-La, and to
Wanda for making my writing better. Lastly, thanks to Chris,
who has taught me so much about storytelling. You're my
romantic hero, and I love you.

ISBN 0-373-79215-8

CAN'T GET ENOUGH

Copyright © 2005 by Small Cow Productions PTY Ltd.

This edition published by arrangement with Harlequin Books S.A.

www.eHarlequin.com

Printed in U.S.A.

1

CLAIRE MARSDEN was late. She hated being late almost as much as she hated brussels sprouts. And she hated brussels sprouts a lot. Traffic inched forward, and she craned her head out her window, confirming that the entrance to the company parking complex was just five car lengths ahead. Unfortunately, there were five cars occupying those five car lengths, and they were all moving as though they were powered by arthritic turtles. She willed them to move faster, concentrating intently on the shiny bumper of the pickup in front of her.

Nothing. So much for any latent powers of ESP she might have.

Might as well use the time to slap on some lipstick. She flipped her visor mirror down and blinked in horror at the too-close image that reflected back at her: eyes red, nose just beginning to peel thanks to too much sun on the weekend and a hefty gob of what her godchild Oscar rather charmingly called "eye booger" in the corner of one eye.

"Aren't you the belle of the ball," she told her reflection.

A dab of moisturizer, some judicious use of Kleenex and a swipe of lipstick went a long way to repairing the damage. She was just completing the last curve of pink-brown lipstick across her lips when the car behind her honked. A jagged lipstick smear raced up her cheek before she could control her reflexes.

Realizing the lane was now clear all the way to the coveted car park entrance, she slapped the visor up, deciding to fix her face later. With an apologetic wave for the driver behind her, she accelerated forward and zipped up the entrance ramp with a spurt of speed.

Now it was simply a case of snagging her favorite spot near the stairwell, and she could still make her first meeting of the day....

She frowned as she pulled up in front of *her* spot. A shiny red sports car gleamed smugly there, light reflecting off its sleek curves. Its owner had gone to the trouble of reversing in—obviously a fan of the quick getaway. The frown creasing her forehead deepened. She knew the owner of this car, and, indeed, he was fond of the quick getaway; at least a dozen women at Beck and Wise could vouch for just how fond.

"Stupid slacker," she ground out under her breath as she threw her car into reverse and began trawling for another spot.

Everyone knew that spot was hers. She made a point of parking there every day. Okay, so it didn't actually have her name on it—Beck and Wise only reserved parking spaces for its very senior executives—but it was common knowledge.

And she knew for a fact that Jack Brook was fully aware of her attachment to the spot; she ignored him every time she passed him on her way to or from her car. Just last week she'd glided coolly past him, not acknowledging his presence with so much as the twitch of an eyelid. So he knew. Oh, yes, he knew.

At last she found another spot, a full five rows farther back than her usual one. She turned into it with more verve than necessary, and had to waste precious seconds correcting the error. The contents of her handbag were spread out across her passenger seat after her ad hoc repair mission in the traffic jam, and she scrabbled around until she'd stuffed them all back into her sleek black leather purse. Like much of her life, it looked perfect on the outside, its chaotic contents well hidden from prying eyes.

She broke into a fast trot as she cleared the first row of cars, but realized very quickly that no amount of training or conditioning could prepare someone for a hundred-yard dash in leather pumps. Slowing to a tight-assed scamper, she spared a glance for the gleaming red affront in her parking spot as she pushed open the door to the car park stairwell.

Jack Brook. Just thinking his name made her grind her teeth. From the moment she'd first laid eyes on him two years ago she'd had his number, and everything she'd heard or seen of him since had only confirmed that initial snap judgment.

Too good-looking for his own good—if you liked tall, dark, blue-eyed, broad-shouldered men.

Too smart for his own good, too—if you admired creative, clever, arrogant, witty minds.

And too damn aware of all of the above, as far as she was concerned.

Most of the women at Beck and Wise thought he was dreamy. Most of the men, too, come to think of it. If they weren't admiring his latest magazine article, they were playing racquetball with him after work, or laughing at one of his jokes.

And he just made her want to spit. Call it an instinctive rejection of a type of man she'd always found incredibly unappealing. Call it the opposite of sexual magnetism. Whatever, it made her back go stiff whenever she caught sight of his dark head, it compelled her to press her full lips into a tight, ungenerous line at the mere sound of his voice, and it switched her clever tongue to take-no-prisoners mode. Not that it did her much good. Usually he'd just smirk at anything she said and throw some off-the-cuff smart comment her way—and damn him if nine times out of ten she wasn't left floundering and feeling stupid. Another excellent reason to avoid him as much as possible.

It wasn't that big a deal, usually. Beck and Wise was a huge publishing company, a media giant that produced hundreds of magazines for the Australian marketplace. Jack worked on a whole different floor to her—when he was in the office—on a whole different selection of magazine titles. If she put some effort into it, she could manage things so that she barely ever saw him.

But now he'd slipped his red penis-compensator into her parking spot, and she couldn't simply assign him to his usual category of "necessary evil" and forget about him.

The automatic doors to the impressive thirty-story Beck and Wise building swished open as she entered, and she glanced longingly across at the foyer coffee shop as a hit of freshly ground coffee beans washed over her. No time for coffee today. She spared a thought for her favorite double mocha latte, eyeing the distinctive steaming cup in the hands of one lucky, contented customer. Her eyes automatically lifted to scan the coffee-lover's face, and she felt her lips assume their usual streamlined position as she looked into Jack Brook's deep blue eyes.

Bastard. Now he had her favorite parking spot *and* her favorite coffee.

She forced herself to look away, concentrating instead on the elevator bank ahead. Checking her watch, she stabbed the up button urgently, then sighed with relief as the doors in front of her opened on a cheery chime. Entering, she punched the button for her floor, then looked up to see Jack bearing down on her, his stride lengthening as he sped up to beat the doors. They made eye contact again, and the corners of his ridiculously blue eyes crinkled as he flashed one of his patented engaging grins at her.

"Could you…?" he called, just a few steps away now.

She moved instinctively, her finger reaching for the button before her conscious mind could approve or disapprove the action. He'd stolen her parking spot, after all. And he had that delicious-looking coffee in his hand…

The doors began to slide shut. Realizing what she'd done, his eyes widened with confusion and then, quickly, annoyance. She tried to despise the little zing of triumph that shot up her spine, but when the doors closed completely she didn't fight the smile that leaped to her lips.

Take that, Smug-boy, she thought.

And then she saw her reflection in the polished steel elevator

doors: a huge smear of lipstick raced up her cheek like some bizarre experiment in modern art. Groaning, she closed her eyes.
Why did Jack Brook always have the last word?

JACK STOOD staring at the closed elevator doors for a full
twenty seconds. What was it with that uptight cow from the
fifteenth floor? Claire Something-or-other, that was her name.
Always frowning. Her lips always squished into nothingness.
Her chin always high and haughty. And what was with the
weird lipstick?

He shook his head, genuinely baffled. To his knowledge, he'd
never done a thing to offend her. Yet every time he smiled her
way she blew him off. It was as if she'd caught him double-
dipping, or cheating on his taxes, or something.

He hated women like that. Women who acted as though every
gesture of friendliness, every joke or helpful suggestion was
about you trying to crack their defenses and get them into bed.
As if he'd be interested in some tightly stitched-up chick who'd
probably just lie there and stare at the ceiling anyway. Thanks,
but he'd rather fly solo.

He stepped into the next elevator car and punched the button
for the seventeenth floor. Claire What's-her-name didn't have
anything to worry about where he was concerned. He liked his
women young—subtwenty, if possible—bubbly and full of life.
Preferably in a bikini, but a one-piece was also acceptable. He
grinned. Okay, so he was exaggerating a little, but if the hat fit...

He took a sip of his latte, then shook his head as the image of
Claire's bestriped face disappearing behind the closing elevator
doors popped into his mind. God, how petty. How stupid and silly
and petty.

And then he got it. He threw back his head and laughed out
loud at exactly the same time that the elevator car slid to a smooth
stop on the fifteenth floor—someone must have pressed the up
button. Heads turned as people looked up from their work, and

he saw Claire's head snap around and her eyes narrow as she spotted him from her office doorway. He grinned and fished in his pocket, pulling his car keys out and dangling them suggestively.

Her lips practically disappeared as she glared at him, and he gave her a little finger wave as the doors closed between them for the second time that day.

She was pissed about the parking spot! He practically giggled as he relished the moment. Imagine being that invested in something so mundane. Imagine wanting to take revenge over something so small and insignificant. Admittedly, the thought that the space he'd reversed into this morning was usually filled by her sensible sedan had crossed his mind at the time. And just as quickly exited at the other end. It would do her good to have a bit of variety, he'd thought. She looked as though she was a creature of habit, always in the same sensible boxy suits, always with her dark, curly hair cut sensibly short. So he was practically doing her a favor, forcing her to break her routine. She might even thank him for the new perspective he was offering her.

Or not. He was still smiling as he stepped out onto the seventeenth floor, raising his latte in greeting at his assistant Linda as he passed by.

"Why are you looking particularly naughty this morning? What trouble have you just stirred up?" she demanded as she followed him into his corner office.

He smiled mysteriously and waggled his eyebrows at her, glancing out the window at his fantastic view of the city of Melbourne. The sky was blue, fluffy clouds floated across the sky… and seventeen floors down, if only he had X-ray vision, he could spot his car…in her spot….

"Jack? What on earth have you done?" Linda asked, real worry in her voice now.

"Relax. It's nothing. Just a stupid…thing that happened. With that Claire girl from Homes and Decorating," he said.

Linda gave him a look.

"Claire Marsden, you mean?"

"Is she the sensible one? With the skinny little mouth?"

"Are we talking about the same woman ? On the short side? Cute as a button?" Linda queried.

He made a dismissive noise, unprepared to think positive things about Claire Marsden right now.

"Well, I think she's very attractive," Linda continued.

"Compared to the Russian women's weight-lifting team, you mean?"

"Whatever did she do to get you so offside?" Linda asked, her eyes wide at his unaccustomed cruelty.

He shrugged, suddenly aware that he'd actually allowed himself to get quite worked up.

"We just had a little…transport dispute this morning."

"I see. Well, she's a nice person. My niece Ronnie spent a week doing work experience with her recently. Claire was very supportive and helpful, and Ronnie is really inspired to have a go at journalism now."

He paused in the act of flipping open the lid on his notebook computer.

"Why didn't you ask me about the work experience? I'd have been happy to have Ronnie up here."

Linda made a noise in the back of her throat. He recognized it as her deeply skeptical grunt and decided he was offended.

"What's that supposed to mean?"

"Oh, come on, Jack. You're hardly the most patient of men. I didn't want you breathing down Ronnie's neck, making her nervous. Besides, you're far too good-looking and Ronnie's far too young and blond for my personal comfort."

He leaned back in his chair, happy for any opportunity to crank his assistant up a little.

"Blond you say? Just how old is she?"

Linda shook her head and slapped his mail down onto his desk.

"Keep your trousers on and read your mail, Mr. Sexy," she said.

He took another big slurp of latte while he waited for his computer to boot up. A dialogue box flashed onto the screen and he typed in his password, flicking idly through the few letters Linda had just given him while the computer logged in to the company network.

Nothing exciting there. In his role as managing editor, he oversaw the production of six monthly magazine titles. It meant he got a lot of mail—most of it dull. Today he had a complaint from one of the tour operators they'd profiled in a recent Travel Time issue, which could go straight in the recycling bin, and a couple of letters to the editor from two of the other titles he managed.

He turned his attention to his e-mail, his eyebrows rising with surprise as he saw he had a message from the Big Kahuna himself, Morgan Beck. He scanned the note quickly, then called Linda in.

"Can you cancel my two o'clock and reschedule it for me? I've been summoned upstairs by God."

"Can do. Anything else?"

He flashed his most disarming smile, turning on the charm shamelessly. To her credit, Linda remained steadfastly unaffected, instead shaking her head ruefully.

"Don't waste your little-boy-lost routine on me. What do you want?"

"Do you think you could also swing past the post office and collect the mail from my personal box? I haven't had a chance to get over there since I flew back into town yesterday."

"Jack, we've been over this. I'm more than happy to collect your personal mail for you every day during my lunch break. Just give me the key to your box and it will be taken care of."

Sliding the small key from his key ring, Jack hesitated before handing it over.

"I feel bad asking you to run personal errands for me," he confessed when Linda made an impatient noise.

"Well, get over it. You're a good boss, you don't treat me like a slave, and I'm happy to help you out however I can."

Overcoming his personal scruples, Jack shrugged and handed the key over. Linda gave him an amused look as she slid it into her hip pocket.

"Don't worry—I'll let you know when you've crossed the line and turned into a heartless corporate shark."

"My deepest, darkest fear. How did you know?" Jack joked.

"I'm psychic. Which is why I suspect it's useless suggesting you tidy yourself up a bit before your appointment with Mr. Beck," Linda said, her tone indicating she already knew his response.

"You *are* psychic, you know. It's uncanny," he said, loving that he could annoy her.

Linda's eyes flicked down to his black, three-quarter-length cargo pants, slip-on sandals and unironed Hawaiian shirt.

"You're lucky Mr. Beck likes you," she said on her way out of his office.

Jack snorted, his mood shifting abruptly as her words triggered a memory.

Luck.

What a concept. What a stupid, random, insane, cruel concept. He was very quiet for a moment as he stared out unseeingly at his view. And then he remembered that big smear of lipstick across Claire Marsden's face and he laughed to himself all over again.

2

BUSY. THE THOUGHT registered somewhere between Claire's third impromptu meeting of the day and the fourth phone call from the client she'd been wooing for the past six months. Now that they'd signed the contracts, Hillcrest Hardware were keen to have their new custom magazine in their hot little hands.

Ironic, if you had the time to appreciate such things. She'd spent so long explaining, and illustrating, and cajoling to bring them to the point of saying yes, and now they were more keen than she was. And she was pretty damn keen.

Despite the fact that it was well past midday and she still hadn't read her e-mail, she paused to appreciate the larger-than-life blowup of the front cover for the launch edition of *Welcome Home* magazine that was leaning against her office wall. Gleaming floorboards reflected light from wide, white-framed windows, and a rustic wood dining setting graced the center of the tastefully decorated room. Color Your World read one of the cover lines, while another claimed Bring Your Garden to Life in an Instant. A little bubble of pride blossomed in her belly. After all the hard work, they were finally a go.

Her own magazine. Based on a concept she'd created. Executed just how she thought it should be executed. It simply didn't get better.

She was the one who had seen the opportunity for a custom magazine within the Hillcrest Hardware chain. She'd watched the growth in demand for decorator magazines, and she'd found a

progressive hardware retailer in the marketplace who was looking for a new way to create relationships with its customers. It
had made sense to her to answer one need with the other, just as
it had made sense to the executives at Hillcrest when she'd
pitched it to them six months ago.

Now she was about to launch a new magazine title into the
Australian marketplace, an important, key part of her five-year
plan. Soon, if she played her cards right, the corner office and
senior management status she coveted would be hers—it was just
a matter of time.

Today was Wednesday; by this time next week, she should
have editorial sign-off from her client, and the magazine should
be well into production. Another week or so later, and the first
edition would be rolling off the printing presses.

A goofy smile still wreathing her lips, Claire clicked the
mouse on the e-mail icon on her computer screen and watched
as her in-box registered way too many notifications. Sighing, she
realized she was going to have to get her assistant to prioritize
them for her, alert her to the urgent ones and print the rest off for
her to read in bed later that night. Another fascinating evening.

It was just as well there was no man also planning on sharing her bed.

She paused for a moment, annoyed with herself. Where had
that thought come from? Parts of her body twitched suggestively,
and she shrugged. Okay, it had been a while. And a bit of frustration release was necessary every now and then, but that was
what George Clooney movies were for. This was more important.
Welcome Home was her baby, and it deserved all her attention.

Besides, it wasn't as though there was a battle going on here
between the magazine and her personal life; apart from her training regime and the actual triathlon meets themselves, she had no
personal life. There was work, and there was the road and the
pool and her bike. End of story.

And it was a nice, uncomplicated, successful story. She was

fulfilled. Really. And hadn't she made it into the state triathlon semifinals thanks to all that focus?

Okay, maybe she was a little horny. But that could wait. Sex would always be there, but this opportunity wouldn't.

A recent memory volunteered itself suddenly—last time she'd visited her grandmother she'd been astonished to learn that her gran was telling everyone in the old people's home that she was a lesbian.

"Just to take the heat off them all wondering when you're getting married and having children, dear," her gran had explained.

So Claire wasn't going to be young forever. But this was important, and sometimes other things had to take a backseat to work. In five years' time, she'd be ensconced in that corner office, in charge of a handful of quality magazines. The sacrifices and loneliness were worth it. For the time being.

Having talked her nether regions into submission, she called her assistant, Tom, in and asked him to sort through the rest of her e-mails.

She was just about to plunge into her in-tray when a familiar figure propped itself against her door frame.

"We still on for lunch?"

Claire stared at her friend Katherine in dismay.

"You forgot, didn't you?" Katherine guessed, one hand resting on her slim hip.

"I'm sorry. I've got so much on, I think I should just work through lunch," Claire apologized.

But Katherine wasn't about to take no for an answer. Swinging around, she called in reinforcements.

"Tom! Get over here and help me convince your boss she needs to eat lunch," she called imperatively.

Tom shot up from his seat as though he'd been electrocuted, and Claire had to stifle a laugh as he stared at Katherine slavishly. At nearly six feet tall with legs that seemed to go on forever and a bust that would put a 1950s pinup to shame,

Katherine was every man's sexual fantasy. The fact that she was funny, clever and worked as editor of a sports magazine were bonuses that most men didn't seem to mind, either. At a tender twenty years, Tom was like a bunny in the headlights of her attractiveness.

"I tell her all the time she should have a lunch break, but she thinks a protein shake is enough," Tom said, sounding for all the world like a worried Jewish mother.

"Are you listening to what Tom is saying, Claire?" Katherine asked, the glint in her eye signaling that she wasn't unaware of Tom's adoration.

Shaking her head at her friend, Claire checked her watch.

"Twenty minutes," she said.

"Done. Thanks for the backup, Tom," Katherine said, giving him a big smile.

Tom just stood there, apparently stunned by such beneficence.

Claire grabbed her handbag and followed Katherine to the elevator.

"You're cruel," Claire admonished.

"How so? I was perfectly nice to him!"

Claire gave Katherine's close-fitting deep red, short-skirted suit and elegant high heels a once-over.

"You ought to be registered as a deadly weapon. Or given a handicap. How are the rest of us mere mortals supposed to compete?"

"You do okay, from what I've seen," Katherine commented dryly.

"Right. That's why I watched three George Clooney movies this month."

The elevator door opened and they exited into the foyer, heading for the coffee shop.

"The opportunities are there, but you choose not to see them."

Claire rolled her eyes—as if she wouldn't have noticed an eligible guy interested in her! To prove her point, a young courier walked straight into a potted palm because he was too busy tracking Katherine's progress across the foyer to look where he was going.

"You see that? Nobody walks into plants for me, I can tell you."

"You don't believe me? What about Cameron Johnson in layout? And that cute security guard on the night shift?"

Claire had to rack her brain to get even a vague mental image of the men. Needless to say, they hadn't walked into a wall, or any other obstacle, the last time she had been in their vicinity—*that* she would have remembered.

"You're deluded."

They settled at their usual table in the far back corner of the coffee shop and picked up a menu each, even though neither of them ever strayed from their normal order—a chicken club sandwich.

"You don't *want* to see—that's your problem. When was the last time you had a date?" Katherine challenged.

Claire studied the menu intently. Why had she even brought this subject up? Hadn't she just decided that she was happy with her work-oriented world at the moment?

"Forget I said anything. I was only joking, anyway," she hedged.

Katherine shook her head sympathetically.

"That long, huh?"

Desperate for some way to avoid the conversation Claire suspected was in the offing, she scanned the coffee shop looking for a distraction. She twitched as she noted Jack Brook propped at the lunch bar, one leg resting comfortably on the foot rail as he chatted to a woman she didn't recognize. He looked so confident and happy and self-assured that she felt her toes curling in her shoes with annoyance.

"You went out with Jack Brook for a while, didn't you?" she found herself blurting.

Katherine looked surprised and she turned to follow Claire's line of sight, quickly spotting Jack lounging at the bar.

The glance she shot Claire was unreadable.

"Yeah, I did. For a few short, spectacular weeks a couple of years ago."

The waiter stopped by their table, and Claire and Katherine both ordered the chicken club sandwich. Silence fell. Aware that Katherine was now thinking completely the wrong thing, Claire felt honor-bound to correct her.

"He parked in my space this morning," she explained. "He's such an arrogant jerk, I just wondered what you saw in him."

"That's simple—pretty much what every other woman sees in him. He's gorgeous."

Claire pulled a face, her eyes sliding across to contemplate Jack's profile.

"He really does nothing for me," she said airily.

Katherine made a small disbelieving noise.

"Then you're officially the walking dead. Whether or not Jack Brook is gorgeous is not a matter of subjective opinion. He has those amazing eyes, and a body to die for—fantastic skin, great arms. And he's a great lover. Really…gifted, if you get what I mean," Katherine said, wiggling her eyebrows suggestively.

Claire shifted in her seat, but she was unable to stop her gaze from sneaking over to him. He was teasing his lunch companion, reaching out to swipe a bit of frosting off her cake. As Claire watched he slid his chocolate-coated finger into his mouth and licked it, his actions completely unconscious and completely erotic. She flicked her eyes away from the blatant display, but, again, they slid back to him of their own accord. Now he was shoving his hand into his pants pocket as he leaned casually on the bar. The fabric tightened across his thighs and, unbelievably, she felt herself blushing as she considered what Katherine had said. Gifted… *What* exactly did that mean? Was that about the finger-licking thing, or the part of his trousers that was holding her attention right now?

"You know, a fling with someone like Jack could be exactly what you need," Katherine said.

Claire jerked her attention back to her friend.

"Are you insane? I wouldn't sleep with Jack Brook if you paid me. He's cocky, conceited, smug—and a complete man-slut."

"I see."

Katherine was smiling knowingly, and Claire bristled. Determined to prove her point, she leaned across the table.

"If you gave me the choice of kissing Jack Brook or punching him in the face, I'd choose the punch every time," she said firmly.

"Ah. So you have thought about kissing Jack, then?"

Claire was about to launch into all the reasons why she considered Jack Brook to be subhuman when Katherine's face suddenly lit up as though she'd just thought of something funny. She laughed, nodding her head as though she'd just worked something out. Claire frowned at her, suspicious.

"What?"

"I just remembered something. I was talking about you with Jack once. He wanted to know why we were friends—he thought you were prissy."

Claire sat bolt upright in her seat and glared across at Jack. What a pig! How dare he call her prissy? What a horrible thing to say—as if she was some dried-up spinster aunt or something. She had the urge to go over and give him a piece of her mind....

"Where does he get off talking about me like that?" she snapped, dragging her gaze away from Jack to find Katherine studying her speculatively.

Claire suddenly felt very exposed under her friend's knowing gaze.

"I mean, as if I care what a jerk like him thinks about me."

Katherine simply quirked an eyebrow disbelievingly.

"Can we please talk about something—anything—else?" Claire asked, fiddling with her paper napkin and cutlery.

To her everlasting relief, their sandwiches arrived.

"You're lucky I'm really hungry," Katherine said lightly. "You're off the hook—for the moment."

TWENTY MINUTES had turned into half an hour by the time they settled their bill and made their way back to the elevator. Claire thought Katherine had let the subject of Jack Brook drop entirely, but just as they were parting ways, Katherine suddenly got serious. Despite Claire's protestations, Katherine insisted on explaining why she and Jack had broken up. Claire listened with arms crossed, determined not to give Katherine any more reasons to jump to ridiculous conclusions about her and Jack Brook. Given that every word her friend said just confirmed her preconceived beliefs about the man, it wasn't hard.

"I just want you to go in with your eyes open," Katherine finally concluded.

"Kat, hell will freeze over before I even consider having a polite conversation with that man," Claire said.

"If you say so."

Claire was shaking her head as she returned to her office, bewildered by Katherine's determination to imagine some sort of...*thing* between her and Jack Brook.

"Not in a million years," she muttered to herself as she began packing her briefcase for her afternoon appointment at Hillcrest Hardware.

"Claire! Oh, my God—I'm so glad I've found you!"

It was Tom, sweaty and excited in her doorway.

"I was checking your e-mails while you were at lunch— Morgan Beck wants to see you at two! I went straight down to the coffee shop, but you'd already left..."

Galvanized, Claire checked her watch, then sighed with relief when she saw it was only ten to two. Plenty of time to get up to the thirtieth floor—if she hustled.

She forced herself to suppress the many panicky thoughts that were suddenly clamoring for attention and equal-opportunity worry time in her mind and instead focused on her schedule for the rest of the afternoon. She'd have to push back that appointment with Hillcrest, then... It was no use—all she wanted to do was fret over this unprecedented call from the thirtieth floor. Why would Morgan Beck want to see her out of the blue like this? Surely *Welcome Home* had been well and truly signed, sealed and delivered? They'd praised her, promoted her to editor, handed the whole project over into her capable hands. What more was there to say?

"Tom, I need you to ring Hillcrest Hardware and tell them I'll be approximately twenty minutes late," she said, slinging her handbag over her shoulder and grabbing her briefcase. "I'll head straight out after seeing Mr. Beck."

Tom was taking notes, loving the excitement of the moment.

"I'll ring the traffic report and leave a message on your cell phone if there are any traffic delays," he suggested eagerly.

"That would be great, thanks," she said, hiding a smile at his action-stations demeanor.

Satisfied that she'd covered all bases, she headed for the ladies' room, her mind working overtime trying to find the reason behind this summons. The mirror revealed that hectic color stained her cheeks and the first thing she did was sluice a great handful of cold water over her face. Patting it dry with some hand towel, she took a deep breath and slowly exhaled.

Be calm. Everything is fine. They can't take this off you now— it's your idea, she told herself.

The mantra appeared to work. Her heart climbed down from her throat and back into her chest to resume normal activities, and she quickly dabbed on some mascara and a fresh layer of lipstick. Wetting her fingers under the tap, she spruced up her short curls, ensuring her face was framed nicely. One final check over, the last-minute realization that she had a blouse button undone flashing her belly button, and then she was out of there and heading for the elevator.

Five to two. She pressed the call button. Even if the elevator stopped on every floor, she'd be on time. Some of the tension eased out of her shoulders and she rotated her left arm a little. It was still sore from last night's workout, but post-exercise soreness was simply the price you paid for getting stronger. And she needed strength if she was going to lift her personal best time and place in the state triathlon finals in two weeks' time.

Claire tried to be objective as she considered her chances of scoring a place in the final three. She'd shaved several seconds off her swim and bike legs over the past few months, but she still needed to build stamina for the long hill runs. She was confident she was getting there, though. Every training session was a gain.

It was one of the things she loved about triathlons—for her, the races were more about beating herself than the other competitors. Each time she went out there, she was competing with her own best times—and success or failure was never a matter of opinion, but objective fact. She liked that, liked knowing that she was getting somewhere, slowly but surely. Becoming the best person she could be. And, of course, it was a great way of burning off all the stress from a hard day in the office.

Despite all the promises she'd made herself, she couldn't stop her mind from thinking about Harry. The closer she got to the finals, the more he crept into her thoughts. Would he come to watch her? She shook her head at her own naïveté—of course he wouldn't. The only reason she continued to invite him to events of interest in her life was out of some bizarre sense of courtesy. It was a little game they played, she and her father, where she pretended he might be interested, and he came up with a palatable excuse for why he wasn't.

The elevator door pinged open in front of her, and she stepped inside and pressed the button for the thirtieth floor, suppressing the little flash of nervousness that usually accompanied any trip in an elevator. The trick was to think about something else, she'd learned over the years.

She was figuring out tonight's training regime when the elevator pinged to a halt just two floors up, and she raised preoccupied eyes and felt her lips instinctively disappearing. She deliberately avoided making eye contact with Jack Brook as he stepped in beside her, but it seemed he wasn't about to let her off so easily.

"Good afternoon," he said cheerily, and there was no mistaking the smug self-satisfaction in his tone.

She tried to manage an acknowledging smile and nod, but she was too busy feeling self-conscious after her lunchtime conversation with Katherine. Suddenly she found herself very aware of how close to him she was standing. She could practically feel the heat coming off his body—was that even possible?—and the woody, tangy scent of his aftershave teased at her. Easing a step away, she searched for something to help restore her usual equilibrium where Jack Brook was concerned. Her gaze fell on his bare toes peeking out from his slip-on sandals, and she found herself seizing on his typically unprofessional office attire as a way to distract herself.

His ridiculous getup had barely registered earlier, but now she gave it her full, disdainful attention. Suits and other acceptable office wear were obviously not cool enough for Jack "The Man" Brook, she noted. He probably thought he was being really cutting edge in those three-quarter cargo pants. And the sandals—how *European* of him. As for the artfully creased shirt…

She smiled minutely, pleased to realize that the strange, self-conscious feeling had evaporated and she was once again in control of the situation and herself. Then he spoke.

"How you doin'?" he asked, lounging against the wall casually, taking up too much space.

Don't respond, don't respond, don't respond, she chanted internally.

"Sleep in this morning?" she asked, eyes flicking over his crumpled shirt.

"Not *sleep* in, no. But I guess I was a little slow rising to the occasion," Jack said provocatively.

She decided she simply would not blush in response to his

suggestive comment. That was what he wanted, after all. And there was no way she would satisfy his juvenile baiting. Except, thanks to Katherine's innuendo earlier, a slow wash of heat already was rising up her chest and into her face. She scratched the ear nearest him, trying to cover her embarrassment.

"Warm today," Jack said, knowingness oozing from every pore.

She ignored him, a strategy she should have stuck with from the start. How on earth could Katherine ever imagine that Claire could be attracted to a man like Jack Brook?

The elevator halted on the thirtieth floor, and she suddenly realized Jack was getting out with her. She glanced at him out of the corner of her eye. He must be talking to one of the financial presidents or something. Trying to buddy-buddy himself an even fatter paycheck, no doubt.

She turned toward Morgan Beck's office suite. Again, Jack followed. She shot him a look. What was going on? There was only one man at the end of this plush-carpeted hallway, and he had an appointment with her.

Jack raised his eyebrows at her, one of those innocent, questioning looks that was supposed to be cute. It made her want to growl deep in her chest.

Pasting a smile on her face, she lengthened her stride and made it to Morgan's assistant's desk ahead of Jack.

"Ms. Bell, I've got a two-o'clock with Mr. Beck," she said, being sure to inject just the right amount of friendliness and respect into her tone. Like a lot of high-powered assistants, Jenny Bell had a bit of a chip on her shoulder about being condescended to by some of the company's executives.

"Of course, Claire. Morgan is just on a phone call. Why don't you take a seat?"

Jenny smiled approvingly at her, and Claire turned toward the waiting area, confident she'd aced that particular obstacle course. Offices were like triathlons in many ways, she mused as she sat, automatically pulling her neat black skirt down over her knees.

If you trained hard, respected the referees and gave thanks to the support crews, you had a real chance of not only finishing, but placing well.

Picking up one of the many Beck and Wise publications displayed artfully on the coffee table nearby, she waited for Jack to explain his presence.

"Jenny, you are looking finer than ever. When are you going to give in and finally come waterskiing with me up at the cabin? You know you want to," Jack teased, his whole attitude one of casual confidence as he leaned against Jenny's forbidding reception desk.

Oh, boy. Jenny was renowned for being a real stickler for protocol and proper office conduct, and Claire almost winced as she imagined the arctic blast Jack was about to receive. Almost, but not quite. Instead, she leaned forward, just in case she missed a single delicious nuance. It was about time Mr. Cocky got the message that the world was not his personal love pit....

"You'd better be careful, Jack. I might just take you up on that offer one day—we'll see how fast you run then."

Claire blinked. Good grief, Jenny Bell was *flirting* with Jack Brook. Actually batting her eyelids and flicking her thick plait of gray hair over her shoulder. Claire slumped a little lower in her seat. Was she the only member of the sisterhood who was immune to Jack's flashy charms?

"You say yes, we'll see what happens," Jack warned her. Claire almost gasped with outrage as he reached across and plucked the pencil from Jenny's hands. "I'm going to keep this as a souvenir," he said cheekily, sauntering over to take a seat beside Claire.

A delighted peal of laughter sounded from Jenny Bell.

"For that you get a coffee while you wait—black, one sugar, right?"

It was like James Bond and Ms. Moneypenny, only he was licensed to make her feel ill. Claire could feel her upper lip curling with distaste.

"How about you, Claire? Would you like a coffee, or tea perhaps?"

This came as Jenny was about to exit, an afterthought.

"No, I'm fine, thank you," Claire managed to choke out, even dredging up a smile from somewhere.

Jenny disappeared into the small kitchen behind her desk, and Claire concentrated on the magazine she'd picked up. She should have paid more attention when she'd grabbed it from the pile on the table—*Big Game Fishing* was hardly her bag. Worse, as she flicked through it trying to find something to grab her attention, her eye was caught by the byline on the major story—Jack Brook. She rolled her eyes. Of course he was into big game fishing. What was she thinking? The man was practically Hemingway reincarnate, with his skydiving and racy car and chain of women and travel writing. He'd probably even run with the bulls in Pamplona.

Out of the corner of her eye she saw him stretch out his long legs, his tanned arm resting on the couch between them. He was amusing himself with the pencil he'd taken from Jenny, rolling it back and forth between his long, strong fingers. She found herself fixating on the dexterous movement of his hands for a beat. *He has a body to die for.* Katherine's words slipped insidiously into Claire's mind. Jack Brook would be an amazing lover, of that she had no doubt. The way he looked at women, the glint in his eye, the casual, animal elegance of his walk—the man simply screamed sex. There would be nothing tentative or uncertain about his technique—he looked as though he knew exactly what buttons to push, and when, and how hard, and…

Claire blinked, stunned at the direction her thoughts had taken. She must be stressed out or something. That was the only explanation for her aberrant thoughts.

Mindlessly flipping the pages, she surreptitiously checked

her watch. What was it with big bosses and the waiting game? In all her years in publishing, she'd yet to walk straight into a superior's office at the time of her appointment. There was always the standard keep-you-waiting ploy to be played out, just to remind you of your place in the pecking order.

A big male hand suddenly grabbed the page she was staring at blankly, pulling the magazine across so that Jack could see what she was reading.

"Thought I recognized that picture," he said, stabbing a neatly manicured index finger at the photo accompanying his big article. It showed a snow-white, luxuriously appointed yacht bobbing on a brilliant azure sea. "Hell of a boat. Crew of fifteen just to run her. Now that's money."

She gritted her teeth.

"Spent a full week on her. Pretty hard coming back to nine-to-five-dom after that, I can tell you."

"I wasn't aware you worked nine to five," she couldn't resist saying. The man was always off on some stupid assignment somewhere.

He narrowed his eyes at her.

"I was speaking metaphorically. You know what that is, don't you? As in—she was as sour as a lemon," he said, and she sat up straighter. What a jerk!

"Actually, that's a simile. A metaphor is more like—his ego was monumental," she returned sweetly.

He was opening his mouth to respond when the door to Morgan Beck's office swung open. Their heads swiveled as one and she didn't need to look to know that Jack's face wore the same friendly-not-too-sucky smile that hers did.

"Claire, Jack. Come on in," Morgan said.

She stood, the smile almost slipping off her face. Up until this second, she'd been telling herself that Jack Brook's visit to the thirtieth floor had nothing to do with her. And she'd almost been believing it. Now she gave free rein to the paranoid feminist within and began imagining half a dozen scenarios where she was shafted royally. Her stomach sunk below knee level as she followed Jack into Morgan Beck's inner sanctum.

"Now, Jack, how much do you know about Claire's new project for the Hillcrest Hardware chain?" Morgan asked, toying with an expensive-looking fountain pen as he leaned back in his well-padded executive chair.

"I understand it's a custom magazine job, a monthly decorator title to be sold only in their stores at a cheaper than usual cover price to create customer loyalty," Jack said.

She resisted the urge to stare at him. How did he know all this? She couldn't have named a single title he worked for. Apart from *Big Game Fishing,* of course.

"Sounds like he's got the important bits right, doesn't it, Claire?"

She nodded, too anxious to trust her voice.

"Before we go any further, I want to acknowledge that this project has been yours, Claire, from the word go. But unfortunately, we've hit a bit of a snag. I've had my thinking cap on, though, and I've come to the conclusion that Jack might be the man to help us out."

She swallowed hard and forced air into her lungs.

"This is a problem from Hillcrest, I'm assuming?" she asked, trying to find her feet.

"Yes, but don't go getting too fussed about it. Old Hank Hillcrest is a dyed-in-the-wool sexist and he's got some pretty wacky ideas. One of those is that the magazine's outlook is too feminine."

Claire frowned. Too feminine? Over half of the magazine's content was aimed at offering heavy-duty building projects to experienced DIYers, along with reviews of new hardware and building products. In fact, the only feminine parts of the magazine were the decorator segments, and a small cookery section which was designed to showcase Hillcrest's kitchen products.

She said as much to Morgan, and he nodded his head sympathetically.

"Claire, I know all this. They know all this. Hell, even cranky old Hillcrest knows all this. But he just doesn't have it in him to let this go without putting his sticky fingerprints all over it. So, as I said, I had an idea.

"You probably don't know this, but Jack started out his career with us in the Homes and Decorating division, writing up projects for our DIY titles. Over the years, he's branched out, moved on. But I bet I wouldn't be wrong if I suggested you still keep your hand in with a bit of DIY work here and there, right, Jack?"

She found herself turning to look at Jack, all the words of protest catching at the back of her throat. She was going to be sick. She was truly going to puke her guts up all over Morgan Beck's polished walnut desk.

"Sure, Morgan, I've got a few projects on the go. But it sounds to me like you've got a done deal with Hillcrest already. And by the looks of things, Claire's put in all the hard yards on this project," Jack said.

Underneath the sick feeling and the anger and the dread, she managed to be surprised at this response from Jack. He actually sounded uncomfortable, reluctant.

"Let's not get ahead of ourselves, people. I'm not suggesting for a moment that Claire be cut out of this thing. We would never do that to you, Claire—please be assured of that."

Morgan took a moment to simply make eye contact with her, his faded blue eyes powerfully sincere. She held his gaze, wanting him to see she had what it took to survive this last hiccup.

"What exactly are you suggesting then, Mr. Beck?" she asked carefully.

"I want to assign Jack to *Welcome Home* as an associate editor for a while—six months, tops. Just so he can have a few meetings with old man Hillcrest, shoot the breeze, all that stuff Jack does so well. It'll be purely window dressing. Jack'll write up a few articles, and then we'll just downplay his involvement until he simply disappears altogether."

She tried to get her head around it. They wanted to give half the credit for her magazine, based on her concept, sold to the client by her, to this crinkle-shirted lothario slouching next to her?

"This…this really…" She struggled to find a way to finish her sentence that didn't have the word "sucks" in it.

"I've got to agree with Claire, Morgan. Surely we can just tough this out? Once Hillcrest have the first edition of their new magazine in hand, they'll be so dazzled they'll forget any objections," Jack said.

Morgan nodded, almost as though he was giving Jack's suggestion some thought.

"We've gone over all this, Jack, believe me. What I'm suggesting is painless, simple and foolproof. I think we can all work together to pull this off, don't you?"

There was no mistaking the sudden glint of steel in Morgan's eyes now. She found herself fixating on the small tufts of hair remaining on his otherwise bald head. She'd always thought of them indulgently as pseudo teddy-bear ears, but now she realized he probably cultivated them to cover the scars from where he'd had his twin horns surgically removed.

"I'll leave the details of all this up to you two, and I know I can rely upon you both to be discreet about this…arrangement."

Somehow she managed to find her feet. Her legs felt numb and heavy, and the distance between her chair and the doors leading back to the reception area seemed a mile off. Morgan leaned forward and shook her hand, again going for the meaningful eye contact. He'd probably look that way as he was pushing her out of a lifeboat on the *Titanic*—deeply moved, but completely committed to saving his own backside.

Anger trickled into her frozen limbs. She lifted her chin, aware she must be looking like a stunned mullet. Although it felt as though her face might crack, she forced her lips into a curve that she hoped resembled a smile.

"I'm sure we can smooth this over," she said, and she was

amazed at how professional and calm she sounded. As she turned toward the door she glanced just once at Jack Brook, and she saw surprise and something else—respect?—in his deep blue eyes before she fixed her attention on the double doors ahead and concentrated on putting one foot in front of the other.

Just get me out of here, just get me out of here, just get me out of here, she begged herself, already aware that her mask of calm was about to dissolve. To show any weakness in front of these men... She'd rather charge at the plate-glass window behind Morgan's desk and take a dive down to the sidewalk.

Jenny looked up and smiled at Claire as she approached, and again Claire dragged her lips into a smile.

"See you later, Claire," the assistant said.

The rest of the office geography assumed the visual equivalent of white noise as Claire honed in on the ladies' sign at the end of the hall and simply walked.

She had no idea what had happened to Jack Brook, but she had no intention of hanging around to discuss details with him—or worse, to listen to some mealymouthed vote of sympathy.

The veneered surface of the restroom door felt smooth and cool beneath her fingers and at last she was alone. She couldn't even look at herself in the mirror, afraid all of her emotions would be painfully obvious: disgust, disappointment, anger, betrayal.

God, when would enough be enough in this world? When would her achievements measure up for these people? When would her skills and talents be acknowledged?

She threw her handbag and briefcase onto the marble vanity and at last faced her reflection in the mirror. To her surprise she looked calm. Cool. Hard. Determined.

She snorted. The great irony of her life was that a childhood of insecurity and disappointment had helped her build a tough fortress of impenetrability as an adult. So now when she was disappointed, no one ever knew. Except for her.

Angry tears burned at the back of her eyes and she clenched them shut for a moment. She would not cry. She hated that when she became angry one of her first responses was to feel tears coming on. It felt weak, ineffectual—a child's response to being thwarted or hurt. If she were a man, she wouldn't be in here being a big sooky-la-la. If she were a man, she'd be off somewhere kicking a hole in a wall or punching up some innocent bystander in a bar.

Inspired, she took a step toward the wastepaper can and gave it a good, solid kick. It slid across the tiled floor and slammed into the far wall, toppling to one side and spilling out a morning's worth of scrunched-up paper towel and tissue.

"Hah!" she said out loud.

As an expression of her anger and hurt and disenchantment, it felt woefully inadequate.

And now there was a pile of tissue all over the floor. Unable to stop herself, she knelt and scooped the scrunched-up paper back into the bin.

Just like a man, she mocked herself.

The outer door swung open and one of the finance directors' assistants entered the room. Claire shot to her feet, smiled awkwardly, then entered a stall as a way of avoiding explanations.

She waited until the other woman had left, then emerged to wash her hands. Patting them dry, she checked her watch: a good five minutes since the meeting had ended. She could head for the elevators now and be confident of avoiding Jack. She could ride the elevator all the way down to the foyer, and just keep on walking. She'd always planned to come back to the office after her appointment with Hillcrest and work late, as usual, but now she impulsively decided to take the rest of the afternoon off. Perhaps if she went for a really punishing run she could lose some of the anger coiling in her belly.

And then she could return to Beck and Wise tomorrow and show them that she wasn't going to let them beat her.

It felt like a plan. If only she didn't still want to scream at someone.

Her hand shook a little as she reclaimed her bag and briefcase, and she took a deep breath before exiting. To her relief, the waiting area near the elevator bank was empty, and she pressed the call button stiffly. A car eased its doors open almost immediately, and she stepped in and pressed the foyer button.

The doors had almost slid to a complete close when a tanned arm shot into the narrowing gap. The doors automatically bounced open, and she gritted her teeth as Jack stepped into the car.

She refused to look at him, but she could feel his eyes on her as the elevator gathered momentum and sped downward.

Silence stretched between them. She kept her eyes glued to the floor indicator, just wanting an out from the elevator, this day, her life.

"Look—" he began to say, but she cut him off.

"Spare me. You've never liked me, and I've never liked you, so don't bother mouthing some empty platitude at me, okay? Of all the unpalatable aspects of this deal, you I find the most difficult to swallow."

She'd planned on exiting grandly into the foyer on these cutting and deeply satisfying words, but all of a sudden the lights flashed once, then blackness descended at the same time that the grinding shriek of metal-on-metal filled the car and the elevator shuddered to a halt.

3

"WHAT THE—?" Jack exclaimed.

"What's happening?" Claire demanded at almost the same time.

"Probably just a freak glitch," he said into the darkness, wishing he felt as confident as he sounded.

"You're an expert on elevator technology now, are you?" she asked sharply.

He couldn't see her, but he rolled his eyes at the corner he guessed she was occupying.

"No, I'm being optimistic. Would you prefer I start reciting the Lord's Prayer and scribbling my will on the back of an envelope?"

Silence. Good. He was sick of her attitude and misdirected anger. As for that dig she'd made just before the elevator went crazy… It had been a long time since someone had told him to his face that she didn't like him. And he was surprised at how much it annoyed him.

An emergency light flickered to life above them and he moved to the control panel. The pale, inadequate glow allowed him to find the compartment which hid the emergency phone, and he pried it open and reached for the receiver.

"Hello? Is anyone there?" he asked, suddenly aware that his heart was pounding faster than usual.

Okay, so this was a bit scary. And maybe he should forgive Claire for being a tad shrill. He glanced across at her as the continuing silence on the other end of the phone sunk in. Her face was pale, taut. Frightened.

"Nothing," he said.

As if she didn't trust him to know the difference between a live phone and a dead one, she crossed to take a listen herself. He leaned against the side wall, elaborately casual as he waited for her to confirm his initial assessment.

"You're right," she said.

"Wow, that must have really hurt," he couldn't resist saying.

She shot him a look that would have turned lesser men to stone.

"What, didn't expect to have to actually stay and cop the consequences of all that mouthing off?" he asked, for some reason feeling really angry with her now. "I know you probably prefer to just hit and run, but unfortunately we appear to be stuck for the short term."

He watched, fascinated, as the color flooded back into her cheeks and her eyes burned with an angry light. Pretty impressive, a part of his brain acknowledged. She even drew her shoulders back and inhaled sharply, and, for the first time ever, he found his eyes dropping to her suit-encased chest.

"It's easy for you to stand there all smug and confident. Did you just have your idea taken away from you and handed to someone completely undeserving? Did you just get treated like some token office bimbo? No. Because you're a man. A racquetball playing, big-game-fishing, bungee-jumping man with a stupid red sports car and the right equipment between his legs to get ahead in this company."

If he'd been a cartoon, his hair would have been streaming back from his head as if he'd just stepped out of a wind tunnel. Whoa, but this was one angry woman. And he could see her point, really he could. But he didn't like the way she was sighting her feminist crosshairs directly on him.

"Listen, I had nothing to do with what just happened in that meeting. You think I want anything to do with this? And if we're talking about tokenism, I'm the one who's being wheeled in as the token male on this project for appearance's sake. How do you think that makes me feel?"

"Don't you dare mock me!" she warned him.

"Then don't you blame your problems on me," he countered. "I can't see why you'd make me the bad guy in all this. Contrary to your belief, I have never disliked you. I barely know you."

She raised an eyebrow skeptically, her whole attitude one of disbelief.

"I know what you said about me," she shot at him.

"Excuse me?"

"You heard."

Genuinely baffled, Jack raised his hands in the air, palms up. "I have no idea what you're talking about. I have better things to do than spend my spare time hanging around talking about you."

That got her! The color was back in her cheeks, and she glared at him fiercely.

"You called me prissy! So don't you dare stand there pulling that Mr. Innocent act," she hissed at him.

Jack frowned. What the hell was she going on about? He'd been speaking the truth when he said that he didn't spend his time sitting around talking about her.

"Sorry, but I think you've got that wrong, lady," he said bluntly.

"Really? We'll just have to ask my good friend Katherine Kirk when we get out of here then, won't we?"

Although his expression didn't change, Jack felt a moment of doubt. Now that she mentioned it, he could vaguely remember having a beer with Katherine some time ago after work. He'd just had a run-in with Claire in an editorial meeting and come out second best….

He made a mental note to thank Katherine for dumping him in it.

Claire was waiting for his response, hands on her hips.

"Well? What do you have to say to that?"

He shrugged. He'd said it, might as well own it. It wasn't as though it wasn't true. "Prissy might have been overstating it. You can be pretty anal, though."

She made a hissing sound, kind of like a kettle about to blow its top, then opened her mouth to retaliate just as the phone rang. They both jumped, startled. Praying this was good news, he reached for the receiver with alacrity.

"Hello?" he asked, feeling her eyes on him, sensing her hopes, like his own, beginning to rise at this contact.

"This is Ted Evans from Security. I'm making contact to ascertain the exact number of persons in lift number six," an officious voice asked.

"Well, Ted, there are two of us, and we'd sure as hell love to get out of here."

Claire made an exasperated noise that he guessed was supposed to signal her wholehearted agreement.

"Two. Right. Well, uh— Who am I talking to?"

"Jack. Jack Brook."

"Right. Jack. You're the one with the red Porsche, yeah? Nice little number," Ted said, his tone all male appreciation. "It's an early 2002 model, right? The one with tiptronic transmission? Very nice."

Jack reined in his frustration. This guy didn't seem to have a real tight grasp on the urgency of their situation.

"About the elevator, Ted," he hinted.

He glanced up as Claire shifted restlessly, a frown creasing her forehead as she no doubt wondered what was going on. He could imagine her reaction if he told her Ted wanted to talk cars.

"Well, we've got a bit of a situation here, Jack. There's been a major power blackout across this whole part of town—something about a fire at the power plant—and most of the building's services have shut down. Air-conditioning, security systems, elevators. You know."

Jack rolled his eyes. Claire shook her head with confusion.

"What's going on?" she asked.

He tried to look reassuring as he returned his attention to Ted.

"So there are other people stuck in elevators?"

"Sure are. Only two of the twelve cars were empty. Elevator four has ten people in it," Ted reported with relish.

Jack grimaced. Ten people would make for a cozy lift compartment. Thank God it was just him and Claire. Out of the corner of his eye, he noted her frown deepening. On second thoughts, maybe a cozy, friendly elevator wasn't such a bad option....

"So how long are we talking here? Half an hour? Ten minutes? What?" he asked, deciding it was time to force Ted to the point.

"Can't tell you that just yet. We've contacted the manufacturer, and they're sending a team out."

Jack tried to control the sinking sensation in his gut.

"So...we could be talking hours here," he said reluctantly.

He could feel Claire stiffen even though she was as far from him as she could get.

"That's not good enough," she said, striding across to pull the receiver from his hand.

"Who am I talking to?" she demanded.

He resumed his lounging position against the wall. He was all for making a little noise if it was going to get them rescued sooner, but he wished her the best of luck up against the remarkably prosaic Ted.

Jack inspected his fingernails as Claire quizzed the security guard, trying to suppress the swell of satisfaction he felt when she returned the receiver to its cradle a few minutes later, her shoulders slumped: she hadn't gotten any further than he had.

"Could be worse. Could be ten people in here," he said lightly, taking in her white face.

She was silent as she crossed back to her side of the space, but he could see her hands were shaking as she brushed her hair back from her face.

Damn. He took a deep breath, then let it out. She was scared. Anyone could see that. And as much as she probably deserved for him to simply ignore her, he couldn't turn his back on her distress.

"Listen, I'm sure they'll have us out of here soon. I think I remember reading somewhere that elevators have manual override functions where they can just winch us down."

He kept an eye on her, noticing her chest was heaving a little now.

"Ah, Claire, you wouldn't happen to be a little claustrophobic at all, would you?" he asked.

She was concentrating fiercely on the carpet in front of her toes, completely unresponsive now.

Okay. He tried to think of something to say or do to help her out. Not being afraid of anything himself, he found it difficult to understand this sort of thing.

"I learned this meditation technique once at a temple in India—" he began to say tentatively, but then Claire slumped against the wall and began sliding down it and he realized she'd fainted.

He leaped across the distance between them, catching her before her head hit the ground. Her hair was soft and silky against his hands, and he could smell her shampoo as he gently guided her onto the carpet. Vanilla. Nice.

A quick once-over revealed that her skirt had ridden up a little, and that her legs were skewed awkwardly, but her eyelids were flickering now and he decided he'd rather stick his head in a crocodile's mouth than be caught adjusting Claire Marsden's clothing while she was semiconscious. Still, he couldn't help noticing that the shortened skirt length belied his previous impression of her legs. Not bad. As a rule, he preferred tall, slim, model-esque women, but Claire's legs were really something of a surprise. Almost as though she could read his mind, Claire made a disgusted noise in the back of her throat, and then her eyes popped open.

CLAIRE CAME OUT of the empty darkness and opened her eyes, blinking rapidly as she tried to reorient herself. Where was she?

What had happened? She felt the ground under her back. And why was she lying on the carpet? And then Jack's face loomed over her and she found herself staring into his concerned blue eyes.

"You okay?" he asked, and it all came flooding back.

They were trapped in an elevator. With no hope of escape for hours. A dizzying tide of fear rushed back up at her and she clamped down on it fiercely. It had been years since she'd allowed this childish terror of enclosed spaces to master her. But while she could suppress it for the short trip up to the fifteenth floor each day, being stuck in a tiny elevator car for several hours was more than her powers of self-control could manage. She'd been grimly hanging on to her calm ever since they'd ground to a halt, but the news that they were going to have to settle in for a long wait had been too much.

"Claire? You all right?" Jack asked again.

He looked funny upside down, she noted, feeling a little detached as she tried to keep her fear at arm's length. Like an alien, his mouth where his eyes should be…

"Hello? Are you in there?" he asked, waving a hand in front of her face.

At last she snapped her attention back.

"I'm okay," she said. "I think."

"Afraid of small spaces?" he asked simply.

"Since I was a kid," she admitted, hating telling him, of all people.

"Ever fainted before?" he asked, clearly trying to ascertain the extent of her phobia.

"No. But this is the first time I've been stuck in an elevator," she said, managing to dredge up a small smile.

He blinked at her, and she realized that this was probably the first time she'd ever done anything except glare at Jack.

"You have lips."

Her turn to blink. "I beg your pardon?"

He shook his head, made a forget-it gesture in the air with his hand. "Nothing."

She narrowed her eyes. Nothing? She didn't think so. "You said I have lips. What exactly is that supposed to mean?"

He sighed, scanned the roof as though looking for inspiration, then shrugged. All of this upside down, him hovering over her prone body.

"It's just that most of the time when you see me you have no lips," he said.

She stared at him. "I assure you, these are not detachable," she said.

He looked skeptical. "Except when you see me. Then they disappear. Like this." He gave an example, thinning his lips into a prim, ungenerous line.

"I do not do that," she said, even as she felt her mouth assuming the usual tense expression she wore around him.

Damn him.

"You're doing it right now."

She stretched her mouth wide and forced her lips to assume a more relaxed expression.

"Happy?"

"That's better," he said approvingly.

She could feel her lips thinning again at his smug response.

"And there we go again," he observed.

She closed her eyes for a moment. This was insane. She was trapped in an elevator with the company's number-one playboy having a conversation about her lip posture while lying flat on her back.

"Feeling faint again?"

She blinked, recognizing that the fear that had been lapping around her knees had receded to toe-height.

"No. I feel…better."

He looked pleased and a little proud. *He's been distracting me,* she suddenly realized. With that thought came an abrupt awareness that her legs were sprawled out inelegantly and her skirt hiked up on one side. She reached a hand down to rearrange her skirt even as she moved to sit up. A heavy male hand landed in the middle of her chest.

"Take it slow," Jack warned, and even though he'd taken his hand away she could still feel the heat and weight of it as she slowly sat upright.

She glanced around the elevator car. Nothing much had changed since she hit the deck: same brushed metal sides, same industrial carpet base, same small, inadequate light.

She knew he was watching her carefully, and she made an effort to appear calm, biting down on the sensation that there simply wasn't enough room, or air, or anything in this tiny little space….

"Okay, this meditation technique I was telling you about," Jack said suddenly, and she suspected that her rising panic might be more than obvious.

"I'll be okay," she said, wishing it were true. Wishing the doors would simply slide open and let her out.

"Humor me. Close your eyes."

She shook her head stubbornly, and he snorted his exasperation.

"For Pete's sake—just let go for a second. That's all I'm asking," he said. "You can stitch yourself back up nice and tight once we're out of here."

She blinked, more stung by his comment than she'd have thought possible. For a moment there she had forgotten what he thought of her, that he was her enemy. Afraid he'd see her reaction, she closed her eyes obediently.

"Great. Now, starting on your next inhalation, I want you to concentrate on your left nostril. Pretend your right nostril is blocked, and concentrate on breathing up your left nostril to the point between your eyes. And then exhale down your right nostril, again concentrating on the sensation. Then, in through the right, and out through the left. Keep repeating it until you feel better."

His voice was slow and calm, and even though most of her

mind was busy being annoyed and hurt and scared, she managed to focus on her breathing. A few breaths later, and she was really getting into it, feeling the sensation of air traveling up one nostril and down the other. A few minutes of this, and a lovely calm was starting to build inside her. She popped an eye open to find Jack had moved back to his side of the car, and was sitting down, his back to the wall.

"This is pretty good. Thanks."

"Nothing to do with me—thank the ancient yogis of India."

"I will, next time I see them. But in the meantime, I really appreciate it."

She maintained some serious eye contact when she said it, wanting him to know that she acknowledged his help, that she wasn't the kind of person she suspected he thought she was. He simply nodded, once, letting her know her message had been received and understood.

Silence slipped between them, and for the first time she became aware of how stuffy it was becoming. She unbuttoned her suit jacket and shrugged out of it. She regarded it for a moment—it was an expensive suit, a treat she'd bought herself for her birthday last year. Oh, well. Sacrifices had to be made if they were going to be stuck in here for hours on end. She rolled it up and placed it behind her, making a pad to lean against. And then she sat, alternately studying her hands, or the tips of her shoes.

It was like being stuck at all of the most disastrous parties of her teenage years rolled into one. She knew she should say something. In fact, a dozen conversational gambits suggested themselves to her, but they all felt wrong. For starters, she'd been arguing flat out with Jack not ten minutes ago. Ten minutes before that, he'd been handed half her project on a silver platter. And then there was Katherine's lunchtime exposé about Jack's… talents. If that wasn't enough to stifle conversation, Claire didn't know what was.

How she wished her friend had kept her insider knowledge

to herself. The last thing she needed was to develop some stupid awareness of Jack as a man. She was stuck in an elevator with him, for Pete's sake. She didn't want to know that he was great in bed, and had a fantastic body. It was bad enough that she'd been mentally undressing him while they waited for Morgan earlier. She flicked a look across at him, but her glance skittered away again when she saw that his shirt was sticking to his sweat-dampened skin, giving her a very nice idea of just how well muscled and proportioned his chest was. She could even see his dark, flat male nipples through the damp fabric....

This man is your nemesis, she told herself fiercely. *He represents everything you loathe in men.* Determined to get over her stupid preoccupation, she deliberately reminded herself that in addition to having a broad, sexy chest, long, strong fingers and knowing, all-seeing eyes, Jack had stolen her parking spot this morning.

A surge of annoyance raced through her. That was better. Suddenly he was just a man again—an annoying man who regularly operated as a thorn in her professional side. She tapped one shoe toe against the other, then followed with a little heel click as she relived that frustrating moment of finding his car in her space. There was no way he didn't know that was her usual spot. He'd have to be either blind or stupid not to know, and she knew he was neither. So—

"Why did you park in my spot this morning?"

She nearly bit her tongue off as she spoke her thought out loud. Now it was out there, however, and there was nothing for it but to pretend she'd meant to challenge him all along.

"I wasn't aware that we'd been assigned parking spaces. Was there a memo sent around? I must have missed it," he said, and she felt her buttocks clench with annoyance.

A memo. Very funny. Any sexual thoughts she'd had about Mr. Annoying receded at a rapid pace.

"You know exactly what I mean. You usually park over near

the pillar in the middle. And I always park near the stairwell. It's a system, a habit. And it works. So why did you take my spot this morning? And don't tell me you didn't know it was mine, because you gave yourself away when you wagged your keys at me this morning."

"You're not serious? You're really all bunged up over a stupid parking spot?"

She sat up straighter at the disbelieving scorn in his voice.

"It's not the spot, it's the principle. Tell me you didn't do it just to annoy me and I'll drop it. But first you have to look me in the eye and say that pissing me off was not on your agenda when you filched my spot this morning."

He rolled his eyes. "Do you know how juvenile you sound? Let me guess—only child, not used to sharing, right?"

She felt a small, familiar stab of regret, and she pushed it down, back into the place where it belonged.

"Look me in the eye and I'll never mention it again," she dared him.

Jack shook his head as though she'd just suggested he pull his underpants over his head and run around making chicken noises.

She simply raised an eyebrow and waited. Finally he got sick of rolling his eyes and telling her she was unbelievable.

"All right. When I parked my car in that spot this morning, pissing you off did not in any way inform my decision," he said, but at the last minute he broke eye contact and his gaze wandered somewhere over her shoulder.

"Huh! You liar! You big fat liar! You *did* do it to piss me off!" she gasped.

"Okay, you want the truth? You're right—I did do it on purpose. You've parked in that spot every single day for the past year. I thought it was time you had a change."

She nearly swallowed her tongue.

He thought it was time she had a change?

"You thought it was time I had a change? *You*—a man who

hasn't yet grasped the basics of ironing—thought it was time for *me* to have a change?"

She realized her mouth was hanging open and she shut it with an audible click.

"Yeah. I did."

His earlier words came flooding back, something about her stitching herself back up nice and tight. Added to his original assessment of her as prissy, it made a pretty unattractive picture. Suddenly she got it—he thought she was some repressed, neurotic career woman. The type of person who had to have routine, made sure she ate all the five major food groups and was never late paying her bills. The idea so outraged her that she couldn't stop the challenge popping out her mouth.

"You think I'm uptight, don't you?"

Her temper increased another few degrees when he simply raised an eyebrow at her.

"Answer me!" she demanded, and even to her own ears she sounded shrill and shrewish. He waited until the echo from her screech had died before spreading his hands as though presenting a fait accompli.

"I rest my case."

She stared at him, very aware of the pulse beating madly at the base of her neck. She hated that she was behaving this way, hated that he could crank her up so easily. Most of all she hated that just five minutes ago she'd been imagining his bare chest, while he was sitting there thinking she was uptight and repressed.

Across the elevator car, Jack yawned ostentatiously, making a show of checking his watch, all of it meant to imply he was waiting for her next "snappy" comeback. Her temper boiled over and without thinking, she slid off one of her imported Italian leather pumps and slung it across the room at him. Unfortunately, hand-eye coordination had never been her strong suit and it simply bounced harmlessly off the wall next to his head.

It did shock him though, which gave her great satisfaction.

"There's another one where that came from, so keep your stupid male chauvinist generalizations to yourself," she warned him.

She started as her shoe landed in her lap with just enough force behind it to make her realize he was much better at ball sports than her.

"That's how much of a male chauvinist I am. I respect you as an equal so much I know you can take what you dish out," he said, and the complaint about him nearly hurting her died on her lips.

Sneaky bastard.

If her first throw had connected, she could have hurt him, and they both knew it. By giving her back some of what she'd dished out, he was forcing her to acknowledge her own double standards—that it was okay for a woman to hit a man, but not vice versa.

A taut silence stretched between them. She bit her lip to contain the hundred and one explanations, justifications and motivations for the way she lived her life, to prove to him he'd got it wrong, got her wrong. She wanted to tell him that her bedroom at home looked as if a bomb hit it, that she laughed at dirty jokes and that sometimes she even drank her beer straight from the bottle. She wasn't uptight or prissy, she was just very professional at work. And very committed to her training schedule.

Thinking all this through helped take the edge off his words. He was just using some pathetic playboy measuring stick to assess her, and because she didn't match his idea of what a woman should be, he labeled her repressed and uptight. Just because she didn't wear tight miniskirts to work and fall all over herself to giggle at his jokes and wear her cleavage like the latest fashion accessory. Just because she was an achiever, and hardworking, and focused.

The truth was, he was probably scared of her. Threatened. It was typical, really—putting her down so he could build himself up. Almost, she felt better. Almost.

Unbidden, a memory popped up: the dinner she'd had with

her old college friends last month. There had been lots of excited chatter as they caught up on the four years since they'd all last hooked up. Sue had been full of her kids' antics, her husband's achievements and her own dream of selling her handmade quilts on the Internet. Georgia had been excited about her upcoming wedding to the fabulous Greg, as well as being quietly proud of achieving partner in the law firm where she worked. And Claire had shared her achievements with the magazine, and talked about her chances of winning the upcoming statewide triathlon semi-final. She'd gone home that night feeling contented and replete after a good catch-up with her old friends. Now she remembered a look she'd caught Georgia and Sue exchanging. Was it possible they'd felt sorry for "poor Claire" and her empty life? When she'd apologetically left the table to take a quick cell phone call from someone at Hillcrest Hardware, had they talked in hushed tones about her being uptight and dronelike? About how alone she was—*still single*—and how she was filling her empty hours with meaningless exercise?

Suddenly Georgia's suggestion that Claire should meet her friend Tony—a *really amazing, laid-back guy*—took on a whole new light.

Hell, maybe everyone thought she was uptight. Miserable, she hunched down against the wall.

She racked her brain, trying to think of the last time she'd done something spontaneous and impulsive. There'd been that time when she'd snuck in the back way at the movies with her boy-friend…but that was when she'd been sixteen, and didn't really count anyway as she'd practically wet her pants with terror she was so worried about getting caught.

What about that time she and some triathlete friends had gone skinny-dipping after a late night beach party? Except that she had been one of only a few who'd chosen to swim in their underwear instead of going the full skinny….

Okay, all right. What about that crazy hat she'd worn to her best friend Jo's party last year? She'd found it in an old magic shop, a top hat with a bunny jumping out of it. She'd won best prize at Jo's party with that hat.

She suppressed a groan and rested her head in her hands. A hat. She was trying to pin her personality on a stupid novelty hat.

She glared across at the man who'd started all this, focusing all her self-doubt and insecurity on him and his big mouth and insensitive comments. What did he know, anyway? Who was he, sitting there with those stupid sandals and his perfect hair and his designer stubble? Just because all of life's doors had swung open for him as he approached, he wrote her off at a glance. So she wasn't one of the beautiful people, and she wasn't gifted with the sort of charm that had eased his way through life.

She'd always thought those things didn't matter—no, she *knew* they didn't matter. It was who you really were, inside and outside, that counted.

But then she blinked, and she felt a tear run down her cheek. God, she hated Jack Brook.

4

JACK STRETCHED his neck to one side and resisted the urge to check his watch, knowing it would only read five minutes past the last time he'd checked. Time dragged as only time could when you were bored out of your mind and stuck in a small, enclosed space with someone who was obviously thirsting for your blood.

He didn't need to be a mind reader to know that Claire Marsden was mentally sticking pins in his voodoo doll doppelganger right now. He'd intercepted one glance from her that was practically dripping with animosity and got the message straight off. Well, she could stew in it, for all he cared. It wasn't his problem.

Except, he couldn't seem to stop glancing across at her every now and then. Just now she looked sad, infinitely sad, as she contemplated the toes of her shoes. He felt a twinge of guilt about what he'd said. Maybe he shouldn't have been so up-front. People had to have their illusions about themselves, after all. And maybe, in her universe, she was a barrel of laughs, the life and soul of the party. Maybe, in her world, with her friends, she was considered a crazy caper merchant in her conservative suits and sensible, safe car. What was it to him, anyway?

A trickle of sweat ran down his back and he became conscious of the increasing stuffiness of the elevator. Without thinking, he slipped open the buttons on his shirt and flapped the two sides to create a breeze. Across the car, Claire glanced at him and then averted her eyes as though he'd just dropped his pants and announced his intention to have group sex with her favorite aunt.

Uptight, that was what he was talking about.

Almost as though she could hear his thoughts, Claire suddenly stood and toed off her shoes. She looked taller from his position on the floor, and he had a mighty fine view as she reached for the hem of her skirt. Instinctively, she must have sensed this and she began turning toward the wall. She hesitated for a moment, an obvious battle going on inside her.

What was she up to? He wasn't sure, but it beat the hell out of not looking at his watch for entertainment.

She glanced across at him, their eyes locking as she wrangled with her better instincts, and then he saw a muscle move in her jaw as she steeled herself. With great deliberation, she hoisted her skirt up in full view of him, reached for the waistband of her panty hose, and tugged them down. He scored a flash of black underwear—lace? He couldn't be sure—before her skirt dropped down discreetly like the curtain at a peep show. Of their own accord, his eyes followed her hands as she rolled each leg of her panty hose down, down, down to the ground where she stepped out of them daintily. Aware he'd just been staring like a horny adolescent, he snapped his gaze away and contemplated the unmoving floor indicator instead.

He simultaneously became conscious of the fact that his heart rate had just increased and he was sweating a little more. And he almost did a visual double take on himself when he realized that another part of his anatomy hadn't been exactly unmoved by her actions, either.

Wow, he must be really bored. This was Claire Marsden, after all, almost the antithesis of everything he considered attractive in a woman: she was brunette, he preferred blondes; she was serious, he preferred giggles; she was short, he preferred statuesque….

His list of his favorite attributes trickled to a halt as he glanced across at her and caught a flash of extremely toned, tanned thighs as she settled down on the floor.

A tan. Claire Marsden had a tan. His mind boggled. He simply couldn't imagine her in a swimsuit. Another assessing glance at her. Nope, couldn't do it. Her long-sleeved, high-necked, roomy blouse defied his attempts to make it disappear, and, for the life of him, he couldn't come up with a mental image of what her body might be like. Well, apart from kind of square and boxy, like her car and her suits. Given his many years of training and expertise in imagining women naked or in their underwear, he decided this was another point in favor of his argument for boredom being the cause of any…interest his body might have displayed over the panty hose incident. Case closed.

Still, her legs were in pretty good shape… He gave himself a mental slap. What, was he in high school again? Could he perhaps think of something that did not pertain to the bare-legged woman sitting opposite him?

He was surprised how much effort it took for him to keep his gaze away from those legs and that tan. Concentrating fiercely, he imagined the next stage in restoring the antique dining table he was working on as a surprise for his mom for Christmas. It would look great in the corner of her living room, and he knew she would love it. Not that he'd be there to see her reaction. His parents were expecting him to fly home to Sydney, but he would send the table instead. He wasn't up for the big family get-together this year. The gruff sadness of his dad, the empty place at the table, the grief in everyone's eyes when they looked at him and saw Robbie. Jack had enough trouble with his own grief without dealing with the weight of theirs.

For starters, there'd be the inevitable kitchen-sink conversation with his mom as she washed the vegetables for dinner. It was her favorite territory for heart-to-hearts, although in a pinch she'd take whatever venue was offered. She'd fix him with her knowing blue eyes and tell him it had been three years now, and he needed to let go. But she didn't know how it felt. None of them did. Then his dad would invite him to tour the garage to check out his latest power tool acquisitions. And in between explaining the clutch on his new hammer drill, he'd make some kind of reference to Robbie and hope that Jack would open up. But that was never going to happen. His grief was like a rock inside him, granite hard and permanent, a part of him now.

No. He wasn't going home for Christmas this year. He'd find somewhere in the Caribbean instead, and go scuba diving and dally with bikini-clad tourists. His parents would understand. They'd have to.

Across the car, Claire shifted and cleared her throat.

"Do you think we should make contact with Ted again, see how things are going?" she asked.

He checked his watch. They'd been stuck in here for an hour now. He shrugged.

"Guess it couldn't hurt."

Standing, he reached for the phone, quickly becoming aware of how much warmer it was in the top half of the car.

"I'll never bitch about air-conditioning again," he murmured as he waited for Ted to pick up.

"What did you say?"

He glanced at her, caught by the arrested expression on her face.

"Air-conditioning. Usually I don't like it—dries everything out. But I'm beginning to understand why it's a necessary evil in a building this size."

She gaped at him, surprise in every line of her body.

"That was true?" she said, something like awe in her voice.

He frowned. What on earth was she talking about?

"What?"

She seemed to suddenly realize what she'd said. She shrugged, elaborately casual, dropping her eyes to avoid meeting his. "Nothing. Is Ted not answering?"

He frowned, aware that something had just happened there. He was about to pursue it, but Ted chose that moment to pick up the phone.

"Yes, number six?"

"Ted, we were just wondering how things are going? Rescue team in action yet? Any news on when the power might be back?"

"Negative on the power situation. Not expected to be up and running until O–one hundred. Rescue team is in place, and setting up. Estimated extraction time per car—half an hour to an hour."

Jack suppressed a smile at Ted's military-style reporting. This was probably about as exciting as it got in Ted's line of work.

"Right. So, when can we expect to be, uh, extracted?"

"Car six has only two occupants, and, as such, is a low priority at this stage," Ted said evasively.

"How long, Ted?" Jack insisted.

A pause.

"Let me check on that for you. Hold on."

He rolled his eyes.

"Because I have so many other places I can be right now," he muttered.

"What's he saying?" Claire asked, hope in her voice.

"Don't get excited," he warned her just as Ted picked up the receiver at the other end again.

"Best estimate is between three to five hours, Mr. Brook."

"Thanks, Ted. Don't be a stranger."

Jack put the receiver down and turned to face Claire. She was standing now, and he saw how short she was without her high heels on. Tiny, really—she barely came up to his armpits.

"Three hours is the minimum, I'm afraid."

He watched her closely, worried she might flip out again.

"Relax, I'm not going to freak out again," she assured him. "In fact, this little experience may have cured me for good."

They sank down into their opposing corners again, and he made a special effort to avoid looking at her as she settled. It didn't stop him from *imagining* her thighs again, of course, but it gave him the illusion of self-control….

Silence took over again, and he replayed the small moment before Ted had picked up the phone. What had really happened then?

"Before, when I was talking about the air-conditioning, you said something," he prompted, watching her face carefully.

She was all surprise, widening her eyes innocently as she *tried* to remember. Pity she sucked as an actress.

"Did I? I don't remember," she said.

"Right. And you never inhaled, either."

His challenge hung between them for a moment, then she shrugged.

"Fine. You want it, you got it. When you broke up with Judy Gillespie from Accounts, she told everyone about how you made her turn off her air-conditioning when you stayed the night, even though she got heat rash if it got too warm. I didn't believe it at the time."

He just stared at her, his mind numbed for a moment by this revelation. She raised her eyebrows at him, obviously expecting an answer.

"Nice to know my private life is public property," he finally managed to say.

She laughed, one of those short, sharp mocking laughs that women use to cut men off at the knees.

"And what's that supposed to mean?" he squawked. He sounded more than a little defensive, and he forced his shoulders to relax.

"Come on. You've dated more than half the eligible females in the building. You think they don't talk about you, compare notes? You think they don't warn every new woman who joins the company?"

Compare notes? For a moment he felt exposed and vulnerable, and then he reminded himself that he had nothing to be ashamed or worried about. He prided himself on the fact that no woman left his bed unsatisfied. If half the women's magazine complaints he'd read over the years were true, he was doing okay.

"Yeah? What do they say?"

He could see his cockiness got under her skin, and he felt on firmer ground now.

"You want the truth?" she asked, daring him.

How tough could it be? Maybe a few complaints about him breaking up with some of them, but most of his office flings had been just that—two adults satisfying a mutual curiosity. He was confident he could handle a bit of woman-scorned bitterness.

"Sure. Hit me."

Her expression should have warned him. She actually looked wary, almost as though she was afraid of what she was about to say.

"They say that you're fun and adventurous, but as soon as anything serious develops you run scared. Also, that you're afraid of commitment, afraid of feelings and impossible to talk to. That even though you're good in bed, they never really felt as if you were really there with them. That—"

"Okay, thanks, I think I get the drift," he cut in, holding up a hand to stem the tide.

A profound silence settled between them as his brain whirled round and round trying to process, adjust and justify her words.

"You did ask."

She actually sounded guilty.

"Hey, don't worry about me. I think I know enough about human nature to understand where those kind of comments come from."

She didn't say a word, but she didn't need to. After just an hour of one-on-one with her, he was becoming finely attuned to her body language. A shift of a shoulder, the sniff of her nose, and she might as well have shouted at him.

"What? Fine, then. Where do *you* think those sorts of comments come from?" he demanded.

Her eyes measured him for a moment before she answered. He fought the urge to squirm.

"You think they're just bitter because you broke up with them, don't you? And you're probably right, I'm sure that's some of it. But there are plenty of them who aren't bitter, just sad."

He couldn't let that slide by.

"Because I broke their hearts? Let me tell you, I am never anything but honest with women. They all know the score."

"They're not sad because you rejected them, Jack. They're sad because for a man with so much potential there's so little on offer. Katherine told me that she'd never met a man who was more afraid of his feelings in her life. She said there was no point pursuing anything with someone who was never going to let himself go."

If she'd quoted anyone else, he would have been able to blow it off as sour grapes. But Katherine… He'd thought they'd had a real understanding. A short, hot fling, an absolute meeting of minds—two people who enjoyed each other, looking for nothing more than a bit of companionship and human comfort. No strings, no hassles.

He frowned as he remembered that she'd been the one to drift away, the one to call a halt before the usual awkward time when the relationship should move into the next stage but was never going to, thanks to his own fierce commitment to being uncommitted.

He tried to shake off the strange feeling of oppression that settled over him as he considered that Katherine's assessment was right.

Immediately he thought of Robbie, and he hardened himself. So, maybe they were right, maybe he didn't have anything to offer on that level. That was simply the way it was. He'd given it all to Robbie, and he didn't have anything left to share.

His thoughts snapped back to the woman sitting opposite. He now knew why she judged him the way she did. A spark of anger sprang to life inside him. She *had* judged him, big-time. She'd listened to office gossip and rumor, and she'd formed her own opinions of him, and decided he was lacking. Hence all that talk about him being the action-man about the office. Hence her thinly veiled contempt for him.

Vaguely, he was aware of how quickly his temper had gone from zero to one hundred.

"And let me tell you, that air-conditioning story is bull. Judy never told me she got heat rash. I said I didn't like the air-conditioning, sure, but she never said she'd get a rash if it wasn't on."

He felt small and stupid as soon as he'd said it. What was he defending himself to Claire for, anyway?

"I told you, I didn't believe it at the time."

Now she was being understanding. She even looked like she was regretting what she'd said to him. He didn't like it that she suddenly seemed to have the upper hand. He was much more comfortable with their normal status quo, where he disdained her repression and she expressed her contempt for his freewheeling attitude.

"I'm surprised you haven't got better things to do than sit around gossiping about me all day. Workload must be a bit lighter than I remember it down in Homes," he snipped.

She rolled her eyes at him. "Spare me. You think I want to stand around and talk about the office stud all day? It's impossible not to pick this stuff up. It's like osmosis."

He sat up straight, bristling.

"I'd prefer it if you didn't call me that, thank you," he found himself saying stiffly.

Can you hear yourself? Now who's uptight?

"I beg your pardon?"

Her incredulity was clear. But he'd drawn a line in the sand, and he had to stand by it.

"Office stud. I find it offensive. How would you like it if I called you the town bike?"

She surprised him by laughing out loud. "Go ahead, see if I object."

For a moment he stared at her, taking in the transformation in her face when she laughed. She looked…nice. Approachable. Attractive.

All just a sugarcoating for her inner shrew, he reminded himself. *Don't forget that. Never forget that.*

CLAIRE PLUCKED at the neck of her heavy silk shirt, trying to get some air between it and her hot skin. Why hadn't she picked a cotton shirt this morning? She pictured the litter of clothes all over her bedroom and declined to comment on the grounds that she already knew why: she was a pig, and she needed to do the laundry.

She spared a glance for the office stud opposite. Now that she knew he hated being called that she'd make sure to slip it into as many conversations as possible. See how he liked being pigeonholed.

His face was closed, quiet, but she could feel his vulnerability. She'd shocked him with her revelations about what his exes and flings thought of him, there was no question. She felt a vague guilt at having spilled so many beans on him. For the first time, she questioned some of the stories she'd heard about him, and some of her value judgments. So, he dated a lot. Was that so bad? And then she remembered twenty-three-year-old Fiona from Legal, her heart-shaped face blotched with tears as she explained how Jack had made an excuse for not staying the night in her bed after they'd *done it*. He'd ended their short romance the next day at lunchtime.

He didn't deserve sympathy. Fiona deserved sympathy—as well as a good kick in the wazoo for letting herself be suckered in by Mr. Silvertongue.

Claire was considering trying to take a nap when movement caught her eye and she looked up to see Jack shrugging out of his shirt.

"What?" he asked defensively. "You want me to ask permission or something?"

What a jerk.

"You can take it all off for all I care," she told him stiffly.

He raised an eyebrow, obviously doubting her. "Feel free to take off whatever you want, too," he said idly, the glint of his eyes giving away the fact that he was mocking her.

She could feel her lips disappearing again and she forced

them to behave before he noticed. He was *sooooo* annoying. She'd truly never met anyone else who could get her so riled so quickly.

What was it about him that got up her nose so much? She studied him through her eyelashes, trying to work it out, and found her gaze drawn to the broad expanse of hairy chest he'd just exposed. All that huntin'-shootin'-fishin' obviously agreed with him because he was in pretty good shape, his pecs nicely defined, his stomach flat, the hint of strong abdominal muscles showing as he breathed. She knew from experience how tough it was to get lean enough to see those ab muscles, and she reassessed her notion of his sybaritic lifestyle. Okay, maybe he wasn't out wining and dining every night. Every second night, probably. He'd need to, just to fit in all his office romances.

It was nice to see a bit of hair on a chest, she decided idly, feeling drowsy in the stuffy atmosphere. Most male triathletes made a habit of waxing their chests to gain a little less drag in the water, and it had been a while since she'd seen a nicely haired male chest. He had a good tan, too, and the hairs looked healthy and dark and springy against his brown skin. Her eyes followed the trail of hair as it narrowed over those taut abs of his until it was just a promise as it disappeared altogether beneath the waistband of his pants. She found herself staring at a point just below his waistband, wondering again about exactly how gifted Jack was supposed to be….

"Can I help you with anything?"

She started out of her daze, suddenly realizing she was staring unashamedly at his crotch. Flaming embarrassment swept up her body in a burning wave, and she was powerless to do anything about it.

She was a good blusher, she'd learned to her detriment over the years. Even her ears glowed when she was totally humiliated. Like now. She felt almost incandescent with heat and she resolutely kept her gaze away from his as she fought to control her own body.

But the more she thought about it, the more she seemed to sizzle and glow, and she tried not to think about how guilty and pathetic she must seem to him.

At last the flush seemed to dissipate, but it left her feeling unbearably hot. Her blouse felt sticky, confining and oppressive. Briefly, she flicked an envious gaze across at Jack's bare chest, only to be caught in the knowing beam of his blue eyes.

A small residual flood of color washed her cheeks as she tore her gaze from him. He was laughing at her! Why, oh, why had she stared at him like that? Was she so hard up that the first bit of decent male action to come her way sent her into zombie-drool mode? Even if that male action was attached to the world's most annoying personality?

She flapped her blouse ineffectually, succeeding only in moving around more hot air.

"Take it off."

It was a dare, not a suggestion. A challenge, and the expression on his handsome, smug face told her that he knew she wouldn't take him up on it.

Her hands were on her buttons before she could think. One button, two, three. And he just sat there, his lips quirked to one side, apparently vastly amused by everything she did. She tried to remember which bra she'd put on this morning. *Not the stretched-out one with the pills and the no-nonsense, no-trim elastic. Please, not that one.* She wanted so badly to peek beneath her blouse to check, but then he'd know. The man was psychic. He'd definitely know.

Four buttons, only three to go now. A patch of black bra showed in her peripheral vision. Maybe if she glanced down casually, just as though she wasn't sure where the next button was? She risked it, sighing with relief when she saw her unexciting but presentable plain black bra. It was a simple, smooth cup style that was more about good design and elegance than frills and see-through bits, and she was damn grateful that she'd put it on this morning. More confident now, she slipped the last button loose, tugged her blouse open and began working on the buttons on her cuff.

He was still watching her, she could feel it. Trying to pay her back for gawking at him earlier, obviously. She could handle it. It was just like wearing a crop top during training, and while she wasn't into showing off her body and flashing it around, she was quietly confident that it was in good shape.

She shrugged the damp silk from her shoulders and slid it off her arms as nonchalantly as possible. Determined to prove she was not the uptight prude he thought she was, she sighed loudly.

"You're right, that's much better."

She even circled her shoulders around, as if she was warming up for a swim. His eyes were glued to her, and she was loving it.

"Yep, that's definitely better," she repeated, mostly just to annoy him.

Smiling sweetly at him, she spread her shirt out on the scratchy industrial carpet, then rerolled her jacket into a tighter pillow.

"I'm going to see if I can get some sleep," she told him blithely.

He was still just sitting there, an unreadable expression on his face. Probably didn't know what to say now that she'd proved him wrong. Typical.

5

JACK CONCENTRATED fiercely on the idea of puppies frolicking in fresh snow. He conjured up an image of a fresh alpine stream, clear water burbling over mossy rocks. He even resorted to imagining a photograph of his grandmother, the one where she was looking very stern and schoolmarmish. None of it stopped the rest of his body from whooping it up over the sight of Claire Marsden in a bra. Whoever designed her suits and blouses was a master of disguise, that was for sure. The CIA should be talking to that guy. Hollywood should be using him instead of all that computer gimmickry they were all so fond of these days.

Because Claire was hot, and Jack had never even suspected it. From the soft, even tan across her chest and torso to the gentle rise of her breasts from one of the sexiest bras he'd ever seen, she was a revelation.

Hot. Damn hot.

It wasn't just that she was built—although that had a lot to do with it. Her breasts were definitely on the generous side, definitely a very nice handful. And it wasn't just the ripple of highly toned muscles on her stomach—although that was pretty damn good, also. It was more that it all fit together so well. She was small but perfect, and generous in all the areas she should be.

In short, hot.

His body seemed determined to worship that hotness in its own very special way, and no matter what he told himself—*she's a shrew, she hates me, she probably irons her underwear*—he was unable to stop it. Thank God he was sitting with his knees drawn up and his back against the wall. Thank God she'd decided to go to sleep, and that she'd rolled to face the wall. Perhaps with those breasts out of his immediate view he could get a grip on himself. Figuratively speaking.

It was a bit disconcerting, really. Not since the uncertain years of adolescence had his body been so at odds with his mind. Because she just wasn't his type. And they didn't get along, at all. And, if he was being completely honest, she annoyed him. She was bossy, and defensive, and too quick with a smart comeback. Too much trouble, all round. So it was very strange to be annoyed and irritated by her, but also wonder what color her nipples were, and if she tasted as good as she looked.

Very confusing. Disturbing, even.

He checked his watch, then returned to studying her back. Damn if she didn't have a nice back, too—smooth, unblemished skin, nicely shaped vertebrae—

He pulled himself up short. *Nicely shaped vertebrae?* Was he going insane?

A little desperate, he cast a glance around his brushed steel cell and then suddenly got it. Stockholm Syndrome, or whatever it was called. That thing where the people were held hostage and started to identify with, and like, and sympathize with their captors. That's exactly what was happening here—Stockholm Syndrome! She was his captor, and he was starting to sympathize with her. Once he was restored to his normal environment, nature would reassert itself.

Relief washed over him. Good old science—always there with an explanation for everything.

Following her example, he decided to try for some shut-eye. If they were going to be in here for another five or so hours, sleeping some of it off was a really good idea. Of course, he wasn't feeling very snoozy, but if she could sleep, so could he.

He lay down, quickly becoming aware that the carpet was the

prickly, unforgiving type that was designed to survive a nuclear holocaust. He sat up and spread out his shirt like a towel at the beach. Once on his back, he stared at the ceiling, his hand automatically sliding down and across his belly and beneath the waistband of his pants to find the long scar that cut low across his stomach and around his side. He couldn't feel the familiar ridge under his fingers without thinking of Robbie, and he made a point of thinking of Robbie every day. It was the least he could do because it was all he had left.

People always talked about feeling as though they'd lost a part of themselves when a loved one dies, but Jack knew with rock-solid certainty that he'd lost the best part of himself when his twin brother succumbed to kidney disease.

Even though it had been three years now, he couldn't think about it without tasting the bitterness and anger again. It should have been him. Robbie had always been smarter, stronger, funnier. Robbie had been the one who'd chosen medicine, while Jack had been just bumming around, trying to find something that held his interest. If fate had to take someone, it should have been him.

"It's so hot in here."

It was almost a relief to be distracted from his own thoughts.

"Not much we can do about it," he replied, knowing it would annoy her. After all, it was what he was good at.

"Imagine if Robinson Crusoe had that attitude. We need to be innovative, think outside the box. Or the elevator, I guess."

His eyes still on the ceiling, he shook his head minutely in exasperation.

"This isn't *Gilligan's Island,* Mary Ann. We can't just bake a batch of coconut cream pies and wait for the Professor to find a way to get us back home."

"Ginger, if you don't mind."

"What?"

"Ginger. I always wanted to be Ginger, not Mary Ann."

That surprised him so much that he turned to look at her and found she was on her back also, and was looking at him. Without his permission, his eyes flickered down to her chest. Her full breasts strained at the fabric of her bra now that she was on her back, and he felt a definite tightening in his groin. What was it with him and those breasts? He'd seen great breasts before. And he'd see them again. Plenty of them, in matched sets. These weren't the only breasts in the world. So why was he suddenly so hot to see them and touch them and taste them?

"Ginger was a redhead," he said, forcing himself to concentrate on the subject at hand.

"So? On the inside, maybe I'm a redhead." Her eyes dared him to contradict her.

"Hey, it's your split personality, not mine."

"Exactly."

Their old friend silence crept back into the elevator. Jack bent his legs and rested one ankle on the opposite knee, for something to do. And to try and distract himself from thinking about her breasts.

He bet they were firm. Firm, and sensitive. He bet if he took her nipple into his mouth, she'd cry out. He had a flash of Claire's eyes clouded with desire, her lids slightly lowered, her mouth open and wet.

"Who would you have been?" she asked suddenly.

"What?" he asked, almost starting with guilt.

"On the island. Who would you have been?" she repeated.

"Mr. Howell."

"You're kidding? Ugh!"

She sounded genuinely disgusted. He had a natural skill in this area, it seemed.

"Come on, think about it. He was rich, he managed to work it so everyone else did everything for him and he still had his main squeeze with him on the island."

She laughed. Another surprise—she had a sense of humor.

"You're the most practical playboy I've ever met," she said.

She was smiling again, her face just an arm's length or so away. It was almost like being in a very large bed, him on one side, her on the other. His body had things to say about the idea of being in bed with this new-improved, friendly, black-bra-wearing Claire Marsden, and he ruthlessly changed the subject. And kept his eyes fixed firmly on her face.

"Okay, Desert Island Top Five," he announced.

"I don't think we need to pretend we're trapped on a desert island, do you?"

She had a point.

"Trapped in an Elevator Top Five, then. All-time favorite movies," he said.

She shot him a look, seemed about to say something, hesitated and then spat it out anyway.

"I thought you were angry with me."

He shrugged. "You want to spend another five hours arguing or sitting here glaring at each other?"

"Good point. Okay. Top five movies. The first one is easy—*The Big Sleep,* definitely."

He couldn't help himself. "Surprise, surprise."

"Excuse me?"

"Everyone picks a black-and-white movie, preferably something with Bogie in it. Gives you street cred."

"But it's my favorite movie!" She sounded outraged.

He made sure there was a heavy dose of doubt in his tone. "Of course it is."

"Wait till it's your turn," she warned him. "Second movie would be *When Harry Met Sally.* I can watch it over and over and it's still clever and funny."

"So predictable, not even worth commenting on."

She threw him an exasperated look.

"You know what's predictable? You not agreeing with a word I say. I swear if I said the sky was blue, you'd disagree with me just for the sake of it."

"Depends."

She snorted with exasperation this time, and he found he was enjoying needling her like this.

"On what, pray tell?"

"If it was nighttime or daytime."

She half laughed at his lame joke, and he tried not to notice how pretty she looked and the way her breasts jiggled invitingly. *Those damn breasts!*

"Okay, third movie. Getting tougher now. Have to have a comedy in there, otherwise it's just way too boring."

She stretched one leg in the air, waggling it around aimlessly as she considered her options. Jack's eyes followed the hem of her skirt as it slid down to reveal more of her thighs. As if her breasts weren't doing him enough damage. But it was impossible to keep his eyes from the sleek, tanned firmness of her legs. She really had great legs. They looked strong, and flexible. Like they could grip a man hard around the hips as he—

"There's Something About Mary!" she said suddenly, and he threw a mental bucket of cold water on himself.

She was watching for his reaction, so he simply looked thoughtful, although he was really quietly impressed. And not a little surprised. The lady didn't mind a good dose of potty humor. Not what he would have picked from her at all. Great breasts, great thighs and fond of puerile comedy. If they hadn't been stuck in this elevator together, she would have taken those secrets to her grave.

"Hmm."

She shook her head and continued. "Fourth movie… Something I can watch again and again, but is still fun… *Con Air.*"

He nearly sat up he was so shocked. "No way!"

"What?"

"You do not like *Con Air.*"

"I think I do."

"No way."

"Jack, I think I know if I like a movie or not. And I want *Con Air* as my number four."

"But—"

She was lying on her side now, leaning on her elbow. Her hand on her face made her cheek squish up, making her look almost cherubic and more than a little naughty as her eyes sparkled across at him.

"What's your problem?" she demanded.

"I was going to have *Con Air,*" he admitted.

"Really?"

"Yeah."

"Wow. Something in common. Scary," she said.

"You're telling me."

"Don't worry, I'm sure it'll never happen again. And you can have *Con Air* on your list, too."

"But then we'll have two copies of the same movie."

She almost laughed at his little gag, the twisting of her lips giving it away.

"Fifth and last movie…*The Wizard of Oz.*"

"The singing munchkins? The wicked witch of the west? You're not watching that in my elevator, I can tell you."

She was getting better at not reacting to his jibes.

"Your turn."

She sat up, rubbing her hands together with exaggerated anticipation, obviously looking forward to shooting him down in flames. He found himself admiring the dancing light in her eyes, and the way she leaned forward slightly, ready to take him on. The fact that her new position also gave him a great look at her cleavage was irrelevant. Completely irrelevant.

"Number one—*His Girl Friday,* with Cary Grant and Rosalind Russell."

He enjoyed watching her indignation grow.

"But you picked on me for having a black-and-white movie!"

"That's just me, I guess. I'm a contrary bastard."

Her eyes narrowed and she made an encouraging motion with her hand. "Keep 'em coming," she prodded him.

"Number two—*Rocky*. But only the first one. I hate sequels."

She rolled her eyes. "Typical. Macho movie about men being manly."

"You finished?"

She smiled brightly. "Not really. But it'll keep."

Boy, she was pretty cute when she smiled. He caught the thought and gave himself a mental slap. This Stockholm Syndrome thing was getting out of control. It was one thing to admire breasts and thighs, but thinking that someone was cute when she smiled was moving into dangerous territory.

"Three—*Raiders of the Lost Ark*."

"Sad, but predictable. Let me guess—you have a secret craving to travel the world, wear hats and be heroic?"

He made a point of looking very patient and forbearing. "Four—*Blade Runner*. Best sci-fi movie ever made."

His look dared her to disagree, but she just shrugged.

"I didn't mind it," she admitted.

"You didn't *mind* it? I s'pose you think the Colorado River is a nice little stream?"

"Number five, cough it up," she said, wisely ignoring his baiting.

He took his time, making a big show of being very thoughtful. She didn't buy any of it, but sat with a look that very plainly said, "I know you're about to be very annoying, and I'm ready for it."

"It's tough, very tough. A couple of good contenders. But I'm going to have to go with *Porkies*."

She managed to maintain a very creditable poker face. "That surprises me. You don't think you're overlooking some of the excellent work in *Revenge of the Nerds?* And let's not forget that seminal classic, *Bikini Shop*."

He played along. "I did consider *Bikini Shop* briefly, but I decided it was too derivative. Plus there are more boob jokes in *Porkies.*"

"Of course. I stand corrected."

The subterranean grumble of his unfed stomach hijacked the rest of the conversation. In the small confines of the lift, it seemed inordinately loud and he found himself staring at his own belly.

"Sorry. I guess I'm hungry."

He hauled himself upright, aware that the waistband on his cargo pants had dropped a little with the movement. He patted his complaining stomach, then watched her eyes follow the motion. A small frown appeared between her eyebrows, just for a second, and when he glanced down he realized his scar was showing. Sighing, he braced himself for the inevitable "Wow, how'd you get that?"

It never came. Instead, she turned to her handbag and started rummaging through it. He watched, perplexed, as her frustration grew until she finally just emptied the whole bag out onto the elevator floor. An enormous array of crap spilled out over the carpeted space between them, successfully distracting him from the increasingly hypnotic power her breasts seemed to hold over him. He surveyed the array of purse-rubble disbelievingly. This jumble of junk belonged to Claire "Crisply Ironed" Marsden?

"Wow. You got a spare Learjet or helicopter in there we could use?" he asked as she began pawing through the debris.

"Trust me, it's all very valuable and necessary," she said, intent on her search.

He leaned forward to pick up a child-size water pistol.

"Very handy with some clients, I'm sure." For an insane moment, he wondered what she would do if he squirted her in the breasts with the gun, and then offered to lick the water off. Before he could so much as tighten his finger on the trigger, she reached up and took the water pistol out of his hand.

"It's my godchild's. Here they are!"

Triumphant, she held aloft a packet of mints as though she'd just found the Holy Grail itself. Very pleased with herself, she offered the pack to him.

"Help yourself," she encouraged him.

She was very proud of her mints, and he didn't have the heart to tell her they wouldn't put a dint in his appetite. So he peeled off a mint, more than a little bemused by this new side to Claire. This godmother-to-someone's-child, lover-of-action-movies, owner-of-a-junk-filled-handbag Claire. It didn't gel with his previous ideas of her at all. If he'd thought about her at all—and he hadn't, thanks to the boxy suits and the efficient way she had of cutting him dead each time she saw him—he'd have imagined her in one of those minimalist white apartments with everything arranged in tidy, geometric patterns. He'd have bet she made her bed with hospital corners, watched worthy historical dramas on public access TV and listened to opera in the original Italian.

Now he knew that at least some of those assumptions were wrong. For starters, those ugly suits of hers had been hiding an Aladdin's cave of earthy delights—exhibit *A* being those spectacular breasts, followed closely by the firm silkiness of her thighs. Plus she had a sense of humor. And she was messy, despite appearances, if her handbag was anything to go by.

Floundering and uncomfortable with this new, far more sexy, human take on Claire Marsden, he tried gamely to cling to his old misconceptions.

"Do you like opera?" he asked, wanting to be able to retreat to familiar, predictable territory. He made a bet with himself that she even knew Italian and had a season's pass.

She poked out her tongue playfully, something he'd never seen her do before. Who was this woman? And what had she done with the real Claire Marsden?

"Hate it. And I know you're going to call me a philistine now and tell me how beautiful and moving it is, but I'm just not into it, okay? So sue me," she said.

She was sucking on a mint, the action puckering her lips a little, and he had to drag his fascinated gaze away from her mouth to respond.

"Bunch of incomprehensible screaming, if you ask me," he said vaguely, beginning to worry again about Stockholm Syndrome.

What if there was no cure? What if he got out of here and this feeling he was beginning to get—this sort of defrosting feeling coupled with a definite physical interest—what if it didn't go away? He didn't want to get to know Claire. He certainly didn't want to *like* her, after all the crap she'd piled on him today. But the niggling thought that perhaps he'd misjudged her kept shouting for attention at the back of his mind. That, and the fact that he had an erection that was becoming increasingly difficult to hide.

HE WAS QUITE entertaining, really. But then, if you were going to be a successful playboy, she guessed you'd have to have a fair line in being charming and entertaining. Stock in trade, really.

The movie talk had been fun. And she'd been surprised by how many movies they'd both liked. Of course, she'd expected him to be prejudiced against *The Wizard of Oz*. Only the truly good and insightful understood how great a movie it was.

She finished stuffing all her bits back into her handbag, and settled once again into her lolling position on the floor. It was getting really warm now. All their talking hadn't helped things any, sucking up all the available air. For a moment, she wondered about how airtight the lift was and imagined running out of oxygen. The walls seemed to frown in over her and all of a sudden she was finding it difficult to breathe again.

"Claire?"

When she didn't answer, he nudged her foot with his, forcing her to look up. He tapped his nose, and she nodded as she remembered to follow his technique.

After a minute or so of nostril breathing, she felt the tension in her chest easing.

"Thanks."

"The nose knows."

She flapped a hand in front of her face, desperate for a bit of fresh air.

"It's just so stuffy in here. Now I know how microwave popcorn feels."

He shot her a look that plainly told her to quit whining.

"I know, talking about it doesn't make it any better. But surely we could pry the doors open a bit, get some fresh air in?" she suggested hopefully.

But he just shook his head.

"Sadly, I left my pry bar at home this morning. Unless you have one in your bag?"

She huffed at him impatiently, already reassessing the good will he'd generated during their movie banter. Amusing he might be, but scratch the surface and he had a solid core of annoying just waiting to be expressed.

Pushing the wet curls back from her forehead, she rolled her head back on her jacket-pillow and stared at the ceiling. This waiting was bringing new meaning to the word *bored*. She remembered seeing some pages from the local paper stuffed in amongst the rubble in her handbag, and she reached for them in desperation. Never had reports on the local school fair or lost dogs seemed so enticing. She unfolded the pages and realized with disappointment that they were from the classifieds section of the paper. She remembered now that she'd grabbed them because she needed to arrange for a plumber to look at her dishwasher.

Still, desperate times bred desperate measures, and she found herself perusing every single ad. Plumbers, gardeners, electricians. She found three spelling mistakes and about a million grammatical errors. But who was counting, right? She was about to flip the page when she saw a small photo ad for a car dealership. The flash of red paintwork caught her eye and she squinted, trying to work out what make of car it was in the tiny photo. A Mustang! And a convertible, if she wasn't mistaken. Excellent.

She settled back to enjoy a good ten minutes' worth of fantasizing about owning a red Mustang convertible. By the time she'd killed a quarter of an hour imagining herself cruising around with the roof off, her practical side was beginning to assert itself. The roof probably leaked, parts would be expensive, and there was nothing at all wrong with her late-model sedan. Besides, she wasn't a red convertible kind of girl. Sighing, she rolled the pages back up and put them to one side.

"Could I...?" Jack asked, eyeing the paper greedily.

"It's pretty dull stuff—but you're welcome to it." She flipped the paper over to his side of the elevator and tried to think of something else to occupy herself. She'd seen an interview with a guy who'd been held captive by South American freedom fighters once. He'd been locked up on his own for months and months, and he claimed he held on to his sanity and his purpose by having imaginary conversations with his family, acting out both sides in his cell.

She slid a sideways look at the man lying beside her. She'd never hear the last of it if she had an imaginary conversation with her father. The idea was so absurd, she almost laughed out loud. Not the least because she couldn't begin to imagine what a real conversation with her father might be like. The familiar feeling of anger twined with rejection stole into her belly, and she steeled herself against it. Harry was not a good investment for hopes, emotions and dreams.

The sound of Jack's stomach growling saved her from further naval gazing.

"Have another mint," she said, tossing the roll of candy across to him.

She returned to her mindless study of the elevator's ceiling, her eyes sliding across the familiar configuration of emergency light, utility access and the ubiquitous expanse of brushed steel.

She allowed her heavy eyelids to close, then sat up straight, inspiration energizing her.

"The utility access!" she crowed excitedly, scrambling to her feet.

Jack was staring up at her from his prone position, a shiny scrap of foil from the mint roll curled on his chest.

"Huh?"

"The utility access, in the ceiling. We can open it, let some of this hot air out. Surely there must be cooler air out there in the elevator shaft?" she said.

He liked the idea, she could tell by the way his eyes darkened to a deeper blue.

"Smart thinking, 99," he said in a really appalling Maxwell Smart voice.

"As an impressionist, you make a great elevator mechanic," she told him playfully, then caught herself up short.

Was she *flirting* with Jack Brook? She looked at him out of the corners of her eyes as he eased himself to his feet and brushed himself off.

She had to admit, she'd come a long way from her initial impression of him. He wasn't as big a swine as she'd always imagined. In fact, he was quite kind, she decided, remembering his deft handling of her claustrophobia. Admitting that Jack Brook was not the devil incarnate she'd always classified him as was like opening herself up to the suggestion that the world might not be flat: too much was predicated on all her previous assumptions and judgments. Their whole past relationship was founded on the basis that she didn't like him, he didn't like her, and never the twain should meet.

"Hinges at one end, catch at the other. I don't think we'll even need that crowbar of yours," Jack was saying, and she snapped her focus back to the current issue and away from the scary thought that more than just her claustrophobia was getting a workout in here.

The ceiling was quite high, she suddenly realized.

"Can you reach it?" she wondered out loud, and he gave her a pitying look.

"I think we'll be fine," he said confidently.

But when he reached casually for the catch they both quickly saw that even standing on the very tips of his toes, he could only just get his fingertips on the mechanism. He didn't so much as glance at her once he realized he'd spoken too soon, so she leaned against the side of the lift and watched as he jumped up and down futilely a few times, his hands flailing uselessly against the catch each time he made contact with the roof. He finally gave up and turned to her, a warning expression writ large on his face.

"Don't say a word."

"Did I even open my mouth?" she defended herself.

"You don't need to. Come on, I'll give you a boost."

She hung back a moment, not really sure how to go about this.

"Come on," he said impatiently.

She stepped forward slowly, deeply reluctant to be in physical contact with him. It just didn't seem…right.

"What should I—" she began, but Jack was already bending forward to grab her around the waist and lift her toward the ceiling. At about the same time her feet left the ground she became aware of his face pressed into her cleavage, and she stared down at his dark head, appalled.

6

"COME ON, I'm not Atlas, for Pete's sake," Jack grumbled, his words muffled by her breasts.

Oh, boy. A thousand and one sensations skittered along her nerve ends and she closed her eyes against the assault. His stubbled cheeks rasped faintly against her skin, and she could feel his breath, hot and moist, with each impatient word. His arms were two strong bands around her body, his chest against her belly, her legs hanging a foot or two off the ground.

He made an exasperated noise, and she belatedly looked toward the ceiling, but it was miles away.

"This isn't going to work," she told him, and the tension in his arms relaxed abruptly and she dropped back down to earth, sliding along his body all the way.

Her heart was beating out of control, and somewhere deep inside, something long-ignored awoke and lifted its head to look around drowsily. *Desire.* His skin had been hot and smooth and hard, and it had been way, way too long since she'd been held by a man. She didn't need to look down at herself to know that through the mere act of talking into her cleavage, Jack had managed to turn her nipples into two embarrassing declarations of arousal.

And for my next act, I shall implode with humiliation, she thought as she hurriedly crossed her arms to hide her traitorous nipples.

How on earth could her body react to Jack like that? It was as though she was suddenly being held captive by some strange alien force. *Come on,* she told her body, *the guy's a poster boy for everything I dislike in a man. We're complete opposites. We have nothing in common. He doesn't even like me. How can you do this to me?*

But her body wasn't taking any calls. Instead, it was resolutely hanging on to the memory of his flesh against hers, his hands splayed firmly across her back, the prickle of his whiskers on her breasts.

"Okay, I'm sure you've got plenty of smart ideas," Jack said, his own arms crossed over his chest now.

Ideas? Boy, did she have ideas. Instantly, her out-of-control body imagined a dozen X-rated scenarios, all of them involving Jack naked, ready and willing. She fought the urge to cross her legs and squirm.

"Um. Sure. You could…you could go down on all fours and I could stand on your back," she finally managed to say past the lump of misguided lust in her throat.

He uncrossed his arms, and she watched, almost hypnotized, as the muscles along his chest and stomach rippled in reaction. *Cool. Make him do it again,* her body urged.

"I know it would probably satisfy some deep inner need for you, but you are not standing on my back to reach for the sky," Jack countered.

"Okay, okay." Desperately she searched around for another idea, anything, before he realized she was acting like a crazy woman, her eyes practically falling out of her head ogling him.

"What about a shoulder ride?" she suggested.

He gave it a moment's thought, then shrugged his lack of objection to the idea. She tried not to get too absorbed in following the ripple of muscle this caused down his body. But she must have been staring, because the next thing she noticed he was giving her a really weird look. The kind of look you give a dog when you think it might have rabies. She almost lifted a hand to check she wasn't foaming at the mouth.

"You want to do this now?" he asked warily.

"Sure."

Concentrate, she warned herself. *Concentrate, and we'll write off the last five minutes as some extremely strange reaction to oxygen deprivation.*

He squatted in front of her, and she froze a moment, staring at his well-muscled back. He really was in fine shape. Most guys who had desk jobs as he did would have let themselves go soft and run to fat, but he either had a truly stunning metabolism, or a natural affection for exercise. For the first time, she understood how Fiona from Legal, and Katherine and all those other women were unable to resist him. He was just plain sexy. Tall, and strong, and handsome, and...

"What are you waiting for, an engraved invitation?" he asked.

She blinked. *What is wrong with me?*

"Let's just get this over with," he suggested, impatience oozing from every pore as he swiveled his head around to look at her.

Slapping every inappropriate thought to one side, she hitched her skirt around her waist, stepped toward him, and slung her left leg over his shoulder. She almost jumped when he immediately enclosed her ankle in a warm, firm grip.

"Other leg, come on," he ordered, leaning forward a little so she could find her balance.

She obediently slid her other leg over his shoulder, and before she could brace herself he'd locked her other ankle in place and was surging to his feet. For a scary moment she teetered on his shoulders, and instinctively she grasped at his head for balance.

His hair was thick and wavy, and she ploughed her fingers into it as she searched for a grip.

"Yow!" he howled, and she immediately loosened her death grip.

"Sorry."

"Can you reach it?" he asked, and she tried not to register the rasp of his stubbly cheek against the tender skin of her inner thighs.

Jack Brook with his face against her thighs? She had trouble even processing the thought, let alone the sensation. Forcing herself to focus on the matter at hand, she studied the catch on the cover a moment, then flicked it open. Tentative, she pushed the cover upward, but it gave way readily, flopping open to clang loudly on the elevator car's roof.

"Done!" she said with satisfaction.

Taking advantage of the opportunity, she shoved a hand up into the opening.

"Much cooler out there. Hopefully it'll make a difference in here," she reported.

She was about to suggest he put her down when he slid his hands up her shins and over her knees to grasp her firmly just above each knee. And then he began jiggling from side to side, causing her to renew her death grip on his hair.

"What are you doing?" she squeaked.

She'd instinctively clamped her thighs tighter around his neck as soon as her balance was in jeopardy, and she could actually *feel* him grin.

"Victory dance," he said, and she held her breath as he twirled them both around in a little circle.

What a goof. But she couldn't help smiling: ridiculous as it seemed, opening a stupid utility hatch felt like an achievement. She smiled as she felt the shifting of his strong shoulders beneath her as he danced a few more steps, and even managed a little bongo-drum accompaniment on his head.

She was still smiling when he announced he was going to let her down. He crouched low, and she maneuvered first one then the other leg off his shoulders, hastily pulling her skirt back down where it belonged before he turned around to face her, a jubilant smile on his face.

He's beautiful. She tried to squelch the thought, to pretend it had never entered her mind.

"Feels better already. Way to go, team," he said, holding his hand up in the classic high-five position.

She slapped his open palm, all the while trying to forget the feel of his hands on her thighs. And his hands sliding up her legs. And his face against her breasts.

Stop it, stop it, stop it.

This had to be caused by some weird combination of claustrophobia and lack of oxygen. That's all this hyperawareness of him was. Hell, they probably did laboratory experiments like this all the time. At NASA or something. The Effects of Enforced Intimacy on Hardworking Female Executives. Or something like that.

Find something else to think about. Her frazzled brain sought desperately for a diversion as they both returned to their opposite sides of the elevator. She found her eyes tracking to the scar that slashed across his abdomen, and before she knew it the words had popped out. "That's a pretty decent scar you've got there."

She wished the words back the moment they were uttered. *How rude! How invasive and nosy and rude!* Wondering what sort of a kisser he was was better than being nosy. She could tell by the way his eyes dropped to the floor that he was thinking of some way to palm her off—which she deserved—and she rushed into speech again.

"Ignore me. I didn't mean to say that. I think I'm oxygen deprived," she blathered.

She could feel him watching her, assessing her, and then he shook his head minutely as though shaking something off.

"It's okay. It's pretty noticeable. Someone once told me it looked like a shark had attacked me."

She made a disbelieving noise.

"Hardly. Unless sharks are getting medical training these days."

He smiled a little, just a quirk of one side of his mouth. Then he said, "I donated a kidney to someone. My brother."

She could tell it had cost him a lot to say it. And she could feel the weight of a long and sad story dragging the words down. This was not a story with a happy ending, she sensed.

"That's pretty incredible. And scary. Your brother was lucky you were a match," she offered, deeply uncertain about what to say.

He'd crossed his arms across his chest, the classic "locked off" signal in body language. She didn't need it to know she was deep in territory he normally kept very private.

"Yeah. Well, not really. We were twins. Perfect match."

His face was so carefully blank, but she could tell. There was a lot of anger and pain pent up in this man, and she guessed why.

"He died?" There was no other explanation for Jack referring to his brother in the past tense.

"Yeah."

"What was his name?"

"Robbie. Or Robert, according to Mom."

She was totally at sea. And she just knew she was going to say the wrong thing any second now. But she also knew she was being given a very privileged insight into Jack's life. No one at work had ever gossiped about this stuff, and she knew absolutely that he didn't talk about it. Normally.

But this wasn't a normal situation, as she was beginning to appreciate more and more with each passing moment.

"I don't have any brothers or sisters," she volunteered. "I can't imagine what it would be like to lose someone so close you. Especially a twin. Was he a writer like you?"

He barked out a bitter little laugh, and she could see so clearly the anger inside him.

I bet you blame the world for Robbie being gone. I bet you blame God, Buddha, modern medicine and anyone else who comes to mind. But most of all, I bet you blame yourself.

"He was a doctor. A pediatrician. He just loved kids, and even though it cut him up when he couldn't help someone, he always stayed in there, fighting away. But them's the breaks, right? Fate, luck, destiny. Whatever. The doctor dies, the writer lives."

The words could have peeled paint. She just let the anger wash over her. It wasn't for her, anyway.

He ran a hand over his face, almost as though he was removing a mask or wiping something away.

"It doesn't matter."

Of course, it did. In fact, it was probably what shaped his life. She cocked her head to one side, considering. All her preconceptions, and observations, and judgments reorganized themselves and settled into a new pattern to accommodate this information, and she suddenly understood why Jack shied away from commitment, and drove a sports car, and skated by on the surface of things: he already had a world of pain to deal with, and he just didn't have the room, or the time, or the inclination to handle any more.

She blinked, and it was as if she was seeing him with new eyes. The lines around his mouth weren't all from smiling and laughing. The spark in those bright blue eyes of his was as much about covering as it was about charming. She felt an enormous desire to cross the space between them and take him in her arms. She actually swallowed at the intensity of it. She wanted to cradle his head on her breast, and soothe him, and tell him that one day he would be reconciled to his brother's death, but first he had to let himself feel it.

It was a bone-deep longing, and it was so powerful she actually sat on her hands, in case they reached out toward him of their own accord. Jack would be horrified if she offered him comfort. In fact, she knew with a crystal-clear prescience that he was going to regret ever having said a word once they were out of this elevator.

And what could she offer him, anyway? They weren't even friends. They didn't even like each other.

But despite all that, she found herself talking. Perhaps because she couldn't offer him comfort, she instead offered him something of herself so he wouldn't feel so exposed.

"I'm the biggest regret of my father's life. He wanted a boy so badly, but my mom died just after I was born. I was his one chance. So Harry tried to turn me into a boy for a while, but I hated the mountains, and I was too scared of falling when he took me climbing. And then one time he had to turn back from an expedition he'd taken me on because I got sick. And that was it. He just kind of…wrote me off."

They were the most honest and painful words she'd ever spoken. In fact, she wondered if she'd even thought any of this through so clearly before. Even as the words tumbled out, she understood why she never acknowledged this stuff: it was like taking her skin off and letting the world see all her fears and ugly places.

Her mind swung around to that damned unanswered invitation for her father to watch her compete at the finals in just over two weeks' time. Why had she put herself in a position where he could write her off yet again?

Jack was looking at her strangely. "Your dad's not Harry Marsden, the explorer?" he asked, amazed.

She simply nodded.

"I never knew," he said.

"I don't exactly have T-shirts made up."

He studied her face appraisingly. "You look like him."

"Not enough, apparently."

A silence, then Jack said, "Thanks."

He held her eyes, and it was the most open and honest contact they'd ever shared. It felt like a fresh start. She smiled, and he smiled back, and all of a sudden all of her lust rolled over her, but this time it was tinged with a desire to ease his unhappiness, to do something without considering the merits and worrying about the consequences.

Could he read her thoughts? It seemed he could, because his eyes dropped to her breasts. She liked that, liked that he'd noticed her that way. She felt her heart skip into overdrive. Had his eyes darkened? Was she getting the message from him that she thought she was? She wasn't sure. Doubt assailed her. He was so much more experienced than her. For Pete's sake, he'd slept with half the building. What would he want with her?

"Claire."

It was an invitation. Wasn't it? She wanted it to be. Very badly. Because she hadn't been this hot for someone for a long time. But he was just sitting there, opposite her. What was he thinking? Should she…should she make the first move? Tentative, she leaned forward, placing a hand in front of herself so she could lean even farther across the space that separated her from him.

His eyes were locked on hers, and she could see something come to life in them. He looked hungry and sexy and very intent. He leaned forward. There was an excruciating moment, a moment between breaths, where she waited for his lips to touch hers. And then they were kissing, tentatively at first, no other part of their bodies touching. His lips were warm, and he tasted of mints and she felt a shimmering *something* unfolding inside her. By some unspoken agreement, they both broke the kiss to stop and stare at each other for a moment. His eyes were very close to hers, and she felt as though she was drowning in the myriad blues of his irises. And then, as if drawn by gravity or magnetism or some force outside of themselves, they came together again. This time she felt a twist of excitement spiral through her as his tongue darted into her mouth for the first time, and then, all of a sudden, it was as though something had exploded inside her. She couldn't get a enough of him, and she sensed the same greedy hunger in him as he reached for her.

His hands swept up her arms, and a shower of heat followed. She clutched at him, off balance, drunk with lust. His skin was smooth and firm, perfectly sculpted over planes and rounds of muscle. She explored him feverishly, measuring the breadth of his shoulders, racing her fingers through the silky hair on his chest. His hands were tracing her face, running down her neck, brushing across the sensitive skin of her upper chest. She sucked in her breath as his hands slid smoothly down and onto her breasts, his thumbs finding her already-erect nipples through the satin of her bra. He plucked at her breasts with a firm, sure touch, and an answering note sounded deep in her belly and she felt herself tighten. As amazing as it seemed, she wanted him. She wanted him right now.

Jack was nibbling his way down her neck now, and she let out a small, excited moan as he brushed her bra straps down her arms and took one of her taut, aching nipples into his mouth. She bucked instinctively, unable to control the urge to push up into something as a storm of sensation raced through her body. His mouth was so hot, and his tongue so quick and firm…

"Jack, Jack—" she whimpered, unable to tell him exactly what it was she was feeling, or what she wanted.

He simply lifted his head to grin wolfishly at her, his eyes shining with desire, and she found herself grinning back at him, glorying in the absolute need that gripped them both. Bold, she reached for the closure on his pants, even as he pushed her skirt up and pressed a palm against the moist heat between her thighs. She could feel how ready she was, was almost embarrassed by how ready she was, but it only seemed to increase his desire as he helped her push his cargo pants down over his hips. His erection was hard and proud against his belly and she reached for it with sure hands. He was big and beautiful and she wanted him inside her as soon as was humanly possible.

He must have been a mind reader, because no sooner had she wrapped her fingers around his shaft than he was dragging her panties off impatiently. She got lost in space and time for a beat as he swept a knowing hand across her mound, his thumb finding the sensitive nub of her clitoris unerringly. A shaft of pure desire rippled through her, and while she was still recovering, he slid his fingers down to the slippery folds of her inner lips. She clenched in anticipation of his penetration, but he held back as his thumb continued to work her clitoris.

"You want me inside you?" he whispered huskily at her ear, his finger circling her slickness now, teasing.

In answer she raised her hand to her mouth and licked her

palm, her eyes holding his as she slid it back between their bodies and slicked her wet hand up and down his shaft, her thumb gliding across the delicate velvet of the head of his penis before sliding down again. As she had before him, he shuddered in response, and she felt a surge of feminine satisfaction as a muscle clenched in his jaw.

"You want to be inside me?" she whispered back, increasing the tempo of her movements, loving the feel of him in her hand.

Suddenly he twisted away from her, grabbing his wallet, finding a condom and putting it on, all before she could protest his leaving. Then she was on her back and he was positioned between her legs, his body weight supported by his formidable arms as he hung above her. There was a split second of thrilling anticipation and then he was plunging inside her, filling her completely, so much so that the base of his shaft ground satisfyingly into her swollen clitoris as he buried his length in her.

She gasped her surprise—it was never, ever this good for her. It was as though he'd been made for her, as though she'd been waiting for this moment for so long that she was on a hair trigger, ready to explode. And then Jack was stroking in and out of her, each sweep driving her crazy. She clutched at his back, his butt, his shoulders, pushed her hips up to him, rocked away, gasped out his name. Straining, wanting all of him, she chased the growing tension inside herself, loving the harsh sound of his breathing as he rode her. Just when she thought it couldn't get any better, he reached a hand between them and found her clitoris again, swollen with need, ready for him. One, two, three passes of his deft thumb and the tension inside her broke in a cascading wave and she was falling apart in his arms, her muscles clenching around him, her hips bucking, his name on her lips.

It was as though he'd been waiting for her, because no sooner had she dissolved around him than he'd stiffened with his own orgasm, shuddering into her, his face pressed against her neck.

For a long time afterward there was nothing but the sound of their harsh breathing. Jack lay on top of her, still inside her, and she tried to pull the fragmented parts of herself back together.

She felt…consumed. There was no other word for it. Utterly, completely consumed by the magic they'd just created together. The best sex she'd ever had. Ever. Hands down. The most amazing sensual experience of her life.

At last Jack raised his head, and their eyes met. He looked as blown away as she felt, his blue eyes incredulous as he looked deeply into hers. A smile softened the curve of his mouth, and he opened his mouth to speak—

The phone rang. They both stiffened. The phone sounded again, and Jack shrugged ruefully.

"I have to get that."

"I know."

He withdrew and rolled away from her in one smooth move, and the sudden loss of skin contact made her feel inexplicably cold and alone. Flushed, she watched as Jack reached for the phone.

"Yeah?" he said, one hand coming up to push the hair back from his forehead. The action hid his face from her momentarily, just when it was very important that she be able to see his face, his reaction. His body seemed tight, defensive. What was he thinking? His hand dropped down at last, and she studied him closely.

He glanced across at her, his eyes flicking down from her face to her still-sprawling body. Suddenly she felt exposed, spread out in front of him with her skirt rucked up, her bra pulled down. With trembling hands she tugged her bra into place and slid her panties on before pushing her skirt down, listening all the while to the cryptic, monosyllabic conversation Jack was having with whomever was on the other end of the phone.

"Great, thanks," Jack said, at last placing the receiver back on the hook.

He reached for his boxers before he spoke.

"Ted estimates about five minutes," he reported, and she nodded her understanding.

It was over. They were about to be rescued, and their enforced encounter was at an end. Neither of them said anything as they shuffled into the rest of their clothes. Claire didn't know what to think or feel. Somewhere, deep in the back of her mind, she was shocked at what had just happened. She felt as though she was swimming in treacle as she tried to analyze her feelings. It had been so good…so intense. She'd never felt anything close to the kind of passion she'd just experienced.

But now it was over, and it was back to the real world, to office politics and maneuvering and executive meetings ad infinitum.

She shot a glance across at Jack, trying to work out what he was thinking. They'd just had the wildest, most uninhibited sex in all the world. Was he feeling as shell-shocked and shaky and amazed as she was?

He glanced across at her, his expression unreadable, and her spirits sagged. Of course he wasn't. She was kidding herself. He was probably thrilled to be getting out of here. As she should be. What had just happened had been an aberration, an insane one-off that would never have happened outside of this very particular set of circumstances. Hell, it probably happened to him every second day—this was the office stud they were talking about, after all.

"They're winching us to the nearest floor," Jack explained belatedly.

They'd pry the doors open there, and then they would go their separate ways. This moment, this incredible, challenging time-out from the normal world, would be gone forever.

Claire found herself reaching into her bag, grabbing one of her business cards and a pen. Urgent, she scribbled her home number on it, not thinking, just feeling. She'd just shared the most extraordinary physical connection with this man. It had been more than great sex—surely she hadn't imagined it? Surely, he,

too, must think that there was something undiscovered here—
something with so much potential that it would be crazy to walk
away from it?

"Here," she said softly, and when he met her eyes she saw
Jack's confusion and amazement and she felt a surge of confidence as she slid the card into his hand.

"My home number," she said huskily.

Before he could respond, the elevator lurched up several feet,
and the sound of screeching metal filled the car. Slowly the doors
slid open to reveal a crowd of onlookers and rescue workers.

She and Jack were swept up by their various assistants and
colleagues, and before she knew it, Jack was heading one way
down the hall, and she was being ushered another. She glanced
over her shoulder once, but he was listening to something his assistant was saying and he didn't see her.

It was almost as though it all had never happened. But she remembered the look in his eyes as she slid the card into his hand.

He'll call, she assured herself fiercely. *He has to after what
just happened between us….*

JACK PROPPED Claire's business card on his hall bureau as soon
as he got home, liking the invitation and potential contained in
that small piece of card. It was a no-brainer, really. He'd just had
the best sex of his life, and she'd told him to call her. What man
wouldn't want more of what he'd just tasted?

Still, there was an uneasy feeling in the pit of his stomach,
and it wasn't until he was shucking his clothes in the bathroom
and stepping into the shower that he realized he couldn't possibly call. Because there'd been that moment afterward, when he'd
still been inside her. He'd looked down into her eyes and seen
so much vulnerability and surprise and amazement in her face.
And he'd felt a weird surge of protectiveness and tenderness that
had nothing to do with hot sex or physical chemistry….

Every survival instinct he possessed screamed "Run." And he

was used to following those instincts—not for nothing had he remained single all these years.

The bottom line was that Claire Marsden intrigued him and attracted him in a way that made him feel distinctly uncomfortable, and every instinct told him that that was very dangerous to his status quo, hot sex or no hot sex.

Even as he acknowledged this and accepted it, his body protested. How could he walk away from something so hot and intense? His hands curved reflexively as he remembered the weight of her breasts, and he closed his eyes for a brief moment and groaned with frustration as he remembered the taste of her and the smell of her and the feel of her. She'd been pure desire, uninhibited, wild. Tight and wet and so responsive, her body seemingly attuned to his naturally.

He made a disgusted noise as he registered that he was now fully erect and aching for round two with Claire Marsden. Brutal, he switched the shower to cold and stood with gritted teeth under the punishing spray for a full five minutes, trying to purge the memory of her silky skin.

Because it wasn't just about animal attraction. There was more—that wasn't the only thing that drew him. He admired her bravery in holding up under the ridiculous conditions Morgan Beck had imposed on her. He thought she was funny and clever. And for some reason, he'd told her about his brother when he hadn't spoken about Robbie with anyone—family included—for more than a year.

And that was the scary part. Because even now he was wondering if she was okay, wondering what she was thinking. Perhaps she was in the shower, too....

He stepped from the shower and swiped at the water on his chest and arms with a towel. He couldn't call her, it was as simple as that. Claire had to be off-limits. He liked her, and he couldn't raise her expectations. He wasn't a forever kind of guy, and she was a forever kind of woman. It was never a good combination, and he didn't want to hurt her.

And she scares the crap out of you, an honest little voice chimed deep inside him.

That didn't mean he wasn't tempted, however, when he passed that taunting white rectangle an hour later. Fortuitously, he had his portable phone in hand, and he almost dialed her number. Almost.

It was exactly because he wanted to call her so much that he didn't. There was something different about Claire, about the way she made him think and feel. And it was distinctly unsettling.

No, she was best set to one side and avoided. Too much at stake, too hard. Too daunting and demanding. Repressing a small pang, he tossed out her card.

He decided to organize some assignments that would take him out of the office, but then the memory of his recent meeting with Morgan rang in his mind. Damn it, he was expected to be on hand to play macho man for old man Hillcrest. How was he supposed to resist having his way with Claire when he was supposed to be her associate editor?

He ran a frustrated hand through his hair, catching sight of himself in the mirror as he paced. He paused, leaned in to look himself in the eye. Could he trust himself to work side by side with Claire and not give in to the impulse to touch her?

Not a chance. Unless certain parts of his body came with an off switch he hadn't been aware of previously, the only way to stop himself from making a fatal mistake was to pull back as far as he could go.

It wasn't as if it was a tough decision, anyway. In many respects, getting to see Claire a lot was the only attractive aspect of the whole arrangement Morgan had proposed.

Who in their right mind would want to be the token anything on a project? Not Jack Brook, that was for sure. He'd been too taken by surprise to put up a good fight when Morgan had sprung the idea on him and Claire today, but he wasn't hot to put his hand up for credit on a project he'd had no involvement with. It was unethical, and unfair to Claire.

He padded into the bedroom, his decision made. First thing tomorrow he'd call Beck and make his position clear.

CLAIRE FORCED HERSELF to go for a run, despite the burning urge to sit by the phone and will it to ring. She had an answering machine, and it would take a message if Jack called while she was out. She only had to repeat this to herself five times before she could force herself out the front door of her apartment. All other considerations aside, she had only two more weeks of training until the finals and she hadn't done all this hard work to blow it off because she and Jack Brook had had wild animal sex in the elevator at work. Every time she thought about it she battled a wash of embarrassment, closely followed by a rush of desire. She was going crazy pacing around her apartment, second-guessing herself, staring at the phone.

So now she was ignoring the burning muscles in her thighs and pushing herself harder up the hill. She forced herself to go past the car dealership where she usually turned for home, then stopped in her tracks for a beat as she caught sight of a red Mustang convertible holding a place of pride in the center of the yard. *Well, hello, old friend,* she thought, remembering the ad that had kept her entertained for a full fifteen minutes that afternoon. The car looked much better in real life—shiny and red and fun. Pity she wasn't a convertible kind of girl, she mused a little wistfully as she pushed on up another hill, her mind almost immediately reverting to its default position of wondering what Jack was doing right now, if he'd called, and what would happen next.

For a second she allowed her mind to flash back to the elevator. A surge of heat swept through her. She could almost feel his mouth on her skin again, feel the wet thrill of his tongue on her breasts. Her body tightened at the memory, and she realized that in a split second she'd undone all the good work her nice, mind-numbing run had done. She briefly considered pushing herself to do another few miles in an attempt to regain some control over her wayward body, but she suspected it would be futile. She'd tasted Jack Brook, and she wanted more—it was as simple as that.

How could a few hours change the way she felt about someone so much? How could she go from thinking someone was incredibly egotistical, cocky and overly confident to wondering if he lay awake at night thinking about his brother?

She had no answers, but she knew that something had shifted forever in that elevator car, and even though in her more rational moments she regretted having given in to the crazy urge to make love to him, and then giving him her home number, she was also glad.

When she got home and saw that no one had called she had to quell a wash of disappointment.

Maybe he had something on this evening.

Like a date.

With another woman.

She pushed the thought away all through her quick post-run shower. There was no way he could turn his back on what had happened between them in the lift. It had been so hot, so intense—surely he was aching to explore what they'd discovered in the same way that she was? Or even, on a more basic level, come back for seconds?

Determined to believe, Claire dumped the entire contents of her underwear drawer onto her bed and searched through the tangle of silk, satin and cotton until she found her best set of underwear—a deep aubergine lace bra with matching panties, very elegant but understatedly sexy at the same time.

She pulled them on, sprayed her wrists and cleavage with her favorite perfume, and spent some time creating a smoky, seductive look with eyeliner and mascara. Surveying herself in her bathroom mirror, she felt a surge of confidence. She was ready for him, ready to pick up where they left off, ready to explore the animal attraction that had sprung to life between them.

The sound of her doorbell buzzing jolted her out of her lust-filled musings, and she dragged on a pair of jeans and a handy T-shirt before padding her way to the door.

"I'm coming," she called out as she approached the door, then felt a little kick of adrenaline in her belly as she wondered if it possibly could be Jack on the other side of the door.

Her breath caught in her throat as she reached for the door handle. Maybe he'd looked up her address, and hadn't bothered with phoning because he just hadn't been able to put her out of his mind, the way she hadn't been able to put him out of hers…. Between her legs, her muscles tightened and she clenched her thighs together, reveling in the thrill of desire that raced through her. If Jack was here, in a few minutes she'd have him inside her again, the firm, delicious pressure of his erection satisfying the ache that had already started at the centre of her.

"Hey there! I've brought champagne and chocolate, and I want to hear all the details," Katherine said as she breezed past Claire.

Claire tried to ignore the leaden disappointment that had replaced the buzz in her blood. Forcing a smile, she went to fetch champagne glasses.

"So, three hours in a lift with Jack Brook. I want a blow-by-blow account of every minute," Katherine said, rubbing her hands together in mock anticipation.

Claire stared at her friend for a horrified second, praying that she wouldn't blush. The last thing she wanted was to dissect what had happened with Katherine—or anyone, for that matter. This was between Claire and Jack, and she wanted to find out exactly what it was before letting the world know anything at all.

Painfully aware that she probably looked as though she'd just sat on a cactus, Claire attempted to shrug nonchalantly. "Nothing happened. We argued, then we talked, then we got rescued. It was an exercise in boredom more than anything."

Katherine sipped her champagne, her pale blue eyes sharp as they quizzed Claire over the rim of the glass. Claire fought the urge to squirm guiltily.

"You realize that half the building was on fire with jealousy? Stuck in the elevator with Jack—my God, it's a whole new genre of erotic fantasy."

Claire took a huge gulp of champagne and wrenched her eyes away from the damned phone.

"Sorry to disappoint, but it was hot and airless and dull. Very dull."

Unbidden, an image of Jack sliding his pants down his hips popped into her mind, the length of him proud and hard and ready for action. She felt a blush stealing into her cheeks, and she shot a look at her friend. Fortunately, Katherine was studying the lid of the chocolate box, trying to make a selection.

"I like the hard-centered ones—something to chew on," she muttered as she plucked her selection from the box.

Claire took advantage of Katherine's distraction to broaden the conversation.

"Do you know who else was trapped? Anyone we know?" she asked, sitting back in her chair and pretending she had all the time in the world.

All the while her mind was working overtime—what if Jack called while Katherine was here? What if he wanted to come over, and she couldn't get rid of Katherine?

"One of the lifts had ten women in it. Can you imagine? Apparently they took turns hyperventilating and freaking out."

Claire forced a smile.

"Wow."

Her eyes strayed to the wall clock over Katherine's shoulder. Eight o'clock. When was Jack going to call?

Two and a half hours later, and she knew the answer to that question: never. Katherine was full of champagne and chocolate, and Claire had sore cheek muscles from forcing smiles she didn't believe in.

Moaning about having eaten too much, Katherine finally rubbed her stomach one last time and called it a night. Claire closed the door on her and turned to contemplate her empty apartment.

It was 10:30. So much for her hot night. The empty champagne bottle and almost-empty chocolate box mocked her.

She felt heavy, a bit dazed. Vaguely she realized she felt humiliated. She dragged off her clothes, and moved into her en suite to prepare for bed. The sight of herself decked out in her very best underwear was a slap in the face.

What had she been thinking, for Pete's sake?

And what on earth had she been thinking when she tore her clothes off and climbed Jack Brook like a cat on a curtain? Had she lost all semblance of self-respect in that tiny, airless space? Suddenly she groaned as she recalled pressing her business card into his hand. She never did stuff like that, ever. All of her life she'd been careful, modest, demure. And now she'd just blotted her copybook spectacularly.

Worst of all, while she'd been sitting here all night, wrapped up in some fantasy world where hot sex equaled spiritual meaning, he'd probably been thinking of the hot blonde he was no doubt taking to dinner.

She stared at her reflection for a beat, forcing herself to face the brutal facts. A sophisticated guy like Jack—he knew the rules. He knew that what had happened in the elevator was a one-off, never to be repeated. He must have been amazed when she gave him her number. She closed her eyes against the wash of humiliation that threatened.

Why, oh, why had she been so stupid?

By the time she'd cleansed and brushed and flossed and crawled into bed, she'd convinced herself it was good riddance to bad rubbish. The man had disaster written all over him. He was a self-confessed commitaphobe with a very short attention span. He was so closed off and protected, she doubted he'd ever let an emotion stronger than pleasure or satisfaction breach his defenses.

Yes, the physical attraction between them had been hot, but that wasn't the only thing in life, right? It certainly wasn't worth humiliating herself over, that was for sure.

Nope, she was very, very lucky he'd never taken her up on her stupid, ill-informed, ill-considered, impulsive, deranged invitation. She thumped her pillow decisively, determined to put the whole experience behind her.

But then she started thinking about work tomorrow. About seeing Jack for the first time. About looking at him, and remembering, and knowing. Her eyes popped open and she stared at the ceiling.

What if he told someone else at work what had happened? What if she walked into the building tomorrow and people stopped talking as she approached? She had a vivid picture of her business card taped up in the men's restroom—*For a good time, call Claire Marsden.*

For a moment she felt sick to her stomach, but then reason returned. She didn't know how she knew, but she knew—absolutely—that Jack wouldn't tell anyone what had happened between them while they were trapped. The realization calmed her. No matter what else she'd managed to misinterpret between them, she knew that she had this right—what happened in the elevator, stayed in the elevator.

And long might it stay that way. Relieved, she rolled onto her side and willed herself to sleep. She was just drifting off when she remembered that she was supposed to work with Jack for the next few weeks or however long Beck deemed it was necessary to salve old man Hillcrest's ego.

That was something of a stumbling block. An Everest-size stumbling block. She sat bolt-upright in bed. If she was honest, she wanted very badly to tell Morgan Beck to shove his stupid arrangement. But that wasn't the way she worked. What Beck had asked from her was wrong, and unfair, and she was still deeply ashamed about sitting through that initial meeting with Jack and Beck without making her feelings clear.

But innate self-honesty forced her to admit that even if she'd had prior warning about the agenda of the meeting, she wouldn't have kicked up a fuss. Her philosophy in her working life had always been to give her bosses what they asked for. While there were limits to this philosophy—both moral and legal—it had held her in good stead until now.

But did her ethos stretch to swallowing this blatant vote of no confidence without voicing an objection?

She shook her head in her silent apartment.

"No. I don't have to just lie down and take it," she told her darkened bedroom.

Tomorrow she'd let him know in no uncertain terms that she wouldn't accept Jack on her project.

She tried to imagine herself stalking into her boss's office and laying her cards confidently on the table. And failed. Miserably.

Perhaps if she really talked it through with Beck, they could come up with another solution. As grown adults, seeing eye to eye. Discussing the issues rationally.

This felt much more her style. It still made her feel nervous, but it was doable.

Of course, sticking up for herself would mean that she didn't have to work with Jack anymore, too. How convenient. She could simply ignore him for a few weeks in the car park and editorial meetings and the elevator, just like old times, and pretty soon he'd forget that Claire Marsden had ever torn his clothes off and had sex with him.

And that was absolutely what she wanted.

So, she was decided. First thing tomorrow, she'd make an appointment with Morgan and see if she could regain control of her life. It should have been the last thing she thought of before she drifted off to sleep. But instead, just as she gave herself up to sleep, memories from the elevator came back to haunt her. The firm, knowing pressure of his clever fingers as he circled her swollen wetness; the sweet, addictive tug of desire between her thighs as he suckled on her breasts; the deep satisfaction of having all of him inside her, and his strongly muscled body tense and passionate above hers.

She moaned frustratedly into the pillow and rolled over. But the memories kept on coming: the wet velvet sweep of his tongue on her neck. That first thrill as he pressed the palm of his hand against her damp mound. The rising excitement as they taunted each other with what they really wanted....

Claire thumped a pillow with her fist. "Get out of my head, Jack Brook," she muttered.

But it was no good. She was too turned on to sleep. Despite every rational reason for disliking the man, her body had other ideas.

She rolled over again, her nipples brushing against the cotton of her sheets. They wanted Jack's touch, the heat of his tongue and mouth, and they sat tight and proud, waiting for something that was never going to happen. Claire slid a hand over each breast and pressed them into her chest.

Stop it, she urged her body. *Forget him.*

But instead of calming her overheated body, the pressure triggered a pulse of desire between her legs. Claire's eyes flickered open, and she glared at the ceiling.

"Damn you," she told an absent Jack Brook.

Then she gave in to her desire and slid a hand down the length of her body and between her legs. Closing her eyes as she slicked a finger over her own wetness, she imagined it was Jack touching her, and that any moment now she would feel the warm, velvet nudge of his erection against her outer folds. As her body thrummed tighter and tighter with tension, she remembered the taste of Jack, and the strength of Jack, and the feeling of being filled by him. The way he'd tugged so tightly on her nipples. The way he'd run his hands over her body as though he couldn't get enough. The feel of him beneath her hands, the hard, smooth power of his body.

She gasped out her release, her orgasm an echo of the one

she'd shared with him earlier. It should have been the end of it, but she lay awake for a long time afterward, angry with herself for wanting a man who clearly didn't want her.

7

"HE SAID WHAT?"

Claire stared at Morgan Beck, aware that she'd crouched forward in her chair and placed one hand imperiously on his desk.

"You heard me, Claire. I know this whole arrangement sticks in your craw but I flatter myself that after thirty years in the business I know what I'm doing. I don't care what sort of a disagreement you and Jack have had, but you're just going to have to sort it out."

Morgan was cranky, his voice hard and his posture aggressive as he glared across the desk at her.

"I just don't understand it. Yesterday the two of you seemed to be in perfect accord, and now this," he said.

You have no idea, she thought. And she tried very hard to get the image of her and Jack doing the wild thing on the elevator floor out of her mind as she held her boss's eye. Now was not the time to get turned on by rogue memories. This was her career she was talking about here. Jack and his perfect penis could go hang as far as she was concerned.

"Wait a minute—are you telling me that Jack Brook has refused to work with me?" she asked, still trying to get a grip on this concept.

"Have I been talking to myself for the last five minutes, Claire?"

She fought back the impulsive urge to tell him to keep his pants on, then blanched that any such urge had even crossed her mind. What was wrong with her? When she'd first entered his office, she'd found him seated with his feet up on his desk. She'd had trouble hiding her smile at his aggressive, I'm-the-boss posture. She'd got control of her unruly mouth, but she'd been appalled at herself—when had she ever felt anything but respect and a faint tinge of fear for Morgan Beck?

"Mr. Beck, this comes as a complete shock to me," she assured him now, neatly sidestepping the fact that she'd come to work this morning with the single-minded intention of finagling her boss into removing Jack from her project. It was one thing for her to reject him…

"Really?"

The single word dripped disbelief. She found herself glaring back at her boss, her temper well and truly firing on all cylinders now. Before she could stop herself, hot and angry words were pouring out.

"Yes, really. Do you truly think I'm so pathetic that I'd get him to do my dirty work for me? I assure you, if I didn't want to work with Jack Brook I'd let you know in no uncertain terms."

Okay, that was a lie, because she'd spent the whole night trying to come up with subtle, nonaggressive ways of suggesting Jack be reassigned. But Morgan didn't seem to understand that she'd spoken out of anger—his eyebrows were rising up, his expression one of pure shock. She tried to remember if she'd ever come close to speaking to him like this before.

No, probably not. Mostly she concentrated on smiling and sounding competent and on top of things when she met with him. Mostly she'd been way too aware of his power and her own desire to win his approval.

But today she was too annoyed to remember any of that. Today she was outraged that not only had Jack left her dangling all night, he'd also pipped her at the post on the work front, too. To top things off, this balding little man in front of her thought she was so wimpy that she'd use someone else as her front man.

"You know, I was prepared to wear all this rubbish about placating Mr. Hillcrest, but I'm beginning to wonder if I wouldn't be better off stepping aside and letting you simply replace me with someone better qualified," she heard herself saying silkily.

Good grief. Give a girl a little rush of power to the head, and suddenly she was the Genghis Khan of office politics!

Morgan had gone pale, but she bit down on the apology that sprang to her lips the moment she uttered her challenge. Instinctively, she understood that much hung in the balance right now.

He needs me, she reminded herself. *It's my project, and he needs me, and he should remember that.*

Except this wasn't her style at all. She was a worker, a quiet achiever. A nonconfronter. And she was going to lose her job. She was going to be escorted from the building by mustached security guards, and she was never going to get another job in publishing. She'd get kicked out of her apartment, and her car would be repossessed, and before she knew it she'd be coming up with catchy names for bad adult movies for a living, titles such as *Ordinary Peepholes* and *Free Willy.* Although, technically, that was no different from the original even if it had a new interpretation. Maybe she'd be no good at this new career, either. Ah— *Three Willy!* Maybe she'd survive, then...

To her surprise, Beck suddenly laughed, pushing himself back from his desk and loosening his tie a little.

"Okay, Claire. Point taken. I apologize."

Her vision of her career in pornography receded and she hoped she wasn't looking as surprised as she felt. *He was apologizing.* Her boss was apologizing. She'd answered back and threatened him and he hadn't had her escorted from the building. A slow feeling of elation bubbled into her blood. She felt... strong. Powerful. Valued.

All these years she'd been toeing the line and working hard and waiting to be acknowledged—and all it took was a bit of mouthing off to get some respect.

"Look, it's a crappy situation we've put you in. I acknowledge that. But if you can swallow your pride for just a few months, I assure you we'll get Jack off your back as soon as we can. And your…flexibility won't be forgotten."

A little drunk with her newly discovered power, she toyed with the idea of making another startling, bold statement. Something such as "I hate that tie," or perhaps, "For God's sake, do something about what's left of your hair," while she was on a roll, but she was wise enough to know when to quit.

"I'm not happy," was what she actually said. "But I'll do it, because I've put too much into *Welcome Home* to walk away."

Her boss nodded.

"Understood. The board knows that magazine is all yours, Claire, don't ever underestimate that. We consider you one of our most talented executives."

She managed to contain the grin that was threatening to stretch her mouth wide. Respect *and* praise, all because she'd lost her temper.

"I trust I can leave it with you to sort things out with Jack?" her boss was saying, shuffling papers around on his desk.

She recognized the meeting was over and she stood quickly.

"I'll take care of it," she assured him.

Once out of Beck's hallowed office, her focus swung around to consider Jack and his sneakery. It was a testament to how angry she was that she didn't even think twice about getting in the elevator and taking it down to Jack's level. She was concentrating instead on what she was going to say to him. He'd gone behind her back and tried to undermine her on her own project. She conveniently swept to one side the thought that she had been about to do the same to him. And she couldn't even bear to think that while she'd been sitting home all night agonizing over why he hadn't called, he'd been planning to approach Beck and get out of working with her.

She steamed out of the elevator and surveyed the open-plan office space confronting her, quickly spotting Jack's assistant at a desk in the corner. Her eyes narrowed as she considered the fact that Jack enjoyed a corner office. One more reason to find him incredibly annoying.

Linda looked up with a smile when Claire stopped at her desk.

"I need to see Jack," she said baldly.

Linda's smile faded as she registered Claire's mood, and Claire immediately felt like a jerk.

Perhaps she was taking this pushy thing a little too far....

"I mean—how are you?" she tried again, summoning a smile of her own.

"Fine. Jack's not in right now," Linda volunteered.

She shifted her gaze to the closed door over Linda's shoulder.

"Is that a he's-in-but-doesn't-want-to-be-disturbed not in, or a real not in?" she asked, trying to keep the annoyance out of her voice.

"He's in a meeting down in Sports," Linda expanded.

"Right." Claire stood for a moment, tapping her toe as she considered her options. She could leave a message for him, go back down to her office, get stuck into some work.

She shook her head. She could just imagine him screwing up any message she left him and tossing it in the bin as he headed out to an executive racquetball game.

"I'll wait," she announced suddenly. Then she pointed to Jack's office door. "In there."

Linda opened her mouth to protest, but Claire sailed past and into Jack's inner sanctum. She did a quick survey of the room, aware that Linda had followed her and was standing behind her.

"Can I get you a coffee while you wait?" Linda asked politely, nothing in her tone giving away her true feelings.

"I'm fine, thanks," she said.

Linda gave a small nod and exited, closing the door behind her.

So she can warn him without me overhearing, Claire guessed. Well, tough. He'd have to come back here some time.

She glanced at the two seating options—a hard-looking chair

at the front of Jack's desk, or a squishy-looking sofa in the corner. She opted for the squishy sofa, throwing herself into it impatiently. It embraced her like an overly affectionate uncle, its cushions giving way alarmingly so that her butt sank low enough to lift her feet off the carpet.

Only Jack Brook could have a bucket-seat couch, she thought, struggling to lever herself up and out of its tenacious hold. She'd worked herself into a sweat and only managed to wriggle her hips forward, finally getting her high heels on the ground, when the door swung open and Jack entered. His blue gaze swung around like a spotlight and she felt the completeness of his scrutiny, becoming painfully aware of her flushed cheeks, the way her skirt was rucked up and the fact that the buttons at the front of her blouse were strained and gaping open because of the way her arms were levered behind her. This was not the way she'd imagined seeing him for the first time after what had happened between them. Neither had she imagined that her body would instantly go onto high alert, eager for any signal from him. Suddenly her breasts felt tight and sensitized in her bra, and she was aware of the brush of her silk shirt against her skin.

She gritted her teeth against the knowing smile dancing around Jack's lips and pushed herself up and out of the sofa with a surge of power. It was like coming out of quicksand, and she staggered a little before finding her balance.

Jack just watched her all the while, one hip braced against his desk, his arms folded across his chest. She stood panting before him, pushing her skirt back down.

"That's the most stupid couch in all the world," she said, aware that any advantage she'd had was long gone.

"I like it," he said simply.

"You would."

She tried to regain the towering anger and feeling of self-righteousness she'd had when she arrived not two minutes ago. Unfortunately, most of her was too busy remembering what it had felt like to be pressed up against his chest, to have his hands on her skin and his tongue in her mouth. A floodgate of sense memories threatened to engulf her—the look on his face as he slid inside her; the small noise of appreciation he'd made when he'd first seen her bare breasts; the moist heat of his breath against the skin of her neck as he shuddered out his climax. She blinked, overwhelmed for a moment by a surge of desire. Fortunately for her dignity, close on the heels of those searing memories came the painful reminder of how humiliated she'd felt when he didn't call last night.

Snap out of it, she told herself, squaring her shoulders and looking him in the eye. The effect was ruined somewhat when one of her blouse buttons popped off, performing a little somersault in the air between them before tumbling to land at his feet. The cool breeze on her torso told her that once again her underwear was on display, and she was unable to stop the flush of heat that was even now flooding her face.

"We really have to stop meeting like this," he drawled, stooping to pick up her button.

She hated him for his casual nonchalance—if his shirt had popped open she would have been bug-eyed and slathering with lust. But he just stood there, cool as a cucumber, completely unaffected by her near nudity. The bastard.

She crossed her arms in front of her breasts but a glance down revealed that this only made them seem to pop up and out over her bra even more. Yesterday in the elevator, and now this. She wanted to die, and as quickly as possible, please.

She could feel his eyes on her, and she settled for holding the two sides of her blouse together with one clenched fist.

"I've just been up seeing Morgan Beck," she announced, determined to win back the initiative.

Perhaps if she just pretended she hadn't practically forced herself on him, it would just go away.

"Figured as much."

His tone smacked so much of casual expectation that she felt her anger heating up all over again.

"Well, thanks for consulting me first. Thanks a lot. I get hauled up there first thing this morning and he practically accused me of making you ask to be taken off the magazine."

He looked surprised. "Where the hell did he get that from?"

"From you, I take it."

"Well, you're wrong. As usual. All I told him was that I had too much on my plate to take on your project, as well."

She puffed her cheeks out to stop from swearing out loud, almost letting go of her blouse she was so furious.

"Take on my project?" she stuttered. "Are you forgetting that you were only ever going to be the token male, wheeled out for meetings to keep that Neanderthal at Hillcrest happy? Take on my project my ass!"

He frowned at her, straightening from his lounging position against his desk. Good. Nice to see him abandon his casual observer stance and wade in at last. She hated the idea that everything she did vastly amused him, that he liked poking her with a stick and seeing what she did next.

If only her heart hadn't leaped as he took a step closer to her, she'd feel almost happy with the turn of events.

"Lady, you have rocks in your head if you thought I was ever going to just roll over and play dead. If I'm working on something, I'm working on it. I'm not in the habit of taking credit for something I didn't do."

"Morgan made the terms of your involvement very clear—it's in name only. You are not sticking your oar into my magazine," she declared hotly.

"Which is exactly why I told Beck I didn't have the time for the project. You should be thanking me instead of carrying on like a harpy."

This made her so angry she needed both hands free to gesticulate at him, and she abandoned her blouse to the Fates.

"You are the most arrogant man I have ever met. I can't believe I actually— I can't believe I didn't implode out of self-defense after spending more than five minutes in your company yesterday." She refused to acknowledge what she'd almost said, instead planting her hands on her hips and glaring at him.

"Ditto. Again, another good reason for us not working together."

"Well, get over it. Because I told Morgan we could sort this out," she fired back at him.

He looked so surprised she almost laughed.

"You did?"

"Someone has to be grown-up about this. And I'm not going to see my magazine stall because of your ego."

"*My* ego?"

He stared at her, but then, almost as if some irresistible force drew his gaze downward, his eyes dropped to her chest. She'd been aware that his eyes had strayed below her neckline more than once in the past few minutes. She felt his gaze like heat on her skin, and she swallowed nervously. Or was it excitedly? She was so confused right now, it was hard to tell the difference. In a split second all her thoughts turned from being furious with him to feverishly anticipating the touch of his hands on her breasts again. She wanted to feel the welcome weight of his body on top of hers. She wanted to touch his smooth, firm skin and hold the strength of him in her hands again. In an instant her panties were damp with wet heat, and her breath was coming short and sharp. She wanted him—but he had to make the first move. She couldn't risk making herself vulnerable again.

JACK COULDN'T STOP his gaze from dropping to her breasts. He ordered himself not to look, but it was useless. What man could resist when fate had handed him such a golden opportunity? She was wearing a cream lace bra today, and her breasts curved lovingly into it, rising and falling with each breath she took.

She was so damn hot. How was he supposed to resist her

when she was running around taunting him like this? He was trying to do the right thing here, trying to be a nice guy and spare her feelings. Because it would be the easiest thing in the world to just sleep with her again, drink his fill, explore the chemistry between them and then move on. He was doing her a favor, damn it—and now she was showing him exactly what he was missing out on.

All he had to do was reach out and pull her to him. His muscles tensed in anticipation. He'd slide her shirt off, then that bra— pretty as it was, it was nothing compared to her unadorned breasts. The pale pink of her nipples, the way they puckered so responsively under his touch, the taste of her, the heat of her skin, the little hitch she got in her breathing when he sucked her nipples deep into his mouth. He'd back her against the desk, pull up that prim little skirt of hers and slide himself into her. She'd get that look in her eye, that glazed but oddly intent look, and she would tilt her hips and tighten her strong, firm legs around his hips—

He didn't need to look down to know that he was rock hard again, his erection straining against the fly of his jeans. Something had to give—and he had a feeling it was going to be him.

"For Pete's sake, how am I supposed to concentrate? Come here," he said, reaching toward her impatiently.

Before Claire could object she'd been forcibly hauled forward by the lapels of her shirt. His body was hard and warm against hers, and for a beat they stood pressed against each other, neither saying a word, their eyes locked together. Her mind was racing. Was he going to kiss her again? God, she wanted him to— even after the humiliation of last night, she wanted him, bad. A muscle twitched in his jaw, and she inhaled sharply, feeling the fullness of her breasts press against his chest. Then he grabbed something from his desk, jamming it between them. A metallic click sounded, and he pushed her away.

She blinked down at her shirt, staring in growing indignation at the staple now holding her blouse together more modestly. Two messy hunks of fabric stuck out on either side of the staple—a five-year-old with bad eyesight could have done a better job.

"This is a Gucci shirt," she said slowly, enunciating carefully so he understood exactly what he'd done.

"I was doing you a favor. I know how uptight you are about public displays of underwear."

She felt a stress twitch break out below her left eye. She was sure that if she had her lawyers introduce the ruined Gucci shirt as exhibit *A* during her murder trial, she could fully justify turning his stupid desk stapler on him till he died the death of a thousand tiny puncture wounds.

She managed to ignore the fact that once again she had been putty in his hands, while he remained supremely unaffected. She could bring that realization out later and really soak up the rejection. But for now, there was her favorite shirt to consider....

He seemed to sense the surge of homicidal feeling rising within her, because he wisely moved away until the desk was between them.

"As much as I enjoy having you carp at me, I do have another meeting in five minutes. So if you don't mind...?" he said carelessly.

She stood there, her hands curled into two tight fists by her sides.

"I'm not leaving this office until we've sorted this out. I need a man to talk golf and football with Hillcrest, and you are a man. But that's all I need. I don't want you writing big-game-fishing articles for *Welcome Home,* I don't want you interfering in the design process and I certainly don't want you having any say over editorial content."

He cocked his head to one side as though he was actually considering it. "Gee, you make it sound like such an attractive gig. No."

She glared at him, reading the determination in every line of his body. He was even breathing a little faster, just like her. He was like her in many ways, she realized, remembering all the things they'd found in common yesterday. And before she could stop herself, she was considering how *she'd* react if he came to her with this offer. What if there was some female-oriented magazine he was working on, and he needed a Trojan horse woman to get him in under the client's radar…?

Some of her self-righteous anger faded as she acknowledged that she'd have told him to stick his stupid offer where only the doctor could surgically retrieve it. Kind of like he just had, after ruining her favorite shirt. Forcing herself to push her personal feelings of humiliation and rejection to one side, Claire decided to be pragmatic. She wanted to get her magazine up and running, and to do that, she needed to do a deal with this devil.

"Okay, what's it going to take?" she asked suddenly, changing tactics midstream.

He eyed her warily. "Don't tell me you're that desperate."

"Jack, Beck has given me no choice on this. So…what's it going to take?"

A significant pause stretched between them. She could see his mind ticking away, no doubt trying to come up with the most outrageous demand he could formulate. She braced herself.

"Give me a project every issue. You've got a furniture-making section, yeah? Give me something in that, and I'll press the flesh and laugh at old man Hillcrest's bad jokes. It's that, or nothing. I can't take credit for something I didn't even touch."

She was aware that her jaw was hanging slackly and she made an effort to not look too witless and stunned. She'd been expecting something offensive at best. This was…well, very reasonable.

"That's it? That's all you want?" she clarified.

"Don't sound so disappointed."

Once again she was on the back foot. Why did that always happen with this man?

"I just…I thought you would… Look, it doesn't matter. The project idea is good. Actually, it'll be helpful. I'm sort of breaking in a project guy, and he's a bit nervous about taking on the full workload," she stumbled, trying hard to regain some kind of professional footing.

A hard task when your most prominent fashion accessory is a stapled cleavage.

"Fine. Can I have my office back now?"

He sounded bored. Her back went up again like clockwork.

"Of course. Just say the word," she said, aware her voice came out hard and tight.

"I thought I did," he drawled.

She blinked at him, aware that his casualness had caught her on the raw. Just when she thought he was a decent human being, he had to go and be like this.

She heard a heavy sigh from him behind her as she headed for the door.

"Claire, hang on a minute. About last night—" he began to say, and she realized with horror that he was about to offer her some sop for not calling.

"It's fine, Jack. Already forgotten," she said briskly.

"I want to explain. I just think that you're—" he tried again.

She spun around, desperate to stop him from saying something about how mistaken she was, how she'd misunderstood him. "Forget it. Okay? I wish the whole thing had never happened. Enough said."

He held her gaze for a moment, and she hoped she looked suitably indifferent. If humiliation resembled indifference in any way, she figured she had a chance.

"Your call," he said, and she shot him a look. Had he meant to choose those words, exactly?

Impossible to tell. She attempted to reassemble a little dignity and self-respect around herself.

"I've got a meeting scheduled with Hillcrest tomorrow at ten," she said coolly, already turning toward the door.

"Fine. I'll be there."

She paused on the threshold of his office.

"And please wear a tie. Hillcrest is a traditional man."

"Hillcrest will have to learn to loosen up a little. Do him

good." He had a dangerous, indolent air, along with a definite "give it your best shot" glint in his eye.

She took a deep breath and reached for some patience. "Jack. Please. Just once. Is it so painful to be conventional, even for just five minutes?"

He shrugged, oozing innocence from every pore. "Hey—I don't even own a tie. So it's irrelevant."

She made an exasperated noise in the back of her throat. He was laughing at her again, leaning against his desk, his broad shoulders silhouetted against his stunning corner-office view.

"Fine. Come in your best holey T-shirt and grass-stained jeans, forget to shave, stink of beer and scratch your furry face through the whole meeting. See if I care."

With that, she wheeled out of his office, slamming the door behind her. Or at least trying to. Except it had one of those nifty pneumatic door closers on it, and all she got was a bit of kick-back when she tried to force the mechanism.

She could still hear his laughter when the elevator doors closed on her. She headed straight for the ladies' room on her floor, and once she was in the safe confines of a private cubicle, she leaned against the wall and threw her head back, closing her eyes against the cocktail of emotions waiting to swamp her.

She felt so weak. Hadn't last night taught her anything? Intellectually she knew that Jack was a disaster area, a no-go zone, even though she'd already been there. But her body could not resist him. Just thinking about how he'd smelled, and the heat of his body against hers when he hauled her close to staple her cleavage—it was enough to get her hot all over again. Claire glanced down and saw that her nipples were stiff and aroused, jutting out against the silk of her shirt proudly. Between her legs, a dull ache throbbed, and she pressed her hand against her mound through the fabric of her skirt.

I don't want this, she ordered her body. *I don't want to feel this way about Jack Brook! Stop it immediately!*

After five minutes of strong self-talk, she emerged from the cubicle. The hectic-cheeked woman who greeted her in the mirror was a stranger, and she shook her head at the gleam of desire that still shone in her eyes.

After a few minutes of wrangling, she managed to extract the staples, but her shirt was ruined. Toying with the idea of sending him the bill, she headed to the nearby shopping mall to find a replacement so she'd be presentable for her afternoon meetings. If only her pride could be salvaged so easily. She had only to remember the way Jack had calmly stapled her to decency to feel a rush of humiliation. She'd spent the bulk of a sleepless night inventing conversations where he explained why he hadn't called, great excuses that meant she could still indulge the fantasy that she hadn't behaved like a total wanton in the elevator. Boy, was she deluded. She'd built up this whole…*thing* between them, imagining a whole lot of stuff she had no business imagining. And all he'd been concerned about was extracting himself from Morgan Beck's assignment.

They'd been stuck in an airless space for several hours. He'd been bored. They'd shared things they hadn't told anyone else, and he'd taken what she'd so willingly offered.

Big deal. She was sure that's what he was thinking. It must have been what he was thinking when he went to tell Beck he wouldn't work with her. And when he decided not to call her last night, despite what had happened.

Bottom line: in the real world, out of claustrophobic elevators where people were forced to strip down to their underwear, men like Jack Brook did not look twice at women like her.

If only she'd known that *before* she'd let him slide her bra off and slide himself into her, before she'd had the best damn sex of her life.

Why had she given him the opportunity to reject her?

She had a sudden flash of Jack sitting on high—Zeus on his mountain—laughing at her as she scampered around at his feet like all the other women in his life.

She was walking past a display in the men's section of a department store, and she almost ran into the young salesman setting it up. She stared down at the colorful array of ties the guy was finessing, and she remembered Jack's refusal to wear a tie to her meeting with Hillcrest.

Suddenly she saw red. It was her meeting, and her client, and her magazine. And he was working with her. The least he could do was respect her reading of her client's sensibilities.

Determined now, she turned to the salesman.

"Excuse me. Which would you say is the most conservative tie you stock? The sort of tie a retired banker might wear, for example?" she asked silkily.

"Definitely something with stripes. Or a royal insignia. That always seems to go over well with our older customers." The salesman helpfully displayed two or three ties for her.

"I'll take that one," she said, pointing to the tie that combined stripes with a royal insignia.

And Jack Brook would wear it if it killed her.

8

JACK WALKED BACK into his office after his last meeting of the day and groaned at the pile of paperwork Linda had left on his desk: afternoon mail, letters to sign, blah, blah, blah. He sighed heavily and dropped into his chair, swinging his feet up onto his desk as he reached for the pile of mail. His feet knocked something to the floor, and he leaned sideways in his chair to peer around the edge and make sure he hadn't broken anything.

His stapler lay on its side on the plush carpet, and he stared at it a moment. Unbidden, unwanted, unwise, a Technicolor image of Claire Marsden's lacy bra popped into his mind. Complete with a memory of how she'd smelled and how she'd felt when he'd pulled her close to remedy the temptation. Because—really—how was a man supposed to have a good, solid argument with a woman when all he could think about was burying his face in her cleavage? And, after that, burying other parts of his body in her, also. He'd been so close to giving in to the need to touch her. If he closed his eyes for more than a heartbeat, images of their time in the elevator flashed back at him. It was the only thing he seemed able to think about. That, and all the other things he wanted to do to her. Once was not enough, he was fast discovering, where Claire Marsden was concerned. At least, that was what his body believed. Intellectually—well, that was a whole other ball game.

Because it was impossible to remember Claire's spectacular body without remembering her spectacular temper. The spark of

remembered lust faded as he recalled her insulting insinuation—
that he'd told Beck she wanted him off the magazine. Man, he'd
busted his ass being diplomatic with Beck that morning, explaining how he was loathe to work on something he wasn't truly
contributing to, pointing out his work schedule was already very
hectic, stressing that Claire was very good and very likely to be
able to soothe savage-beast-Hillcrest all on her own.

And she reads that as him setting her up! Which was the problem with her, when he got right down to it. She was always ready
and willing to read an ulterior motive into everything he did.
More trouble than she was worth.

Insidious and undeniable, the memory of her simple but sincere sympathy for him snuck into his mind. She'd said exactly
the right thing, and she'd even anted up with a confession of her
own so he wouldn't feel like a complete dick when the doors
opened. So she wasn't an absolute lost cause....

And then there was the sex. He kept coming back to that. Had
he ever been that hot for a woman? Surely in his teens he'd had
encounters that were that hot...but he couldn't quite remember
with whom or when. In fact, all past encounters paled into in-
significance beside what had happened yesterday. It was even
beginning to worry him a little, the way his mind would automatically drift to those few precious memories of the smell of
her skin, and the sound of her excited breath in his ear, whenever he let his guard down. He'd nearly embarrassed himself several times in meetings today. One moment he was discussing
deadlines and feature stores, and the next he was fighting off
sense memories of tanned skin and the wet, voluptuous slide of
his body in hers. And as for how his body had reacted when her
shirt had popped open... It had been a close-run thing, and he'd
been forced to seek refuge behind his desk to hide his desire. The
last thing he needed was for little Miss Uptight to know the potential hold she had over him....

He started as Linda stuck her head into his office doorway.

"I'm going now. See you tomorrow," she said.

He grunted a goodbye, deliberately pulling his attention back to his pile of mail.

Stop thinking about Claire, he ordered himself. He'd already laid her ghost to rest last night, when he'd decided not to call her. So why did she keep rising to the surface of his mind?

Here he was again, reverting to thinking about her as soon as all other distractions were gone! He'd already walked down this road, and it was a dead end. Time to move on. With a real force of will, he focused on his mail, sorting through more than half of it until he came to an internal mail envelope. Like most internal mail envelopes, the previous recipient had crossed their name out before reusing the envelope for another message. He stared at Claire's crossed-out name for a second, then squeezed the bag, frowning. It felt bulky, not like paperwork. Mystified, he broke the sticky-tape seal and pulled out a small shopping bag. The cool slither of silk on his hands clued him into the bag's contents before he'd pulled the tie out. It was striped, with some sort of lion and crown etched into it. The sort of tie his grandfather had always been fond of. He stared at it, genuinely dumbstruck for a moment.

She was a real piece of work. Not content to have the last word, she'd gone out and bought him the perfect response to his claim not to own a tie.

Well, she could whistle Dixie as far as he was concerned— there was no way he was wearing a stupid tie. Especially not this particular stupid tie.

Thank God he hadn't called her last night. He'd regretted it earlier today, even after their fight he'd found it in himself to regret it, because there was something about her that drew him... But after this? No way. He and she were chalk and cheese. She'd drive him crazy. He tossed the tie negligently to one side.

He actually snorted his exasperation and disbelief out loud as he reached for the folder Linda had filled with his personal mail from his post office box. There were a handful of bills, but one envelope caught his attention. That was his Mom's handwriting scrawled across the front of the pale lavender rectangle. A dead, dull weight settled on his chest as he lifted the flap on the envelope, knowing full well what was inside: a birthday card.

Just like his Mom. She never forgot birthdays, even though he'd made his feelings clear on the subject. He almost laughed out loud. He'd been mostly successful in ignoring the march of time this year. He'd figured that if he was very careful and skimmed along through November, he could skip over his and Robbie's birthday.

But he'd still known that it was coming up, just the same—otherwise he wouldn't have felt that instant weight upon seeing his mother's card. Otherwise he wouldn't have this well of grief opening up inside him so readily and easily.

Liquid heat threatened at the back of his eyes, and he pushed himself to his feet, dropping the card onto his desk, ignoring all that needed to be signed for tomorrow. He had to get out of there, right now.

THERE WAS A CALL waiting on her answering machine when Claire got home from work that evening, and she despised herself for the little thrill of anticipation she felt as she noted the flashing message light. Maybe Jack had called after all. Maybe he'd felt as angry and frustrated and disappointed as she had after their argument.

Then she gave herself a mental slap. There was no way Jack would have called after the fight they'd had in his office. Or, if he called her at all, it would only be to give her hell for having foisted a tie on him, despite his insistence that he wouldn't wear one.

But it was her father's voice on the answering machine. She stared at the small black appliance as he told her that he was in town unexpectedly. Would she like to catch up for dinner?

She hadn't spoken to her father in months. She sent him

e-mails on a regular basis, mostly because she was determined
to do all that she could to have some kind of relationship with
him. Occasionally he replied, but he rarely commented on her
news. Instead he concentrated on his latest expedition or project, his letters reading more like press releases than missives from
a father to his only child.

Warily pleased, she called the hotel number Harry had left. His
voice sounded unfamiliar and distant when he answered the phone.

"Dad, it's me, Claire," she said.

"Oh, hello, Claire. I take it you got my message?"

As usual, the cool matter-of-factness of his manner stopped
her from saying any of the things she instinctively wanted to
say—that it had been a long time, that she'd been thinking about
him. That she was hoping he could make it to her triathlon final.

They quickly arranged for her to meet him at his hotel for dinner—he was disinclined to let her take him out to any of her favorite Melbourne restaurants. In a city that was well-known for its food
and wine culture, Harry preferred to chance the hotel dining room,
and she felt unequal to the task of convincing him otherwise.

She settled for a scaled-down version of her training session
for the evening, and it was only as she was discarding the third
top she'd tried on in ten minutes that she acknowledged she was
nervous.

Ridiculous, really—but he was her father, and their relationship was uneasy at best. Still, he'd made the effort to get in contact while he was in town. That was something, a change. She
allowed herself to hope that maybe all her hard work in main-
taining contact had perhaps gotten through to him on some level.

She was surprised at how old he looked when they met up in
the foyer of his hotel. At sixty, he was very active and still organized expeditions, even if he didn't lead them himself anymore.
But his hair had thinned, and was now completely white, and his
eyes seemed faded somehow. She had to fight a surge of emotion
as she realized that time was running out for them to reconcile.

"Claire. Good to see you," he said, leaning forward stiffly to kiss her cheek.

Ignoring his formality, she hugged him, pressing her cheek close to his.

"How are you?" she asked warmly.

"Good, good. A little annoyed at having to make this extraneous trip to Melbourne when we're so close to heading off, but these things happen."

Unsure of what he was talking about, Claire followed him into the dining room and waited till they had been seated before venturing further.

"You're organizing another expedition, I take it?" she asked.

Obviously her father was unaware that he hadn't communicated with her for some time.

"Yes. It's a joint Australian-Swiss assault on Everest. We were supposed to leave next month…but I don't want to bore you with the details. How is work? And your marathon thingy?"

She blinked with surprise. Her father never tired of talking about his work, and he never enquired after her life. She struggled to pull her thoughts together. "Work is good. Busy, but good. We're very close to launching our first edition of the magazine. And my triathlon training is coming along well. Just two weeks to go now."

He made the appropriate noises as he studied the wine list, while she studied his face. Was this truly the breakthrough she'd been hoping for all her life? Or, if not that, exactly, perhaps the beginning of a thaw?

"This is the magazine that you devised, the hardware thing?"

Another surprise—he'd read her e-mails, actually remembered their content.

"Yes. It's more home renovation and decoration than hardware, really. But you've got the basic idea." .

He shot her an assessing look, then indicated her menu. "Better hurry up and decide—I can't stand waiting around for my meal," he said, already signaling for the waiter to come over.

There was a momentary hiatus in their conversation as Claire hurriedly decided on a salad as entrée and fish for her main, and the wine waiter poured some wine into her glass—a red, her father's choice.

"So, I guess this Beck character who runs all those magazines of yours must be pretty pleased with you, then."

"Well, he's certainly happy to have landed a new client."

She took a mouthful of her wine, wondering that her father even remembered what company she worked for.

"But you know him, yes? You've spoken with him?"

For the first time she registered that this was more than just polite interest from Harry. What was going on here?

"I've had several meetings with him, of course. Have you met him somewhere?"

Her father shook his head vigorously, tearing his dinner roll apart. "No, but I will tomorrow. Just trying to get a bit of a feel for the man. What do you know of him? Is he a sports man?"

Claire sat back in her chair, baffled and bemused. Why would her father care what she thought of her boss, or what he thought of her? And why on earth would her father, renowned explorer, be having a meeting with Morgan Beck, millionaire publisher?

And then she got it.

"Is he thinking of funding one of your expeditions?" she asked flatly. She watched her father's face closely, feeling that this moment was pivotal somehow. It was possible she was wrong, that her father truly had found some smidgen of sentiment in himself as the years rolled by and was genuinely interested in his daughter's life.

"As a matter of fact, yes. It's a bit of a difficult situation, actually. This Beck character was interested in getting involved right from the get-go, but then we had a better offer from the Swiss side of things. Now our Swiss guy has dropped his bundle, and I'm hoping to talk Beck into renewing his offer."

Harry was animated and enthusiastic as he explained his situation to her, describing the details of the assault, the makeup of the team, the differing experience levels, the problems he'd had and overcome.

And she sat there, watching his face light up with passion for his subject, for the only thing he'd every really loved, the bitter taste of disappointment in her mouth.

Who had she been kidding, really, when she thought that her father had suddenly become all Brady Bunch?

Harry seemed to sense her preoccupation, and he broke off his recital to consider her. "Is something wrong, Claire? Don't you like the wine?"

She stared at him for a beat, tempted to just let things slide like she always had. But suddenly she couldn't bear the thought of pushing her own thoughts and feelings down again. Yesterday she'd admitted to Jack that she was the disappointment of her father's life. But it didn't have to be that way. She wasn't a bad person—she was just different from what he'd wanted in a child. But did that mean she had to accept the crumbs from his table for the rest of her life?

"You know, I thought you'd asked me here to spend time with *me,* because you wanted to see *me,*" she said.

"Yes, of course, and that's exactly what we're doing," her father said, the picture of surprise.

"No, it's not. We're having dinner because you want something from my boss. You're not really interested in my magazine or my triathlon or anything else in my life."

She tried hard to keep the tears out of her voice, but they were lurking there, giving her a husky vibrato. Her father was pulling an exasperated face, and shaking his head.

"I don't know where you're getting all this from, Claire. I was in town, I asked you to dinner—it was as simple as that."

"Really? Fine, then tell me when my triathlon final is. I told you earlier, when you asked, because you were so interested in my life, so it shouldn't be any big stretch for you to remember what I said."

She held her father's eye, challenging him.

"I can't recall the exact details, but I know it's soon…" her father began, and Claire pushed her chair back and stood up.

"I am your daughter, and I love you, but I am not going to be the only one participating in this relationship. I call you and e-mail you and offer to fly to visit you for Christmas every year, and you can't even remember a conversation we had five minutes ago."

Slinging her handbag over her shoulder, Claire turned to leave.

"You let me know if you're prepared to put a bit of effort in, because I'm not going to make it easy for you anymore," she said over her shoulder.

She walked straight out and didn't look back.

She was proud of herself all the way home in the car. Then reaction set in. He would be so angry with her, she probably wouldn't hear from him for months and months. She never, ever caused a fuss with him, because she knew how he hated having to deal with emotional messes. She understood, deep in her heart of hearts, that if she didn't keep up the contact with her father, she would never hear from him. Whatever faint connection that existed between them would fade and shrivel, and she'd be utterly alone.

It was a scary thought, but she refused to take it to bed with her. She was a grown, adult woman. She had an exciting, vibrant life of her own. She was about to launch a new magazine. She had a real chance at winning the state triathlon finals. And she'd had dirty, wild elevator sex with the office playboy not twenty-four hours ago.

Never did she think that she would turn to those stolen, wanton moments with Jack as a source of comfort, but the world was a strange and amazing place. For some reason, thinking of him, going over their argument today, and the discussions they'd had in the elevator, made her feel a whole lot better. She had stuff going on in her life. She didn't need her dad.

Inevitably her thoughts turned from what she and Jack had talked and argued about in the elevator to what they'd done, and before long she was imagining what might have happened in Jack's office today if he'd kissed her again instead of stapling her shirt shut. What if he'd slid her shirt off, and then her bra? She would have reached for his jeans, because she'd been thinking about having him inside her ever since he'd withdrawn from her. Maybe she would have sunk to her knees and taken him in her mouth, loving the look on his face as she laved him with her tongue. And maybe he wouldn't have been able to stand it for long, and he'd have pushed her onto that stupid, squishy couch in the corner and reached down between her legs to push her panties aside—too impatient to remove them entirely—then he'd be inside her again and—

Claire was panting into her pillow. Very resolute, she got out of bed and rummaged through her drawers until she found a pair of pajamas. She always slept naked, but these were desperate times. Pulling on underwear, and then the pajamas, she slid back into bed.

No more fantasies about Jack Brook, she warned herself.

Armored in cotton and determination, she finally drifted off to sleep.

THE NEXT MORNING she was feeling distinctly jittery about having cut off communication with her father and about seeing Jack again. First, there was that irritating thing her heart did whenever Jack was in the room—it was almost as though it missed a beat now and then, lurching around inside her chest like a drunken sailor. Then there was the powerful physical awareness she seemed to have developed for him ever since they'd gotten down and dirty. You'd think that jumping on each other would have put an end to any sexual tension, but, if anything, it was worse. Now when she looked at his strong thighs and long fingers and broad shoulders she knew exactly how devastating they could be. And, to her shame, she wanted to be devastated. Badly. Hence the fact that he suddenly had top billing in all her sexual fantasies. Slowly but surely, he was driving her crazy.

Combine that with the fact that she was almost one hundred percent certain that he wouldn't be happy about her gift tie, and she had plenty of justification for the butterflies winging their way around her midsection.

Then there was her father. Why had she laid down the gauntlet like that? Why couldn't she have just eaten her dinner like a good girl and maintained the status quo? Really, it was getting to the point where she shouldn't be allowed out without a keeper.

She spent the time before her first meeting with Jack and Hillcrest Hardware looking up whenever anyone walked near her office, and jumping every time her phone rang. She felt like a sitting duck, waiting to be ambushed by Jack from one side, or her father on the other.

By a quarter to ten, she had talked herself around to a reasonable state of calm. If her father was going to make contact with her, it wouldn't be for some time. He'd want to leave a nice long buffer between her angry words and any future conversation to ensure she was calm and over whatever madness had had her in its grip. As for Jack— Well, she had no choice but to be ready to face him, tie or no tie.

Except he didn't come. As the time drew closer to 10:00 and her appointment with Hillcrest, she had to use stronger and stronger arguments for not reaching for the phone to confirm Jack's presence. She had to trust him; he was a successful, experienced executive; he wouldn't bail on her. On the last count she couldn't be so confident, however. They'd fought almost every time they'd been alone together for more than five minutes. There was a chance he'd see this as an extension of their battle of wills.

At 10:00 on the dot her assistant Tom told her that the Hillcrest executives were in the foyer. Caving at last, she reached for the phone and called Jack's office. The moment Linda picked up the call she knew Jack had hung her out to dry.

"Jack, is that you?" Linda demanded anxiously.

Claire took a moment to remind herself not to shoot the messenger. "No, Linda, this is Claire Marsden. I have a ten o'clock with Jack and Hillcrest Hardware, but I'm guessing that I'm going to be handling this alone…?"

There was a slight pause on the other end of the phone, then, "I'm sorry, Claire, but your appointment isn't in Jack's diary. I guess you made it with him directly. Otherwise I would have called you earlier to let you know…he seems to be running a little late today…."

The usually competent and professional Linda sounded extremely rattled, but Claire didn't have time to deal with the other woman's concern for her no-good, lazy, sneaky boss. The big rat was probably relaxing somewhere, lazing around enjoying his self-appointed long weekend.

Ending the call as nicely as possible, she headed in to take on Hillcrest and his honchos.

It wasn't a pleasant meeting, mostly because Hank Hillcrest managed to convey his deep skepticism about the appointment of Jack Brook to the magazine. The old man's repeated references to the "so-called Jack Brook," as though she and Morgan had made him up, became almost more than she could bear during the one-hour torture session. Somehow she managed to placate her client, spinning a yarn about Jack flying back in from a big-game safari in Africa and his flight being delayed. By the time she'd finished, Hank Hillcrest was so intrigued she began to suspect she'd have to cough up a genuine lion's head trophy just to shut the man up.

At last she shook hands with the now-cheerful Hillcrest executives and saw them out into the foyer amid assurances that she would bring Jack out to meet them at their head office next week.

No sooner had the elevator doors closed on them than she let her smile drop. She couldn't remember ever being so furious with anyone. She was so angry, in fact, that she was a little scared of herself, and she deliberately took the stairs to Jack's floor in order to give herself some time to calm down. Her shirt was already clinging to her thanks to the tense meeting, and she slung her jacket over her arm as she exited the stairwell and made her way purposefully to Linda's desk.

Linda was looking harried, and she glanced up at Claire distractedly. Almost as though she was talking to herself, Linda explained that she'd managed to reschedule all but one of Jack's meetings, but she still hadn't heard from him.

"Probably too scared to turn up now," Claire suggested coolly.

Linda gave her an impatient look.

"You don't understand. Jack has never ever done anything like this before. I know he looks casual and laid-back, but he's always punctual, he always meets his deadlines and he always lets me know what's going on. I've worked for him for two years now, and this has never happened, ever. I'm worried."

Which made two of them, because as Linda spoke an awful image of Jack's stupid red sports car wrapped around a tree popped into Claire's brain.

"I take it he's not answering his home line or his cell phone?" she ventured reluctantly.

"His home line just rings out, and his cell phone goes straight through to his voice mail."

She saw the worry in Linda's eyes and patted the other woman's arm reassuringly.

"Have you checked his office? Maybe he left a note or something in there and forgot to put it on your desk."

"I had a quick scout around, but nothing struck me," Linda said doubtfully.

As one they turned toward Jack's closed office door, and, at Linda's nod, Claire stepped forward and pushed it open. Jack's desk was a mess, which didn't seem too unusual, but she couldn't fail to see the tie she'd sent him strewn on the floor like an old sock.

She automatically bent to pick it up, smoothing the silk through her fingers as she continued surveying Jack's desk. Linda frowned at the tie, curious.

"What's a tie doing in Jack's office? He never wears a tie. I wonder if…?" Linda's startled eyes connected with Claire's, and Claire could see the other woman was busy constructing an Agatha Christie plot.

"It's okay. I bought it for him," she explained.

Linda's eyes went round with surprise, then her hand snuck up to cover her mouth. She was laughing, Claire realized.

"I'm sorry. I was imagining his face. It's just…Jack never wears a tie. I don't think he even owns one."

"I know. That's why I bought him one. For the Hillcrest meeting."

Linda shot her a speculative look, and Claire guessed what the other woman was thinking. "Oh, no—it's nothing like that. I was just trying to annoy him," she hastily explained.

Linda looked unconvinced. "Right."

"No, really. I wanted him to wear a tie to the Hillcrest meeting, he said he didn't have one… It was just a joke, really."

Linda nodded, but Claire got the distinct impression that the other woman didn't believe her. Unwilling to dig a bigger hole for herself, she began surveying the desk again. Linda joined in straight away, but Claire was aware of her lingering scrutiny and she kept her face carefully blank.

"I don't see anything, do you?" Linda said after a futile few minutes.

Claire was shaking her head, about to agree with Linda, when she spotted the discarded birthday card.

Frowning, she plucked it from amongst the mess and flipped it open.

Dearest Jack, thinking of you on this special day. Please be kind to yourself—our love is with you. Don't feel as though you have to go it alone. Lots of love, Mom and Dad.

She turned to Linda, urgent now. "Did this come yesterday?"

Linda shrugged. "How could I know? He may have had it for weeks. Except— Hang on a minute."

Linda scuffled through the papers until she found the torn lavender envelope. Matching it to the card, she nodded once. "Yes. This definitely came yesterday, because I remember the purple envelope. It was in the mail I collected from Jack's personal mailbox. Claire, what's going on? What's this about?"

Claire closed her eyes briefly. This had to be it. Jack's birthday was Robbie's birthday. She opened her eyes, even more worried now than she was before.

Because what on earth happened to a man when all the grief he'd stuffed down deep inside threatened to escape?

She grabbed Linda's arm, imperative. "I need Jack's home address, pronto."

HE LIVED IN A HOUSE. Another surprise. A big old rambling house with a yard and trees and a white picket fence. Parking her car in front, she felt a moment of shame for all the clichés she'd ascribed to Jack. She'd always imagined him in a penthouse apartment, with lots of gleaming chrome and black leather furniture and mood lighting.

Girding her loins, she made her way up the path to the front door and leaned on the doorbell. Nothing. She waited, then tried again. Still nothing. She tried knocking next, and when this was still ineffective, she stepped back and surveyed the house. It was possible he wasn't here at all, of course. Lord, he could be anywhere. But his car gleamed redly at the end of the drive, and she had a gut instinct about this—Jack was very private, and she doubted he'd take his grief to a public place.

She tried the front door, but it was solidly locked, so she headed boldly up the drive, emerging into a beautifully landscaped backyard. Fruit trees and roses, climbing jasmine on the fence and a rustic outdoor setting created a little oasis of calm and tranquility. She smiled at the laughing Buddha statue half-hidden in amongst some irises, then frowned as she saw the back door open and swinging in the breeze.

Well, at least she wasn't breaking and entering....

Feeling a little more tentative now, she stuck her head in the darkened doorway and glanced up and down the hallway. In front of her, old floorboards gleamed all the way down the central hallway to the front door.

"Jack? Jack, are you here?" she called out.

Nothing. Sighing, she stepped properly into the house. The kitchen was on her right. It was old but serviceable, and Jack was obviously in the process of renovating it, with half the tiles removed and the wallpaper stripped down to bare plaster.

Two empty tequila bottles lay on their sides on the kitchen table. *Oh, goody.* Nothing like a tequila hangover.

She found him in the living room, slumped on the couch, his posture defeated and closed. At first she thought he was asleep, but he lifted his head when she put her hand on his shoulder, giving her a minor heart attack.

"Jack!" she said, startled, and he blinked up at her owlishly.

"What are you doing here?" he slurred, and she pulled back from the truly impressive haze of alcohol he was exuding.

Amazingly, he still managed to look dangerously attractive, despite his bleary-eyed, bestubbled, incoherent state.

"I was worried about you," she said, not bothering to edit herself. She'd be stunned if he remembered any of this.

"Were you? That's nice."

His head sank back down, and she allowed herself a small moment to simply rest her hand on his head, feeling for him. He held too much to himself, blocked himself off too much....

"Jack, I think we should make you some coffee. And some food. You feel like some food?" she suggested, forcing herself to take her hand off his silky, springy hair.

"Don't want anything," he said, childishly.

"I'm sure you don't. But I promise you'll feel better if you eat some food."

"Don't want to feel better."

I bet you don't. She stared down at his still-bowed head, then made a decision. "Why don't we get you in the shower?"

He didn't respond to this, and she crouched down to peer up into his face. "Jack? Jack?"

Slowly he opened his eyes again.

"Don't want shower."

She nodded as though she was agreeing with him. "Sure. But you trust me, don't you? And I think you should have a shower," she said.

He just stared at her, and she leaned forward and slid her arm around his shoulders, bracing herself and ensuring a strong grip on his well-muscled side.

"Come on, now. Let's stand."

It took a few more minutes of coaxing and some serious counterweight balancing to get him to his feet. She cursed herself immediately for not having done a bit of recon and worked out where the shower was before she got him standing, but he was swaying on his feet so much that there was no way she could trust him to stay upright if she went for a quick scout.

So they staggered up the hallway, and she found the bathroom behind the second door she tried. She tried to make him understand she wanted him to sit on the edge of the tub while she took off his boots, but he just stared at her blankly.

"Jack, how much have you had to drink?" she asked suddenly, beginning to wonder if he'd had the whole two bottles of tequila. How much did it take before a person got alcohol poisoning? She didn't have a head for drink herself, and the thought of so much strong spirit made her wince.

He shrugged, clearly disinterested, and she was forced to get down on her knees and lift his feet up one at a time to drag off his expensive-looking boots. The rest of him could go in the shower as is, but the boots just looked too good to ruin, and she knew he wouldn't thank her if she destroyed them. Hell, he was unlikely to thank her anyway, but she was here now....

She'd just tugged his last boot off when Jack swayed alarmingly and staggered backward. There wasn't far for him to go in the small space; his legs kicked forward, catching the heel of the boot she held and flicking it toward her face, and he slammed against the tiled wall and slid down until his butt was in the tub and his legs were dangling over the edge.

White light exploded behind her eyes as the boot connected with her right cheekbone, and she reeled backward from her crouching position, connecting with the wall behind her.

Claire just breathed through the pain for a moment, then pressed a hand to her face, probing her cheekbone tentatively. Nothing felt broken or wrong, and she guessed she'd be looking at a bruise and nothing more. Still, it hurt like hell, and she took a couple more deep breaths.

"Claire? You okay?"

She looked up quickly to find Jack staring at her, his eyes more lucid now; perhaps the impact had knocked a bit of sense into him, sent some adrenaline into his system to counteract all that alcohol.

"I'm fine."

She pushed off the wall behind her and stood up.

"Come on, let's get you into the shower," she said.

She had to brace herself to help drag him up out of the tub, but he seemed much more aware of things as he sank down onto the edge of the bath and cradled his head in his hands.

"Did you knock your head?" she asked him, worried about concussion now. She leaned over him, reaching behind his head to probe the back of his skull for any bumps or blood.

Suddenly Jack's hand shot out and grabbed hers, and she found herself being pulled down so that she was kneeling in front of him.

"Let me see," he was murmuring. "I hurt you."

He was determined and way too heavy for her to move around without his cooperation, so she let him have his way when he tilted her face up to examine the throbbing mark left by his boot. She tried not to look into his intent but bleary eyes, focusing instead on the tiled wall behind him.

"I hurt you," he repeated, one large hand cradling her chin as the other brushed delicately at her cheek.

She had to swallow against the rush of feeling and memory his tender touch evoked, and she took herself to task firmly— the man was five parts drunk, incoherent and morose, and she was more hard up than she'd ever imagined if this was all it took to move her these days.

"It's okay, Jack. It's just a bruise. You didn't mean it. It was an accident," she reassured him, trying to turn her face away from his probing scrutiny.

"I still hurt you. I'm sorry, Claire, I'm so sorry," Jack said, his voice very low and gruff now.

She froze as both Jack's hands cupped her face and held it steady as he stared intently into her eyes, his own face just a foot away.

"I'm really, really sorry," he said, and she watched as tears welled up in his amazing eyes and spilled over his stubbly cheeks.

"I didn't mean to hurt you," he repeated, the tears still falling.

"Jack, it's okay," she said, tears welling in her own eyes at his misery.

His hands slipped from her face and dropped lifelessly into his lap. His shoulders shuddered, and then he seemed to crumple in on himself and she caught him in her arms as he leaned forward. A cry of anguish that seemed to seep out of his very bones echoed through him, and then he was gripping her back with a terrifying strength as he cried and cried and cried.

His weight pulled him forward off the edge of the tub and onto his knees on the floor, and she knelt with him, her heart aching for him as he wept in her arms.

She soothed a hand down his back and up again, making encouraging noises and wincing a little because he was holding her so tightly.

They stayed like that a while, until well past what her knees were happy with, but she waited until his sobbing had tapered off before soothing a hand down his back one last time and pushing him back from her.

"How about that shower now, Jack?" she suggested.

His eyes were swollen, and he needed to blow his nose, and she had to look away from the raw vulnerability in his face. *This is why men don't let women see them cry,* she realized. Suddenly Jack seemed infinitely fragile.

She got him to his feet and into the shower, and was about to turn on the taps when he caught her hand again.

"Hang on."

With one shoulder wedged against the wall, Jack reached for the waistband on his jeans and she found herself following the movements of his hands with an unnatural fascination as he slipped the stud from its buttonhole and unzipped his fly. He hooked his thumbs into the waistband of his jeans next, and with a smooth motion he shucked them down. She gulped as she realized he'd taken his underwear with the jeans, hastily averting her eyes.

Because to do anything else would be an invasion of privacy, right? But Jack was really, really out of it, and the odds of him remembering any of this with great clarity were pretty damn slim. Almost against her will, her eyes lifted above his ankles where he was even now stepping clumsily out of his jeans and boxers, past his knees, up his well-muscled, nicely haired thighs, until she hit the money shot and swallowed a sudden lump in her throat.

Whoa!

The sight of him was enough to make her thighs tighten instinctively. It had been so hot and intense in the elevator, a lot of the details sort of blurred into one blood-stirring memory. But the sight of him made her remember what it had felt like to be completely, achingly filled by a man. She swallowed, aware that her breathing was a little shallow.

But even though she knew it was rude to stare, and that she shouldn't be indulging these sorts of fantasies, especially with Jack Brook, she couldn't seem to stop her eyes traveling back down to where all the action was, even as she accepted the T-shirt he'd shucked, and pulled his jeans out from around his feet.

Of its own accord, heat pooled low in her belly, and her heart thrummed against her ribs. She really wanted to touch him. She really wanted to get her hands on the solid, thick length of him, to feel him against her body, *in* her body.

It would be so easy just to step into the shower beside him. To peel off her clothes off and press herself against him and let herself have more of what she'd tasted.

She gave herself a shake at this last salacious thought. The man was not in his right mind. And they had been down this road before, and that way lay rejection and embarrassment.

"Right," she said, more for herself than for Jack, who was leaning against the tiled wall, his eyes closed. "It's going to be cold, okay?" she warned him, shooting one last wistful look downstairs—not even Jack Brook, with all his apparent talents, could withstand the rigors of an ice-cold shower.

She twisted the cold tap on full and leaped back as Jack reacted like a scalded cat despite his drunkenness.

"What the hell?" he demanded, suddenly standing tall and angry and naked, glaring belligerently at her.

"It's for your own good," she squeaked, shutting the shower door between them with a slam and pressing her palms against the glass. "You really need to sober up."

Jack seemed to take in what she said, but she noted that he reached for the hot tap just the same. The wary glance he shot her made her realize the cold had shocked him far closer to sobriety than she'd imagined, and she suddenly felt very uncomfortable.

"Um, I'm going to make you some food," she mumbled.

He just stared at her through the water-beaded glass, then turned his back on her and reached for the soap.

9

SHE MADE HER WAY back into the kitchen and pulled out a chair, sinking into it gratefully.

Maybe she shouldn't have come. But then she touched her shoulder where not even half an hour ago he'd been clinging desperately as his grief poured out, and she couldn't regret a thing. In her opinion, that crying jag had been a long time coming, and if she'd helped him open up some of his pain, then it didn't matter that he was probably going to hate her for it once he sobered up.

Because while she might not be the most amazingly perspicacious reader of men, she knew enough to know that Jack would rather throw her off a cliff than bump into her every day in the office knowing that she'd seen him so vulnerable.

Well, tough. He'd seen her passed out from some stupid, babyish fear of small spaces. If she could hack it, he could, too.

Now that she'd bolstered her own courage somewhat, she felt free to register the throbbing ache of her cheekbone. Before she did anything else, she needed ice.

She could still hear the shower running as she wrapped a handful of ice cubes in a clean dish towel, pressing the impromptu ice pack to her cheekbone with a sigh of relief.

"Much better," she told the empty kitchen.

Now—something to eat for a man who'd been drinking all night. She opened cabinet doors randomly until she found a stash of groceries. Here, at last, Jack Brook conformed to her idea of a bachelor—salt, pepper, a packet of noodles and some bottled sauces. Otherwise, that was it.

While she considered herself a decent cook, these kind of ingredients were beyond her. She tried the fridge, and found a package of sausages, some potatoes in the crisper, milk, butter and an onion that looked just about to sprout.

"Okay, now we're talking."

It was twenty minutes later, and she had the onions on the back burner, the sausages already cooked and put to one side, and the potato masher in hand when she registered the fact that she couldn't hear the shower running anymore.

For some reason, this made her feel nervous, and she took her feelings out on the innocent potatoes awaiting her in the saucepan. She added butter, milk, salt and pepper, and concentrated very hard on making the mash lump-free, rather than giving in to the urge to grab her car keys and leave Jack to it now that he was up and about.

You're just feeling guilty because you had a look in the candy shop without permission, she told herself, but it didn't stop her heart from picking up a little.

"This is a surprise."

She swung around to find Jack in the doorway, one shoulder propped against the door frame, a towel slung low around his waist, his eyes clear and dangerous-looking.

Water glistened on his skin, and the hair on his chest was coiled in tight, dark circles. He looked good enough to eat, damn him.

She tried to find a smile, but managed only a nervous grimace.

"You didn't turn up for the Hillcrest meeting. Linda was worried…and I saw the card from your mom," she explained hastily.

He frowned suddenly.

"What happened to your eye?" he asked, starting forward.

She stared at him. Was it possible he'd really forgotten everything so quickly? Then her gaze slid to the two empty bottles of tequila. Despite appearances, it would be stupid to assume he was anywhere near sober now.

"I had an accident. It was nothing," she said, edging away from him. The last thing she needed was for him to know how much his near-nudity was affecting her. She'd already given him more than enough opportunities to laugh in her face.

"So you came over to play nursemaid to me, did you?" Jack asked as he pulled out a chair and sat down.

Her eyes slid down the tanned planes of his chest, and she took in the apparently loosely cinched towel around his waist nervously. Why didn't he go dress? And why did she find it so hard to keep her eyes off his chest?

"I thought you might need a friend," she said.

His eyes narrowed, and she smiled weakly. He was making her feel very nervous. Something about the way he was looking at her. As if he was hungry.

"I made you something to eat," she squeaked, desperately wanting to distract him. "Sausages and mash."

"I'm not hungry."

"But you should eat. You've had a lot to drink—"

"But I'm not hungry," he repeated, and the way he was looking at her made all other protests die in her throat.

He shifted, and the towel moved a little, and she found herself staring a little breathlessly at the hard-muscled thigh now on display. Okay, this was bad. The chest she could handle, but that thigh was well nigh irresistible. She was only flesh and blood, after all. Trying to get a grip, she fought a serious, no-holds-barred battle of wills with her baser self, and finally managed to wrench her eyes away. Only to discover Jack was well aware of her preoccupation.

"See anything you like?" he asked.

She swallowed, turned back to the stove.

"This'll get cold. If I serve it up now, you can eat it later. Just heat it in the microwave…" She trailed off as she heard his chair scrape against the floor, and she spun around to find him approaching her.

She felt like a bunny in headlights. Here was the man she'd been fantasizing about for a solid forty-eight hours, walking almost-naked toward her. She only had to close her eyes to remember the feel of his body under her hands. They'd been on fire in the elevator—and now, here he was, looming over her, obviously thinking the same kinds of things she was....

"I tried to stop thinking about you, but I can't get you out of my head. And now you're here and even if it's a stupid mistake and work sucks afterward, who cares? I want you right now," he said.

She stared at him wide-eyed, conscious of the rush of heat that whooshed down into her thighs at the phrase *I want you.*

He's drunk, you're an idiot, and this should not be happening, she warned herself.

He was in front of her now, not a foot away. She could feel the heat radiating off his body. Or maybe that was her own heat. She had to get a grip. She should get out of here, walk away from this disaster-in-the-making.

Remember what happened afterward, she told herself. But all she could remember was how much her body had ached, how bereft she'd felt when he'd pulled away from her to answer that damned phone.

"I've been thinking about your breasts... I have to taste them again. Take your shirt off," Jack murmured, one hand reaching for the opening of her blouse.

Oh, boy. She watched his hand come closer and closer, and knew that, more than anything, she wanted to give in and let herself have this moment. There was no one to stop them, no earthly reason why they couldn't have at each other and end all the wondering and the lust and the wanting.

But she'd been sensible for too long to be able to ignore all the voices of reason clamoring for attention in the back of her skull. He was too drunk to know what he was really doing, and she didn't go in for casual sex, and he wasn't offering anything else, and they were work colleagues, and he hadn't even bothered to call after what happened between them in the elevator, and he was hurt and looking for something to make himself feel better….

She made herself step backward, no matter how much she wanted to just stay put and have it all. The stove was behind her and she felt the saucepan handle digging into her back.

"This is probably a really bad idea," she said faintly, aware that she'd sound a lot more convincing if her voice wasn't thin and breathy.

"Who cares?" he said, and then he ducked his head and his mouth was on her neck.

A shudder rippled through her from heel to crown as his tongue laved her neck.

Oh-boy-oh-boy-oh-boy. Her thighs felt as though they were going to explode and she could feel her breasts swelling within the confines of her bra.

He's going to regret this in the morning, she thought, and then her flailing hand connected with something and she grabbed it and pushed him away with all her strength, brandishing the object at him.

"Just keep your distance, buddy, okay, or I'll—" She paused a moment to contemplate her weapon of choice: the potato masher.

"Just…don't move," she corrected herself.

"Come on, Claire, live a little," he tempted her.

She couldn't prevent her eyes from dropping below his waist to where the evidence of his arousal was making a very respectable tent beneath his towel.

Oh, please, let's go camping! her wanton half begged, but it was hard to give up the habits of a lifetime.

"I think we need to be calm and rational about this. You've had too much to drink, and I think that you're just channeling your grief into some sort of sex thing with me. You don't really want me. I'm not your type. Plus, I'm really not into this kind of thing. I know after what happened the other day you might think I am, but, honestly, that was a one-off, and—"

She froze as his finger descended on her lips.

"Just, for once, shut up," he said huskily, then he smiled, an I'm-going-to-eat-you-up smile that made bits of her jump up and down with excitement.

She dropped the potato-encrusted masher as he closed the gap between them and then he was up against her, one hand reaching around her back to pull her close, the other sliding down over her butt to lift her against him.

She gasped as his mouth descended on hers, which was just as well because she forgot to breathe as he kissed her with a thoroughness that made her realize that, as spectacular as her recollection of the other day had been, her memory had done him a serious disservice—this man could kiss!

His other hand was doing something tricky behind her back, and then she felt a slight give around her torso and knew he'd released her bra catch through the fabric of her shirt. Wow, what a professional.

If she hadn't been so busy reacquainting herself with the curves and dips of his chest and back, she'd have been worried about just how professional he was. Instead she was grunting with satisfaction as he lifted her off the ground and turned to prop her on the edge of the kitchen sink. One impatient, very male hand swept her skirt up, and then his hips were between her knees and she found herself spreading her thighs and urging him forward so that all of his hardness could press up against her where she needed it the most.

It felt so good—especially because she'd effectively been waiting for this moment for more than two days now. Two days of tortured, argumentative foreplay. But what a payoff.

She had no idea how he got her shirt undone, she just blessed the gods that he did because then his mouth and tongue and hands were on her breasts and she threw back her head and bit her lip and tried not to explode.

His stubble scraping against her skin, his hot tongue teasing her nipple, the firm pressure as he ground his hips into the heart of her…it was almost enough to stop her noticing the tinge of alcohol on his breath. Almost, but not quite.

She managed to think for just a second as he switched his attention from her left breast to her right.

This was wrong. This was folly of the most enormous order. She would regret this if she let it go any further. Worse, she'd be like those other women in the office, the ones who took what little Jack offered, but secretly wanted it all. She knew he wasn't going to call after this. She knew exactly how this encounter was going to end, how bad and stupid she'd feel afterward, and how much she'd regret it.

"No!"

It took great determination to utter that single word and push him away from her. It took even more determination when his towel chose that exact moment to loosen completely and slide to the floor. The very impressive evidence of his arousal tempted her even as she tried to catch her breath. His blue eyes were dilated, his breath coming fast, a frown forming between his eyebrows as he registered that his toy had been taken away from him. She saw him tense to start forward again, and she held up a hand.

"I'm sorry, Jack, I should never have let this get started. But let's stop things before we do something we'll both regret."

She grasped the edges of her shirt and pulled it shut over her still-aching breasts, sliding off the edge of the sink and back down to earth. He seemed to register the finality of her actions, and he ducked to pick up his towel.

"Why'd you come, then?"

She could hear the frustration and rejection in his voice, and paused in the act of buttoning her blouse, aware her heart was still racing out of control and that her hands were shaking.

"Not for this, if that's what you're thinking."

"Really? Could have fooled me." He was almost sneering at

her, and she resumed buttoning her blouse, her fingers shaking from hurt and anger now, not lust and frustration.

"You're drunk," she told him quietly, smoothing both palms down her skirt.

"And you're uptight. And scared."

She stared at him. He was like a schoolboy who'd been banned from watching TV for a week.

"Eat something. And try not to choke on it," she told him, sweeping up her purse and car keys on her way out the door.

She stumbled on a crack in the concrete driveway as she half ran to her car. Her bra was hanging loosely around her ribs, and she kept her arms wrapped around her body until she got into the car.

Once locked inside safely, she slammed a hand against the steering wheel and swore loudly. She was a complete idiot. She could not believe she had almost had dirty drunk sex with Jack Brook, the office lothario. Hadn't her bout of dirty elevator sex taught her anything?

His demand rang in her ears. *Why'd you come, then?*

Because I knew you were hurting.

But she could have left him in the shower. She *should* have left him in the shower. And she wasn't ready to consider why she hadn't.

WOODY WOODPECKER had taken up residence in his skull and was working on an extension to the facilities. It was the first thought that staggered across Jack's mind as his eyes flickered open early Saturday morning. He lay still and stared at the ceiling for a moment, aware that a headache roughly the size of a small planet was waiting to descend on him. He forced himself to sit up, and the headache descended like a banshee. Cradling his aching forehead in his hands, Jack took his tongue on a tour around his mouth. Not good. If he didn't know better, he'd suspect some poor woodland creature had crawled in there and died last night.

Slowly he stood and made his way to the kitchen, wondering

vaguely along the way why he was naked. The kitchen faucet drew him like a magnet and he stuck his mouth beneath it and simply drank until he could hear water sloshing around inside himself.

Then he turned and leaned against the sink, trying to hazily recollect where he kept the aspirin these days. His eyes fell on the two empty bottles of tequila on the kitchen table, and he grimaced. Why on earth had he chosen such a lethal poison?

His gaze tracked to the left and he found himself contemplating a mess of saucepans on the stove. Frowning, he stared at the congealed food: mash, sausages, onions. And then memory flooded back and he closed his eyes in sheer self-defense.

Claire. She came over because…that bit he couldn't quite grasp. But he remembered her being hurt, remembered touching her face… Hell, he'd hurt her. The memory of overbalancing in the bathroom was vague, but he got the gist of it.

Great. He was such an asshole.

Hard on the heels of this revelation came another: he'd cried. He'd cried like a baby, like a little boy who'd lost his puppy.

Like a man who'd never grieved for his dead twin.

His first impulse was to writhe with humiliation. Of all the people to witness his self-indulgence, Claire Marsden was almost the worst he could imagine. Perhaps only Mike Tyson rated higher.

But the memory of being held and soothed in her arms washed over him then, and he could almost feel her empathy and calm as she waited him out.

Maybe she hadn't been such a bad choice, after all. It didn't escape his attention that after a long time of not daring to say Robbie's name out loud, he'd chosen to tell her about his brother the other day in the elevator. And now he'd blubbered all over her….

But try as he might, he couldn't find a way to reconcile himself to such a display of emotion and helplessness. Way too revealing. Way too emasculating. And he never cried. Never. Not at Robbie's bedside. Not at Robbie's graveside.

Yet all it took was a few gallons of tequila and Claire Marsden and he was howling like a pro.

In case he'd forgotten, his headache stepped things up a notch and he groaned. Before anything else, aspirin was required. In large, industrial doses.

He headed to the far cabinet, but the feel of something soft and mushy underfoot stopped him in his tracks. A dozen suggestions flitted across his mind, none of them pretty, before he steeled himself to glance down.

Mashed potato? He laughed with relief, and then sobered suddenly as the last jigsaw puzzle piece of memory slotted into place.

Claire Marsden, sans bra, sans attitude, all hot, wanton woman, on his kitchen sink. It was enough to make parts of him salute with respect.

How in hell had that happened?

And—more importantly—why had it stopped? Because it had been good. Very good. Even his tequila-soaked memory of it was good, very good. He'd been determined to keep his distance after their last intimate encounter, sure that he'd made the right decision. But, for some reason, he'd abandoned his game plan and succumbed again. It was becoming something of a habit, in fact. A scary, addictive habit.

An accusation leaped to mind out of the blue. *You're drunk.*

Only Claire Marsden could be responsible for the inflection he was recalling so vividly. And, indeed, he had been drunk. Really, stinking, rotten, putrid drunk. That probably explained his lack of impulse control. And the dismal quality of his memory of the whole thing. He cursed himself—at least if he wasn't able to repeat the experience in reality, he should be able to repeat it in the privacy of his own mind. His own messed-up, confused mind.

He downed a couple of aspirin and visited the kitchen faucet for one last monumental watering before staggering back to his bedroom. Throwing himself on the bed, he slung a protective arm across his eyes and began regretting the last twenty-four hours in earnest.

He'd been feeling…well, he'd been *feeling,* bottom line. So he'd tried to drown it in a tequila bath. Or vat, more likely, given the way his head was throbbing.

Hell, when was the aspirin going to kick in? He groaned a little, just to compound his self-inflicted misery.

His eyes felt gritty, dry. *That would be from all the crying, you big girl,* he told himself in disgust. Why had he bawled in front of Claire? His toes curled at the very idea of revealing himself so completely to a woman who had already judged him and found him wanting, and he groaned out loud again.

If he was given the moment all over again, he might actually choose Mike Tyson to witness his breakdown over Claire—that's how much he regretted it.

Hard to regret the other part of her visit, however. He'd wanted to touch her and taste her again so badly. She'd been the elusive star of his erotic dreams. And now the faint memory of the press of her body against his teased at him. She'd been up for it. He could still feel her hands gripping his shoulders, pulling him closer.

How had they leaped from mutual antagonism to mutual lust in the space it took a drunken man to traverse his kitchen? And why did it keep happening? First in the elevator, then the near miss with the stapler and now this. When was he going to learn to stop playing with fire?

Even now, lying here hungover and messed up, he only had to think of her to send blood rushing south of the border. It was as though he had no control over his own carnal desires where Claire was concerned. He didn't want to want her, every logical, rational brain cell argued that she represented nothing but trouble. Yet his penis had very definite views on the subject. He lifted his head and glared at the offending organ.

"Down, boy. You have no idea what you're asking for."

One thing was for sure—Claire had regretted what had happened between them almost instantly. If he closed his eyes, he could actually relive her pulling her blouse closed across her bared breasts. He tried to freeze-frame it on that bit of the memory, but it inevitably tipped over into revealing the hurt and disappointment on her face as she gathered herself together and headed for the door. And she was already pissed at him for not calling her after their last encounter....

More bad behavior such as this, and he'd be on every feminist hit list in the country—and he could guarantee that Claire would never even glance his way again. And that was a good thing, a really good thing. Wasn't it?

CLAIRE STEPPED OUT of the shower, toweling her body roughly. It was useless, however. No matter what she did, anything that touched her skin reminded her of Jack's hands on her body.

And it wasn't as if she needed prompting to remember her ill-fated visit to Jack's home. For starters, she had a huge, shiny black eye to mark the occasion. And whisker rash on her neck from where he had... Well, it didn't really matter what he'd done. It was more that she wished it all undone. Please.

She dropped the towel abruptly, padding out into the living room. For a moment she simply stood there, aware that her back and most of her legs were still wet. And that if she looked down, she'd see her nipples were erect.

Damn Jack Brook!

And damn herself. She'd had a long, uninterrupted, sleepless night to consider just how delusional she'd become over the past few days. She'd come to the only sane conclusion: she'd put her hand into the wolf's mouth, and he'd tried to bite it off. Twice. She shouldn't be surprised that the wolf had acted according to instinct—that was what wolves did, after all. But she had to wonder why she was traipsing around offering herself up at every possible opportunity like an almost-out-of-date platter of hors d'oeuvres.

That bit she hadn't been able to work out. She didn't know what was going on inside her convoluted, messed-up mind at the moment. If someone had asked her what she thought of her life and herself a few days ago, she would have been able to say confidently that she was happy, satisfied, settled. But today, at this moment, standing naked in her apartment, she would respond very differently.

Now she felt like every certainty in her life was up for grabs. Hell, she wondered if she even wanted to keep doing *Welcome Home*. But she couldn't for the life of her work out if that was because it seemed now to be inextricably entwined with Jack, or because Morgan had taken all of the glow and shine out of it for her. Or perhaps it was both…

She also wasn't talking to her father, and probably wouldn't be for the near future.

Truly, her life sucked.

She tugged her swimsuit crop top on, grimacing as the lycra clung to her damp skin. This was her second-last weekend before the triathlon final, and she had to focus. She hadn't trained for all these months for nothing. She wanted to win. Jack and her messed-up feelings for him didn't matter. Her father and the fact that he'd probably removed her number from his Rolodex didn't matter.

What she needed was some punishing exercise, and that flashy memory-wiping thing Will Smith and Tommy Lee Jones used in *Men in Black*. Then she could forget all the nice things she'd learned about Jack over the past few days and consign the memory of his hands on her skin to the dustbin of time.

Nice idea. Shame about the reality.

10

HE HAD TO APOLOGIZE. Somehow Jack had to stand in front of Claire and apologize for crying on her then nearly molesting her. It was a conclusion that was waiting for him, fully formed and unavoidable, when he woke up for the second time that Saturday morning.

It wasn't going to be easy. Or pretty. But it had to be done.

He managed to push the consideration to the back of his mind during the rest of the day, what with nursing the mother of all hangovers and then catching up on all the work he'd let slide while he had his meltdown. By the time night was falling, he'd come up with a raft of reasons for putting it off, any time it swam to the front of his consciousness. For starters, he didn't have her phone number. And, really, that sort of thing should be handled face-to-face.

By midmorning on Sunday he admitted to himself that he wasn't going to call her. He didn't know what to say. He hadn't asked her to come over to his place. He hadn't asked to be trapped in the elevator with her. And she had something on him now. She'd seen him cry, for Pete's sake. Even his mother hadn't seen him cry since he was seven—and that was only because he broke his leg in two places jumping off the roof of the shed.

And—deep, dark honesty here—he felt too raw to face her just yet. He wasn't quite sure why he'd let rip with all his grief for Robbie the other night, but he was still sorting through it all in the back of his mind somewhere. Maybe when he understood what had happened he would know why he'd confessed all to a woman he'd barely known a week ago, but who now held sway over most of his subconscious. Damn her and her silky breasts. And damn the raging hard-on that kept rearing its persistent head whenever he so much as thought her name.

Then it was Monday, and he couldn't put off the apology any longer. He rehearsed a couple of very rational, mature explanations in his head as he showered. Somehow, every scenario kept sliding to the same conclusion—Claire, sans clothing, assuring him that one night of unbridled, no-strings-attached sex with him was the only recompense she could possibly accept for his shabby behavior.

Like magic, the die-hard boner that had haunted him all weekend was back. Jack groaned out loud. He had to get this woman out of his system. The way he was going, he'd walk into her office to apologize and Mr. Stiffy would want to join in. No, it was time to deal with his body's stupid fascination with Claire. Reaching down between his legs, he very deliberately pictured a sexy blond woman he'd dated a few months ago. She'd had small, high breasts and long legs….

But try as he might, the only face and body he could summon up out of his subconscious was Claire's. A couple of hot encounters, and he was turning into a stalker. Great. Especially when the chances of actually achieving any kind of satisfaction again on that front were extremely slim. She and he were about as compatible as…as chilies and ice cream.

Clenching his eyes shut, he tried to imagine anyone else—Angelina Jolie, Halle Berry, Naomi Campbell…but no dice. Claire Marsden remained centre stage in his brain. With a despairing groan he surrendered himself to the demands of his body, giving himself up to the heat of the shower and his dangerous fantasies. Undressing Claire again in his mind's eye, he watched her face transform with desire, reveling in the little hiccup in her breathing when he bit gently on her nipples. He could almost feel the weight of her breasts in his hands, and the smooth curve of her butt as he lifted her and plunged into her wetness. He imagined the feel of her skin beneath his hands, and the slick, tight heat of her wrapped around him…

Too quickly he shuddered out his release, then sagged against the tiled shower wall.

"That's it," he told his rebellious body. "Now leave me alone."

In a feeble attempt to ease his way into an apology, he decided to go to the trouble of dressing well. The iron was dragged out of its dusty hidey-hole, and he even toyed with the idea—briefly, just briefly—of wearing the tie she'd given him. But a man had his principles, after all.

Now he stood in front of his bathroom mirror and practiced a smile. The man smiling back at him looked sick and insincere.

Great. He couldn't even fool himself.

He had planned on going straight to her office to apologize the moment he got into work, kind of like swallowing his medicine really fast and pretending he couldn't taste it. But he found himself diverting instead to the foyer coffee shop. A good dose of caffeine, and then he'd be ready. And he was not avoiding the situation. Not at all.

But somehow, when he got in the elevator he found himself punching the button for his floor, not hers. He'd just check his e-mails, and make sure there were no urgent phone calls. And then he'd do it. Definitely.

MONDAY MORNING. Claire sat in her car and tried to pretend it was like any other Monday for a full ten minutes, but she still couldn't force herself to get out and face the working week. She didn't ever want to see Jack again. She certainly didn't want to see him while she was sporting this lurid black eye. Apart from purely aesthetic reasons—and she didn't care about him thinking she was ugly, she really didn't—it made pretending that last Friday never happened impossible.

Why had she let him kiss her? A whole weekend of pounding the pavement, swimming lap after lap and riding her bike till her backside felt like it would never be the same again, had not even put a dint in her regret and self-recrimination. She'd spent nearly two years ignoring the man and telling herself she was superior to the other women in the office who fell all over him, then he'd barely glanced at her and she was ripping her clothes off in an elevator for him, and writhing around all over his kitchen sink. Just the thought of it made her flush with humiliation. And remembered desire. Which only made the humiliation more humiliating. Did she have no self-respect whatsoever?

Which brought her back to how to handle the current situation. She was still discarding options when the elevator pinged to a halt on her floor. She adjusted the enormous Jackie-O-esque sunglasses she'd bought on the weekend, then began weaving her way through the warren of workstations on the way to her office.

She was braced to cope with stares and shock when people saw the shiner—she'd dealt with it all weekend—but most people were too busy to notice her, and Tom wasn't at his desk. She slipped virtually unnoticed into her office and for a cowardly second toyed with the idea of keeping on the glasses all day. But she knew that it would just add fuel to the fire if she tried to hide her eye. The trick to pulling this off with the minimum of fuss and bother was to brazen it out.

She'd decided on a nice, innocuous explanation for her eye—she'd had an accident while training. No connection between her and Jack. No need for either of them to bring it up, even if he remembered. And he might not, right? He'd had a lot to drink….

She grunted with self-disgust.

Like he didn't remember. As if she could get that lucky. How on earth was she going to look at him? And why had she felt it was her responsibility to save him from himself in the first place? Lastly, why had Beck foisted Jack, of all people, onto her project?

Feeling ridiculously exposed and vulnerable, she turned on her computer, then carefully slid off the sunglasses. Her in-tray was groaning with mail and memos, and she dragged it toward herself gratefully—anything to stop her mind from running in circles like a mouse in a wheel.

She was engrossed in paperwork when Tom entered loaded up with muffins and take-out coffees from downstairs.

"Now, I knew you wouldn't have had time to have breakfast, as usual," he said brightly.

She lifted her head to thank him, and he almost lost his grip on the coffees as he registered her damaged eye.

"Good golly Miss Molly! What on earth happened to you?" he squeaked.

For a second there she'd forgotten about the eye.

"Bit of an accident out training. Looks worse than it is," she said, hoping she sounded dismissive but instead sounding nervous.

She tried to smile calmly as Tom came closer, his face screwed up with a mixture of fascination and disgust as he studied her bruise.

"Man, that is *sooooo* bad. I have never seen a worse shiner in my life. Does it hurt? It looks like it hurts."

She felt her smile slip a little. If she couldn't even cope with Tom, how was she going to face Jack?

"It's fine. Really. And it'll be gone in a few days' time."

"Are you kidding? That thing is going to go yellow and brown and purple and green—you just wait."

Her smile felt as though it was set in concrete, and she reached for the muffin bag Tom had dumped unceremoniously on the desk.

"Don't suppose there are any blueberry in here?" she asked, desperate to divert him.

But Tom was still hyped about her eye. He leaned out of her office doorway.

"Hey, Kirsty, Helen, Roy—come check out Claire's shiner! It's unreal!" he hollered.

It was going to be a long day.

As Tom herded his colleagues into her office so he could show her off like a sideshow freak, she was vaguely aware of a stir on the other side of the floor. A hushed quiet, closely followed by lots of feminine discussion. But Tom was pointing out the many different colors of purple in her bruise to Kirsty, and she didn't see the human bouquet until it appeared in her doorway.

Jack was holding the largest bunch of flowers Claire had ever seen. A veritable riot of color, so large that only his head and legs were visible at either end of the damn thing. Tom and Kirsty and Helen and Roy all looked from her to Jack and back again, then smiled knowingly.

She didn't need to be a rocket scientist to work out what they were thinking. Or to understand why her heart was suddenly racing. Damn him.

A sudden memory of how his stubbled cheek had felt against the soft skin of her neck flashed across her brain, and a wave of heat followed quickly in its wake. She felt dizzy, and unbearably transparent. He could probably read every thought crossing her mind. She could just imagine him laughing with his buddies over the uptight chick at work who'd turned to butter the moment he'd crooked his little finger.

"Um, did you want to see me, Jack?" she managed to say finally. Her voice came out squeaky and breathy, and Kirsty and Helen nudged each other meaningfully.

Jack was staring at her face, a small frown creasing his brow. "Jack?"

He blinked, then looked from her to the flowers to the interested spectators crowded around her desk.

"Yes. Yes, that would be good," he said awkwardly.

She waited for her uninvited guests to slowly, reluctantly ease from the room. Tom lingered the longest, shooting one last speculative look over his shoulder as he exited.

She waited till they were all gone before crossing to the door and closing it. Taking a deep breath, she turned to face Jack.

HE'D GIVEN HER a black eye. Jack couldn't believe it. He'd given women a lot of things over the years—flowers, chocolates, orgasms. But never a black eye.

He didn't know what to do. He'd come down here with a game plan—hand over the flowers, apologize for leaving her high and dry with Hillcrest and manfully skirt around the topic of having sobbed his heart out on her shoulder. But now she was sporting a painful-looking shiner and all bets were off. Guilt and regret swamped him. He'd hurt her—she'd come around to be his friend and he'd hurt her.

"This is really awkward. I've never given a woman a black eye before," he heard himself say.

Very smooth. She was staring at him as if he was a few chromosomes short of being fully human.

"What I mean is…I'm really sorry. I didn't realize. These flowers were for bailing on the Hillcrest meeting, and for, you know, the other…thing. But that eye…I'm really sorry."

She'd gone pale. She broke eye contact with him, her gaze shifting over his shoulder. Why couldn't he just say what he meant? Why couldn't he say that he wouldn't hurt her for all the world? That seeing her like this, knowing he'd done this to her, made him feel sick to the stomach?

"It's fine, it was an accident. There's no need to talk about it. Really," she said.

Of their own accord, his eyes found her breasts. She was wearing a high-necked, dark red blouse, but he knew what lay beneath her librarian's wardrobe now. It was amazing that he'd never noticed before, really. She was a very attractive woman. And passionate. He couldn't forget the way she'd responded to his touch.

He wrenched his eyes away from her chest. What was he doing? This was a woman he'd blubbered all over like an idiot. A woman who'd made her feelings about him pretty clear. A woman who was sporting a glowing shiner thanks to his drunken grief. He shouldn't be thinking about pushing her up against the desk and lifting her neat little skirt. It was too late, however—the erection he'd thought he'd tamed that morning was back with a vengeance.

Confused and angry with himself, he thrust the flowers into her arms.

"Here. I'm sorry," he said, ready to make a run for it.

But she just stared at the bouquet, her eyes shifting over his shoulder again.

"I can't take them," she said, thrusting the flowers back at him.

This wasn't how it was supposed to go. She had to take the flowers. She had to accept his apology, because he was not having this hanging over him. She already had enough on him, she wasn't having this. It was bad enough that he couldn't get her out of his head, that she peopled his dreams and haunted his subconscious.

"But they're yours," he insisted, shoving them back at her.

"But I don't want them."

Back to him.

"You have to take them."

Back at her.

"Do you have any idea how this looks?" she pointed out, thrusting the flowers back at him one last time and then retreating behind her desk.

"It looks like I'm giving you flowers. Or it would, if you could stop being so damned uptight for ten seconds," he snapped.

She sucked in a breath and her hands found her hips. He willed himself to not look at her breasts, and had to be content with snatching a quick look before glancing away.

"Take a look over your shoulder," she snapped at him.

Frowning, he turned and saw that half the floor was standing watching their little interplay through the glass wall of Claire's office. Did these people have no lives of their own?

"Think for a minute, Jack. You, the office playboy, bringing *me* flowers. And I have a black eye. What do you think people are going to make of that?"

He tossed the flowers on her desk, his temper really firing now. Did she have to sound so disgusted by the prospect that people might think there was something going on between them?

"I don't care what people think. And I thought we'd agreed I don't like being called the office playboy."

"Maybe you should have thought about that before you did all those laps of the typing pool."

He made an exasperated noise. She didn't like that. Her lips went all thin, and her nostrils flared.

"I'm serious, Jack. I don't want to be another notch in your bedpost. Now the whole office thinks we're sleeping with each other, thanks to these stupid flowers."

"Sweetheart, I never make the same mistake twice, so don't get your hopes up."

It was out before he could think, a jibe straight from the school yard, and he'd have to be blind to miss the flash of hurt in her eyes before she put on her game face.

"Don't flatter yourself. I prefer my men a little more sophisticated, not to mention sober."

He'd deserved that, but it still made him see red.

"For a moment there I forgot who I was dealing with, but thank you for the reminder, Little Miss Hospital Corners."

Before she could say anything else he'd flung her office door open.

"Excuse me, your attention please."

He waited until the whole floor had stopped what it was doing and turned to face him. For a split second his impulse control kicked in, but by then his mouth was fully engaged.

"For the record, Claire Marsden and I are not having sex."

He heard her horrified intake of breath and spun around to face her.

"Happy now?"

She could only stare at him. He managed to make it all the way to the elevator before the remorse and guilt hit him. But by then it was too late to do anything except keep going.

SHE STOOD FROZEN in place for a full minute after he'd gone. It was only when Tom came and knocked awkwardly on her door that she found her spine.

"Can I get you anything? Coffee? An aspirin?" he asked helpfully.

She groaned and dropped into her chair.

"Do I look that pitiful?"

Tom just smiled weakly, obviously not wanting to lie.

"Should I…should I get a vase for these?" he asked, gesturing toward the flowers Jack had all but thrown at her.

"Hell, no. Take them away. Give them to the assistants, or your girlfriend, or whoever. I never want to see them again," she said.

Tom eased them out from under her nose, and she made a show of getting on with business so that the rest of the prying eyes in the office would have nothing to feed off. She made a phone call, checked her e-mail, opened some letters. All the while, her mind was a careful blank. Somewhere, deep inside, was a tsunami of humiliation just waiting to swamp her. But she was damned if she would give Jack Brook the satisfaction of giving in to it with half the office watching.

"Okay, let's go."

She looked up to find Katherine in her doorway, a determined look on her face.

"Sorry, what?"

"Claire, I've just had no less than three phone calls from people on your floor telling me that Jack Brook just brought you flowers and told the whole building that you're not having sex. Come on, we're heading out."

It didn't feel like a request, more like a demand, and because she was still reeling from Jack's very public display, Claire meekly collected her purse and followed Katherine to the stairwell. A few heads turned and someone sniggered. Katherine sniffed haughtily and lifted her chin high, true friend that she was, but, despite all her determination, a hot tide washed up Claire's chest and into her face.

Katherine led her down a floor before stopping and sitting on a step. Claire obediently followed suit, feeling completely out of her depth in this undiscovered world of office romances.

"Okay, what's going on between you and Jack?" Katherine asked bluntly.

"Nothing. I mean, we've been forced to work together, but that's all."

"Right. Which is why he's just told the world that he's not sleeping with you. Where there's smoke, Claire…"

Katherine was regarding her intently, and Claire couldn't quite meet her eye.

"Something might have happened the other day in the elevator. And again the other day at his place."

"Did he do that to your face?" Katherine asked, her expression tight.

Claire guessed what her friend was thinking and hastened to reassure her.

"It was an accident, he was drunk—"

"Right!" Katherine stood, six feet of pure, angry woman. Realizing she had the wrong end of the stick, Claire grabbed her ankle before she could barge up to Jack's office and give him what for.

"It wasn't like that. I was helping him take his boots off, and he tripped. It was my fault as much as his," she explained.

Katherine froze, then some of the tension dropped out of her and she sat beside Claire on the step. Silence stretched between them for a beat. Then, "So you're seeing him, huh?" Katherine asked, her expression unreadable.

Claire shook her head, then winced when it made her eye hurt.

"Uh-uh. Things just got out of control. We don't even like each other."

Although, that wasn't quite as true as it used to be. Even humiliated and angry, she had to admit that there were aspects of Jack that she liked and admired.

"I keep hearing this from you a lot lately. Love and hate are just opposite ends of the same spectrum. You know that, don't you?"

Claire stared at her, genuinely horrified. "Are you kidding? There is no way I feel anything close to…*that* for Jack Brook. We just got stuck with each other, and we were bored. It's kind of a power thing. That's all."

She almost convinced herself. Katherine sighed and stood, brushing her skirt down.

"Well, good luck. He's a hard nut to crack," she said ruefully.

Claire looked at her sharply. "Did you—did you love him?" she asked hesitantly, picking up on something in Katherine's voice.

"Of course not, we barely lasted more than a week or two. I just think he's a good guy, underneath it all. Kind of the one that got away, you know."

Claire nodded her understanding, and Katherine squeezed her shoulder briefly before heading down the stairs to her own floor.

"Oh, and forget about the gossip. That time I got busted with the Xerox guy in the photocopier room? A five-day wonder. Something else will come up, and you and Jack will be old news, I promise."

Claire smiled weakly, but as soon as her friend was gone she dropped her head into her hands and sighed heavily. She could honestly say she'd never been more humiliated in all her life. She'd worked so hard to project a certain image at Beck and Wise. She had a reputation for being hardworking and serious, and she liked that. It was important to her to get ahead, to secure her own future. She'd learned the hard way that the only person you could rely on in life was yourself.

And she'd stupidly dropped her guard and allowed herself to

feel something for Jack. After just a few brief hours in an elevator, she had written off a lifetime of caution and carefulness and
given in to her baser instincts. And look where it had got her—
the whole building was talking about her.

Perhaps this was why she'd always kept Jack at arm's length—
because she'd known, deep down inside, that he was her nemesis, romantically speaking. A force with the power to scramble
her thoughts, hijack her libido and drag her focus from the things
she truly considered important, like her sport and her career.

Katherine was a good friend, but she was wrong about Claire
and Jack—there was no love-hate thing going on here. For some
strange reason, they had discovered a sexual chemistry. That
was it, pure and simple. And Claire wasn't about to let it ruin her
life. A lot of things that were really important to her were coming to fruition in the next few weeks. She wasn't about to let Jack
distract her from her dreams.

She sat up, then stood. Goodbye, easy-to-bait, slightly infat-
uated Claire.

She smoothed her skirt, adjusted her cuffs. Hello, cool, polished professional who could cut through Jack's flirting and bra-
vado like a hot knife through butter. From now on, she gave him
nothing. And if that meant it was back to the cold-war status that
had existed before they were trapped in the elevator, fine. Because she wasn't letting him get the better of her again.

HE'D GONE TOO FAR. That much was obvious. He'd gone down
there intending to apologize, and he'd wound up being nasty. All
because she'd gotten all prim and proper about people thinking
they were sleeping together.

It wasn't as if it was a big deal that a man and a woman might
want to have sex with each other. It had happened before in the
history of time. Sure, it was unlikely that it would ever happen
again between him and Claire, but it was nothing for her to be
getting her knickers in a knot over. Boy, was she uptight.

And probably mad as hell with him. Beck had had no idea what he was doing when he'd forced the two of them to work together.

Jack groaned and spun around in his chair. Clouds scudded across the bright blue sky in the world outside, and he wished he was out there instead of stuck inside having to deal with the repercussions of his actions.

Why had he given in to the impulse to humiliate her? A little voice whispered something deep inside, but Jack stomped on it mercilessly. He didn't want to think about how mad he'd gotten when it became clear that Claire was embarrassed about having had sex with him. That she *regretted* their encounters. While he'd been tossing and turning and fighting to retain control of his subconscious all weekend, she'd been cleaning him out of her memory and her life. For some reason, it rankled very deeply that she could dismiss him so easily. So he'd lashed out. And the rest would go down in office history, no doubt.

Of course, they were beyond apology now. You couldn't apologize for an apology that had gone wrong.

All that was left now was retreat. Which was no bad thing, when push came to shove. Because he was spending way too much of his day thinking about Claire. Ever since their time in the elevator she hadn't been far from his thoughts. And that was not on.

He knew what he wanted out of life. Uncomplicated friendships with women. A successful career. Travel. Excitement. Freedom.

And the absolute guarantee that he would never again feel as bereft as he'd felt the day his brother died.

So, it was decided, then. No more enjoying himself teasing Claire. Definitely no more checking out her butt or her breasts, or imagining what it would be like to make love to her again, no holds barred, in the privacy of a bedroom. Long and slow, hard and fast and lots of ways in between. And forget trying to make her laugh. No, it was back to basics—work, work and more work. He'd just grit his teeth and get through this stupid alliance Beck had manipulated, and that would be that. From now on, professionalism was the name of the day. Coolheaded professionalism and self-control.

CLAIRE CHECKED her watch and resisted the urge to drum her fingers. Jack was late. Again. It was Thursday, three days since the Flowers Incident. Three days of calm and focus as she got back on track with work and training. Her event times were good, the magazine was coming along nicely and she'd managed to live down the sniggers and gossip generated by Jack's impromptu announcement. She was even coming to terms with the fact that there had been nothing but a very speaking silence from her father. She was in the zone. Cool as a cucumber.

Sure, she hadn't actually come face-to-face with Jack yet. She'd organized this meeting between him and Hank Hillcrest through the nice, safe mechanism of e-mail—but she'd done it. It had only taken her an hour or so to compose a suitably terse, chill note explaining about the store tour that Hank Hillcrest wanted to take them on today. But that was all part of the new attitude—terse and chill. A lean, mean business machine. With a central oasis of cool confidence.

Except now Jack was late, and her confidence and cool were beginning to curl at the edges. If he didn't show a second time, if he left her standing outside the building waiting…she would seriously have to suppress murderous urges if he let her down again.

The low, throaty burble of a sports engine cut across her thoughts and she turned to find Jack cruising to a halt beside her in his red Porsche. Her stomach contracted nervously and she told herself it was because he'd startled her. No other reason.

Don't give him an inch. She had to remember that.

"You're late."

"There was a pileup on the freeway."

She inclined her head minutely to indicate she was willing to accept this.

"We'd better get a move on if we don't want to be late getting out to Hillcrest headquarters," she said, all brisk business.

"Not a problem," he said, leaning across to open his car door.

It took a moment for her to realize that he wanted her to get in.

"I think we should take my car," she said, balking at the idea of being stuck in such close confines with him for the better part of an hour.

"Sure. If that's what you want. Except my car's all ready to go."

She gave him a sharp look. He sounded very…cooperative. Not a characteristic she associated with him at all.

And, of course, now she couldn't insist on taking her car without looking like a royal pain.

Businesslike. Professional. She had to take her personal reactions out of the equation. What would she do if he was any other business colleague?

Damn it. She'd really wanted to have her own car, to feel in control of this outing.

She pulled the car door open a little wider.

"If you're sure you don't mind driving…?" she asked hopefully.

"Not a problem."

She slid into the low bucket seat, dragging her hem over her knees. His aftershave wrapped itself around her and she stiffened, suddenly unbearably aware of everything about him. The crisp curls on the back of his hands. The way his faded jeans hugged his thighs as he changed gears. The faint stubble darkening his cheeks.

"Take the southeastern out of town," she instructed, riveting her gaze on the hood and refusing to acknowledge all the little messages her body was sending her.

He nodded, and a tense silence fell.

She should have insisted on separate cars. Definitely.

IF HE HAD TO MOUTH one more polite, bland, nothing-burger phrase, Jack truly was going to scream. When had small talk become so excruciating? It was like being stuck in a car with a robot. She looked like Claire Marsden, she smelled like Claire Marsden. She had Claire Marsden's softly curling hair and cute turned-up nose. But all other human qualities had been stripped away to leave nothing but a polite business machine.

Which was how he wanted it, of course. It suited his own agenda absolutely. Except...

He couldn't help remembering the sound of her laughter when they'd discussed their favorite movies. Or the soft curve of her mouth just before he kissed her. And the way her eyes dilated with desire when he touched her just so....

Which was truly disturbing, and enough to renew his determination to keep her at arm's length. He didn't want her haunting his dreams. He didn't even know where to begin negotiating a place for her in his world.

"Just turn left here," she said, indicating a street up ahead.

He turned the corner, immediately spotting the enormous Hillcrest building. Easing the car over a speed bump, he slid into a parking spot and pulled on the hand brake. Silence filled the car as he switched the ignition off.

"Any last-minute things I ought to know before we go in?" he asked.

Anything to fill the void.

She was gathering her things, checking her papers in her briefcase.

"I don't think so."

She was cool, dismissive. He matched her.

"Let's go then."

They got out of the car and began walking toward the front entrance of the huge glass-and-steel building. He stood aside to let her precede him into the building, and just for a second he let his eyes drop down to caress her butt as she passed him. He could remember what that butt felt like in his hands, could remember how he'd held her to him and she'd rubbed herself—

He had to remember. Today was about business. Strictly business.

11

CLAIRE STARED at the polished timber tabletop in front of her and tried to stave off the urge to yawn. Boring did not begin to do justice to the tedium of a day spent talking hardware retailing with Hank Hillcrest. And it was still going, even though the store tour was well over. They'd long since returned from admiring paint departments and lumber yards, and for the past hour they'd been ensconced in Hank's private meeting room enjoying what he referred to as a "good old chin wag."

The entire day had been a unique form of torture for her. Despite her determination to ignore Jack and her traitorous body's reaction to him, she'd had to give herself a severe private talking to several times. Once Jack had stepped backward in the warehouse to make way for a forklift, accidentally walking into her. She'd been seriously incapable of coherent thought for a full ten minutes afterward. And then they'd been forced to sit next to each other in the back of a company car while one of the Hillcrest executives drove them to a store so Jack could "get a feel for the business." His thigh had been pressed against hers the entire time, and she'd been unable to stop the thoughts and sensations that had flooded her. Every inch of her body had felt highly sensitized by the time they'd stepped out of car, and when Jack had put his hand on the small of her back to guide her into the store, a rush of damp heat had pooled between her thighs. This, just from a hand on the small of her back! If things kept up like this, she was going to have to carry a spare pair of panties around with her in simple self-defense.

She'd spent the rest of the afternoon going to insane lengths to keep as many people between them as possible.

Giving up on the intricate wood grain of the table's surface, she tuned back into the conversation Jack and Hank were having. Something about advances in electric drill technology. She studied Jack as he talked. She had to hand it to him, he'd been fantastic today. Patient, intelligent, funny. With Hank and his executives, that was. With her, he'd been cool, brisk, businesslike. Exactly what the doctor ordered, of course. Except she couldn't help feeling a bit piqued when she saw him being funny and charming with everyone but her. All she got was dry business chat and polite observations about the weather. Not that it had made any difference to her body's reaction to him, of course, but it added a nice fillip to her humiliation when he didn't spare her so much as a glance while she was turning to goo at the very sight of him.

A sudden stiffening in Jack's posture alerted her that something was up and she tuned back into the conversation again.

"…was wondering how you found the elephant populations in Kenya when you were on safari? Last time I was over there they were very positive about herd numbers."

She froze. Jack was staring blank-faced at Hillcrest. As well he might, given that she'd failed to fill him in on her cover story for his absence from last week's meeting. Probably because she'd forgotten it herself. Fortunately, Hank Hillcrest hadn't. Lucky her.

A frown wrinkled Hillcrest's formidable forehead as he waited for Jack's response. She felt sweat break out on her own brow. She should say something. Something witty and clever that would save the day. But her mind was a complete blank. And any second now she knew that Jack was going to open his mouth and deny any knowledge of Africa or safaris and she was going to look like the world's biggest liar.

The silence stretched. Jack's eyes flickered across to her, and she tried to signal him with her eyes. Unfortunately, she hadn't quite mastered the art of eyebrow semaphore. He probably thought she was having a facial spasm.

Then he turned back to Hillcrest and smiled. A big, confident, broad smile. "I think they're pretty happy with the herd populations at the moment," he said carefully. His eyes flickered across to her and she nodded encouragingly to show him he was on the right track.

"Claire was telling me that you like to stay with the local tribes rather than in the tourist facilities…?"

She closed her eyes for a brief moment. She'd been under pressure last week, and the most enormous crock of rubbish had come pouring out her mouth. God only knew what gem Hillcrest was going to remember next.

When she opened her eyes again Jack was giving her a very pointed look.

"Claire told you that, did she?"

She smiled weakly. Jack settled back into his chair, slipping easily into raconteur mode as he began regaling Hillcrest with tales from his African adventures. Such as the time he drank fresh cow's blood with the Masai tribe he was staying with. And how he'd gone on a hunting party looking for a rogue lion that had been attacking the tribe's herds.

She sat on the edge of her seat throughout, barely believing that he was pulling this off, torn between admiration and disgust at what a good liar he was. And terribly, terribly aware that she now owed him. Big-time.

Finally the meeting was over. Now that he and Jack had the whole African continent in common, Hillcrest was filled with bonhomie and he escorted them all the way down to the foyer. A last round of handshakes and back pats for the men, a restrained handshake for her, and then she and Jack were angling across the lot toward his car.

There was silence between them for a beat as they settled into

Jack's low-slung Porsche. She held her breath, waiting. Then Jack turned to her.

"Safari? That was the best excuse you could come up with for me not being at a meeting?"

She winced apologetically. "I'm sorry. I'm a terrible liar."

"What was wrong with simple sickness? A nice, normal bout of food poisoning?"

"He was in a bad mood. I kind of got carried away," she admitted.

"Boy, are you lucky I watched *Tarzan* so much as a kid."

And suddenly they were both laughing. All the tension of the meeting poured out of them as they howled for a good five minutes. The car resounded with their wheezy breathing as they both tried to regain control, but she only had to make eye contact with him and she was off again, and the sight of her crumpled face seemed to have the same effect on him.

Finally they managed to calm down.

"Oh, man," he breathed, rubbing his face. "My face hurts."

Still giggling a little, she fumbled in her handbag to find a tissue, and dabbed at her wet cheeks.

"That was almost better than sex," she said without thinking, and Jack shot her a look.

Why did she say that? To *him,* of all people? She gave herself a mental kick. He probably thought she was obsessed with sex. It was too humiliating.

"I mean—I mean, you know, kind of a release," she found herself blathering.

Great. Sooo much better.

She risked a glance across at him and he was watching her broodingly, all trace of laughter gone from his face.

"Last week—" he began, but she rushed to cut him off.

"Is best forgotten, don't you think?"

He was still watching her. Steeling herself, she pretended a calm she didn't feel and met his gaze square on, even managing a little questioning quirk of the eyebrow. She couldn't read his expression, but she got lost in his eyes. They were so blue, the exact, amazing blue of the sky on a perfect summer's day. When he was like this, laughing and open, she forgot all the reasons why she shouldn't like him. She remembered the intimacy of the elevator, and the feel of his arms tight around her as he cried out his pain. And what it was like to have his skin against hers…

Desire blossomed in her belly. She wanted to kiss him again. She didn't care about the flowers, or the regret that had been plaguing her for days. Suddenly she wanted to throw the rule book out the window and wing it.

His eyes dropped down from hers. Was he looking at her lips? Did he want to kiss her as much as she was aching to kiss him? He had to make the first move this time. She'd put herself on the line and been rejected by him too many times before. She held her breath, hoping, waiting.

"You've got some stuff on your cheek," he finally said, gesturing vaguely toward her face.

She blinked, trying to shake off the fog of lust she'd sunk into. "What?"

"On your cheek. Some, you know—stuff. From your nose. From when we were laughing."

She groped in her handbag and found her compact. Flipping it open hastily, she stared at the reflected image of herself, complete with something that was definitely not tears. She wiped it off with a trembling hand, and blew her nose for good measure.

Great.

Another round to Jack Brook.

A WEEK LATER, Jack leaned back in his chair and tried to restrain the impulse to look at his watch. He was tired. His eyes were gritty, his patience was wearing thin, and he was seriously considering punching Morgan Beck in the face. That, or dragging Claire off her prim little ass and having his way with her, damn the consequences.

He'd been stuck in this meeting with Beck and Claire for four hours now as they discussed a last-minute advertising problem with the magazine. It was a common enough occurrence to have advertisers drop out just prior to the cut-off date, but usually the client didn't get involved. Hank Hillcrest was a law unto himself, however. He'd heard about the advertiser's change of heart, and waded in, and now they had offended advertisers on all sides.

And every time they got close to hammering out a solution, Hillcrest came up with another objection. Jack was beginning to think the first edition of *Welcome Home* would never even get out of the starting gate.

It wasn't so much the frustration and annoyance of dealing with crusty old Hank that was getting to him. Sure, that was irritating, but it didn't crank up his stress levels anywhere near as much as the fact that he was fast developing an obsession with Claire.

It had been a long week since their visit to Hillcrest headquarters. A week of working together, of cozy chats and working lunches and brainstorming as they cobbled together the last few magazine departments before putting the first edition to bed. A week of staring into Claire's wide brown eyes, of laughing at her quick one-liners, of breathing in her spicy-sweet perfume.

What had started out as a sort of reluctant attraction had fast become a raging fascination. She was such an enigma, with her high-necked blouses and her sexy, toned thighs. Not that he got to see anything of the latter, of course. But he could remember them. Oh, how he remembered them….

He'd tried sticking to his game plan of remaining distant and professional. But he couldn't work with someone every day and not warm to her. Or come to like her. Even admire her.

He lifted his attention from the doodles he'd been scrawling across his notepad, his eyes narrowing as he studied Claire. She was discussing something earnestly with Morgan and she leaned forward slightly in her chair, her hands gesticulating fluidly. There was a slight flush on her cheekbones, and a determined glint in her eye. And the way she was sitting made her skirt ride up, just a little. Not enough for his liking, but enough that he was going to embarrass himself if he had to stand in a hurry.

It made him angry and desperate in equal measures that apparently he had no control over himself where she was concerned. He didn't want to want her. Hell, he didn't even want to like her. Life had been far, far easier before he'd been stuck in the elevator with her and seen beneath her defenses.

If only he hadn't kissed her and touched her. Perhaps then it wouldn't be so bad. Because now he knew, and, knowing, he wanted more. He knew he shouldn't, that it was the worst idea in the world—but it didn't stop him wanting.

She glanced up, and caught him staring. For a moment their eyes locked, and he realized that she knew exactly what he was thinking. Well, not exactly, because she probably would have run screaming from the building. But she had some idea that he was thinking about her, and him, with as little clothing between them as possible.

She blushed and looked away. And then looked back at him, as if seeking confirmation of what she'd just seen. There was a question in her eyes, and he was so frustrated and angry and aroused that he didn't bother trying to hide his desire. He was sick of it. He'd had a week of pure torture, sitting opposite her, playing nice, keeping his distance.

They both started as Morgan suddenly stood.

"I've got to call my wife, tell her I'll be late home," he said, heading for the door.

Then they were alone in the big executive boardroom. Jack's gaze swung to Claire. She was making notes on her files, apparently engrossed in work. He stared at her, willing her to look up, but she kept her head down.

He returned his attention to his notepad. Probably just as well. Every other time he'd given in to his lust for Claire he'd just wound up in trouble.

CLAIRE STARED at the incoherent jumble of words she'd written. What was wrong with her? It had taken a single week of Jack's company to reduce her to a gibbering wreck. She couldn't concentrate, her analytical skills were a joke, and only by sheer dint of will alone had she managed to sound remotely coherent for the past four hours. If Morgan had any idea of the thoughts that were chasing themselves around her head, she'd be pursuing that career in pornography sooner rather than later.

Given the direction and tone of her thoughts, it was probably just as well. Because she could not stop thinking about sex. More specifically, sex with Jack. She thought about him at home. While she was out running. During gym workouts. And now.

Oh, boy, was she thinking about him right now. About how he'd looked in the shower—before she'd turned the cold water on. About the hard plane of his belly. And the firmness of his muscled, male butt. And the way he—

She gave herself a mental slap. This was ridiculous. She had to stop doing this to herself. Especially at work. At home she'd virtually given up on trying to stop thoughts of Jack creeping into her mind. But at work, it was just wrong to be sitting opposite Morgan and have nothing in her head except visions of herself tearing Jack's clothes off.

Except, of course, Morgan wasn't sitting opposite her. He'd just gone to phone his wife. Which meant she was alone with Jack.

She flickered a look across at him. He was making notes. Of course he was, because he was a professional. While she was sitting here marinating in lust, he was applying his mind to the matter at hand. Damn him.

She'd hoped she'd learned her lesson after that moment in the car. But where Jack was concerned, it appeared she was a glutton for punishment. She simply could not stop herself wanting him.

For a beat she wished she were like Katherine, who seemed

to be able to throw herself at a short-term fling, take her passion where she found it and move on unscathed.

But she wasn't. She was Claire Marsden. And, if the past few weeks had taught her anything, they'd taught her that she definitely wasn't Jack's type.

She stood abruptly. Jack lifted his head, and she found herself staring into his mesmerizing blue eyes.

"Coffee," she blurted, which was a miracle, really, because the only words in her mind were "Take me."

"I'll get it," he said, standing in one powerful movement. She tore her eyes away from his thighs.

"It's fine, I'll do it," she insisted, moving toward the coffee station at the far end of the room. Out of the corner of her eye she could see he was walking down his side of the table. They met at the coffee machine.

"Really, I'm happy to get you a coffee," she assured him.

"You made the last one," he insisted.

She reached for the coffee can, but he got there ahead of her. A spark of annoyance burned its way through the lust clouding her brain.

"No one's keeping count," she said, reaching out to take the can from his hands.

He twitched it out of her reach.

"Fine, so I'll make it, then," he returned infuriatingly.

Suddenly she found she was really, really angry. She wanted to rip the coffee can from his hands and then beat him about the head with it.

"Look," she said, trying to sound rational and calm, "just hand over the coffee."

"No."

She glared at him, and he glared back. She felt like a thwarted five-year-old. Before she could stop herself, she lunged forward to try and snatch the coffee from him. He was gripping it with both hands now, holding it tight against his body, and they swayed back and forth for a beat, both clutching at the small silver can.

She could smell his deodorant and aftershave, and his fingers were warm on hers as they both scrabbled for purchase on the coffee can. And then, all of a sudden, her fury twisted inside her and she realized her nipples were hard and that she was so turned on it was a wonder there weren't dogs howling at the moon all over town.

She broke away from Jack, confused, hot for it, panting with desire and the exertion of their tug-of-war. They stared at each other for a beat, Jack's own breathing harsh, his face tense. Then he seemed to make a decision.

"To hell with it," he said suddenly, tossing the coffee can to one side and lunging toward her.

Then he was kissing her, his tongue demanding in her mouth, his hands sliding under her jacket and onto her breasts.

She wanted to touch all of him at once. She returned his kisses greedily, her hands roaming across his back, dipping down to grab his butt, then racing back up again to traverse the width of his shoulders.

This was so good—so much better than her memory of that day at Jack's place, better even than in the elevator since she'd had all this time in between to anticipate his touch. Better even than the many fantasies she'd concocted.

He ducked his head to kiss her neck, working his way down into her cleavage. She writhed with pleasure, then snaked a hand between their bodies, feeling a deep and intense satisfaction as she found the rigid length of him, hard and straining against the faded denim of his jeans.

Jack groaned into her mouth, and suddenly he broke away from her, picking her up and turning to place her on the board-room table before moving to assume a position between her parted thighs. They stared at each other briefly, panting, hot.

His eyes locked with hers, Jack slid a hand under her skirt, and she bit her lip as his fingers stole up her silk-covered legs. The shock as his hand found her naked thigh made her gasp, and he seemed startled, too, that he was suddenly touching bare skin.

"Garters?" he guessed.

"Stay-ups," she clarified, and Jack pushed her skirt up roughly so that he could see her unencumbered. His breathing quickened as he studied her, legs spread, black stockings in stark contrast to the tanned expanse of her upper thighs.

His eyes glinting dangerously, he ducked his head to her breasts again, suckling at her nipples through the thin silk of her shirt, the hunger in him almost frightening. As her head dropped back helplessly, his hand completed its journey, gliding up her thighs to land unerringly on the part of her that needed him the most.

"Yes," she breathed as he rubbed her already swollen mound through the silk of her panties.

And then he was hooking a finger into the elastic, sliding her panties down over her hips. She felt mindless with need, the thought of being one with him again driving out every other consideration. She reached for the stud on his jeans, but Jack simply shook his head at her. Before she could protest, her panties were off and Jack was ducking down to blaze a trail of kisses across her lower belly. But she was aching for him now. She needed him inside her, and she was struggling to tell him just that when he dropped lower still and silenced her with one lightning sweep of his tongue.

"Oh!" she moaned, reaching for the edge of the boardroom table and hanging on for dear life.

His tongue was hard and hot and firm, and she felt overwhelmed by the spiraling desire that was drawing tighter and tighter inside her. She forgot to breathe as he lapped at her, delicate then rough, slippery and deft as he tongued her clitoris again and again. She could feel the faint friction of Jack's stubbly cheeks against her sensitive inner thighs, and the firm, delicious pressure as he parted her slickness and slid a single finger inside.

"Oh, yes!" she cried, writhing, uncontrolled. She was so close, so close—

Then a faint, foreign sound intruded—a phone ringing in the next room. Vaguely Claire registered the rumble of someone talking on the phone through the wall. And suddenly she recalled exactly where she was, and what she and Jack were doing, and just who was likely to walk through the boardroom door any second now.

Was she insane? Had she lost it completely?

She stiffened and Jack's head lifted at the same time that they both heard the distinct sound of Morgan talking to Jenny just outside the door. Claire's heart leaped into her throat, and she pushed Jack away and slid off the table in one clumsy move. Breathless, disoriented, she tucked her shirt in and pushed her skirt down. The feel of the silk lining of her skirt against her bare butt reminded her that her panties were lying around here somewhere, and she spotted them on the floor at the same time that the door began to swing open. Jack had been busying himself with buttoning his own buttons and tucking his shirt in, but he spotted her panties at exactly the same moment and suddenly lunged forward.

Claire held her breath as he scooped up the offending triangle of black silk and stuffed it into his jeans pocket just as Morgan stepped into the room, his attention still on Jenny, unseen outside the room.

"…that should be fine. Make the booking for eleven," he was saying.

Her heart pounding, Claire ran a shaky hand through her hair and shot a look at Jack. To her horror, she saw he had her lipstick smeared across his face, and she gestured urgently for him to wipe it off. He, in turn, gestured for her to pull her jacket closed, and she looked down to see twin wet patches on her shirt where he had been sucking her nipples through the silk.

Fingers fumbling, she tugged her jacket closed just as Morgan turned to face them properly. Attempting to be casual, Claire smiled brightly. Out of the corner of her eye, she could see Jack doing the same. There was a fraught, stretched moment as Morgan stared from one of them to the other. Then he frowned.

"Is everything okay in here?" he asked.

Claire didn't dare look at Jack.

"Sure. Absolutely. We were just having a coffee break," she said, only then realizing that the coffee can she and Jack had been arguing over was lying abandoned on the carpet in front of them. All three of them stared at the can, then Jack laughed.

"To be honest, Claire and I were having a bit of a wrangle over whose turn it was to make the coffee," he said lightly.

The frown creasing Morgan's forehead deepened, but he turned back to the other end of the table.

"I see. Perhaps we should finalize these last matters and call it a night."

Claire forced herself to walk back to her place at the table, horribly aware of how hot and flustered she felt and no doubt looked. If that phone hadn't rung in the next room… She felt sick to her stomach as she listened to Morgan drone on for the next five minutes. Jack was very quiet, also, and eventually it became clear that nothing of great value was going to be achieved this evening.

Shooting each of them an exasperated look, Morgan slotted his expensive pen back into his expensive folder and closed it decisively.

"Well, I have to say I'm very disappointed," he said heavily.

Claire twitched. Out of the corner of her eye she saw Jack stiffen.

"The Hillcrest account is very important to our client-based magazine division. I had hoped that I would have the undivided attention of two of my top editors on this project."

He looked from one to the other, and Claire just resisted the urge to toe the carpet and hang her head.

"Was I wrong in thinking you were the right people for the job?"

"No, Mr. Beck," she said.

"No, Morgan," Jack said.

Morgan eyed them both for another beat or two.

"Well, perhaps we should call it a night."

Claire nodded her acceptance of his decision, and concentrated on shuffling her papers into her briefcase. Issuing them both a curt good-night, Morgan exited. Silence stretched as Claire finished sorting out her briefcase. Then she cleared her throat.

"Could I have my panties, please?" she asked tightly.

She couldn't look at him, but out of the corner of her eye she saw Jack tug her panties from his pocket. He slid them across the table to her, and she scrunched them into a ball and stuffed them into her briefcase.

Then, horribly aware of the cool breeze on her bare derriere, she headed for the door. She couldn't bear the thought of waiting for the elevator, so she bolted for the stairwell. Once the plush-carpeted halls of the thirtieth floor were behind her, she let out a strangled moan of despair, the sound of it echoing up and down the stairs. When was she going to learn to stay away from Jack Brook?

12

THE NEXT DAY was a Friday, and the triathlon final. Claire awoke with a single image burned into her mind's eye: her, sprawled across the Beck and Wise boardroom table, Jack Brook between her thighs, her self-respect and dignity nowhere to be seen.

It was enough to make a girl dye her hair, change her name and emigrate. How was she ever going to look Jack in the eye again? And as for Morgan Beck… Lord knows what he thought had been going on. Something, obviously, hence his little lecture.

Although, really, she should thank her lucky stars that he'd come back when he had. Anything could have happened. Another few minutes, and she and Jack would have been on the floor, oblivious to anything and everything.

Deep down inside, a tiny, forbidden, depraved part of her wished that they'd had those few extra minutes. She'd been craving Jack's hands on her body for days. Was it wrong that she couldn't find it in herself to truly regret what had happened, no matter how humiliating the circumstances?

She rolled over and buried her face in her pillow. She couldn't think about any of this now. She was supposed to be building herself up for the challenge of the race, not reliving each second of her humiliation in psychological Technicolor.

She rolled out of bed and trotted into the bathroom, amusing herself by mentally reviewing her résumé. She could resign by e-mail and never actually have to see Jack Brook or Morgan Beck

ever again. Tom could clear out her desk. For five blissful milli-
seconds, it felt like an option. Then she passed by the answering
machine and her eye was caught by the blinking light. She'd been
so overwhelmed with shame last night that she hadn't noticed
she'd missed a call. She backtracked to press the play button, then
froze as an awful thought occurred. *Please don't let it be Beck.
Or Jack. Or Katherine. Definitely not Katherine—she'd be able
to tell what happened in the boardroom just from the sound of
my voice.*

"Claire, it's Harry. I just wanted to let you know it looks like
I will be in town for the final tomorrow. I'm assuming you'll have
an early start, so I'll make contact with you at the race."

She stared at the machine, all thoughts of Jack and finding another job pushed to one side. Her father was coming. She'd given
up on him, really she had. But he was coming, he was coming
to watch her race.

Almost two weeks of silence, and now this!

A little flare of hope sprang to life inside her, and she immediately told herself not to be naive. This was her father, after all.
Even if he was coming, it didn't necessarily mean anything. She
shouldn't get her hopes up.

But would it be completely self-delusional to think this might
be a step in the right direction? That she'd told him how she felt,
and he'd been moved to take action after her outburst?

As she turned on the shower, she told herself to stop specu-
lating. But it was no use. She'd been worrying about this for too
long to set it to one side. She dressed quickly in her competition
swimsuit, smoothing suntan lotion into her arms and legs, and
putting sunblock on her nose. And all the while her mind was
working overtime, hoping that this contact from Harry might signal a change for the good.

She grabbed up her backpack, water bottles and bike helmet
and headed out the door, aware that there was a new thread of
excitement burbling through her veins, not just the usual prerace

jitters or the normal adrenaline buzz that came from anticipating competition.

She realized that she really wanted to win this race.

Of course, she really wanted to win every race—that was the point of competing, right? But this race…she really, really wanted to win this race.

She paused on the next to last step down into the underground garage.

Because of her father?

An image of herself streaking across the finish line, her father watching, flashed into her mind. Yes, because of her father. Because she wanted to prove to him that he'd been wrong about her, to show him that she was a success in her own right and that his approval didn't matter to her at all.

She'd put the bike rack on last night, and her competition bike was already suspended above the tailgate. She threw her helmet and other gear onto the passenger seat, and swung herself into the car.

Her father was coming, and she wanted to win for him. She wanted him to see her win, more correctly.

And she wanted to pretend that she'd never kissed Jack, that they hadn't almost been busted by her boss and that she didn't remember every second of their encounter in the finest detail.

Great mindset to take into a race you've been aiming for all year. Just great.

JACK SPENT a sleepless night going over and over those few heady moments when he'd had Claire in his arms. And his mouth. Those black thigh-high stockings—he'd almost exploded when he saw them. And the way she'd given herself over to the moment. The noise she made as he touched her—that, alone, was enough to make him hard.

Of course, he quickly realized that that way lay torture, and a long, long cold shower later he was finally able to drop off to sleep.

She took over his dreams, too, however. But his subconscious surprised him—his dream wasn't hot and heavy. Instead, he kept seeing the embarrassed color in her cheeks as she made her hasty exit from the boardroom. In his dream he followed her, making her stop and listen to him as he explained—

He awoke with the alarm sounding in his ear and the sense that he'd just missed out on learning something profound.

Maybe it was the dream that made him detour via her office on the way into his own the next morning. He told himself he simply wanted to offer her the sense of solidarity—after all, it had taken two to tango. Or whatever dance it was they'd been considering before Morgan so rudely interrupted them. The S.O.B.

To his surprise, she wasn't there. He didn't examine the surge of disappointment in his gut too closely—that was what his subconscious and those dreams were for, after all. Instead, he stood staring at her empty chair, aware of all the noise and bustle of a normal business day going on behind him. Maybe he should wait for her….

"Can I help you?"

He spun around to find a small, nervous-looking young guy staring at him. The stare was a tad belligerent, and he realized he was standing fully inside Claire's unattended office, hovering over her paper-strewn desk. Bad office etiquette.

Smiling engagingly, he took a step forward until he could lean against the door frame, and some of the alertness in the other guy's face eased.

Territorial little devil.

"Yeah, I'm looking for Claire," he said.

Intense brown eyes flickered up and down his body. "I see." His tone implied that he didn't like what he saw.

Jack gave the little guy back some of his own attitude. "You want to tell me where she's at?"

"I'm not sure I should."

Jack blinked with surprise. "Unless Claire's on a mission for the FBI, I think I'm a pretty low security risk."

To his further surprise, Mr. Intense suddenly moved forward, ushering him back into Claire's office and shutting the door.

Jack frowned. Who was this guy? Surely not Claire's *boyfriend?*

"I just think you should know that I know about your reputation. Everyone does."

Jack stared at the earnest young man quivering in front of him. "Yeah? And what's it to you?"

"Claire's a really nice person. One of the best."

Okay, not a boyfriend. Anyone who'd spent any time with Claire would not describe her as *nice.* Hot, maybe. Damn sexy. But not nice—nice was for hand-knit socks Granny made for you at Christmas.

"And?"

"And she doesn't deserve to be chewed up and spat out by a guy like you."

He actually blinked with surprise. For a brief second he considered grabbing the little guy by the ankles and hanging him upside down out of a window for a while. Then he remembered the feeling he'd had in his chest when he'd woken from that dream this morning.

It was kind of nice that Claire had people looking out for her.

"We're working together. End of story, okay, pal?" he found himself saying.

There was a tense moment as the little guy seemed to consider this. Then he said, "She's competing today." He opened the door, moving toward the desk stationed outside Claire's office.

Suddenly Jack twigged—Claire had a male assistant. He tried not to smile—*of course* she had a male assistant!

A male assistant who'd gone to the trouble of having his name engraved on a little plate to sit on his desk.

"Listen, um, Tom, you want to help me out here? Where exactly is Claire competing? Some magazine thing somewhere? What?"

Tom threw him a you're-weird look.

"No. Why would she be doing that? She's got the semifinal for her triathlon. They had to make it a Friday because it's impossible to shut the beach down on a weekend. If Claire places in this, she gets into the national final and has a chance to go to Hawaii for the Pros," Tom said proudly.

He just stared. Triathlon? Claire was a triathlete?

"This is at St. Kilda beach?"

Tom nodded as though he was dealing with an idiot. Which was quite possible, Jack reflected.

"That's right, near the pier."

"Thanks."

Jack headed for the elevators, completely preoccupied. How had this not come up in all their time in the elevator or all the time they'd spent working together over the past two weeks? It explained why Claire looked nothing short of sensational in her underwear, of course, but it didn't explain why they hadn't discussed what was apparently a major part of her life.

He pulled his cell phone out of his back pocket as he headed toward the car park.

"Linda? Hey, it's me. What have I got on today?"

"No appointments until three, and that's just my yearly review."

"Cool. I'm out of the office for the day, then. By the way, did you know Claire Marsden is a triathlete? Am I the only person in the office who didn't know this?"

Linda's sharp intake of breath gave away her annoyance, and he braced himself for a lecture.

"We'll do your review on Monday, I promise," he offered, trying to head her off at the pass.

"Forget the review, Jack. Just be kind to Claire, okay? She's a really sweet girl, you remember that."

He stared at his handset for a moment. Okay, this was getting ridiculous. Did he have a biohazard warning label painted on his back or something?

"What's this all about?" he asked, annoyed.

"Look, I know you, Jack. Claire's a really nice person."

Again with the nice. He felt his frown deepen.

"That's the second time someone's said that to me today. Am I not a nice person, is that it? And what exactly do you imagine I'm going to do to Claire, anyway, Linda?"

"Don't go getting all snippy on me. It's not that you're a bad person, Jack. It's just you're a... Well, you treat women like they're disposable napkins. One use and they're gone. I've seen you work your way through the office, and that's totally your business, but I get the feeling Claire isn't the kind of woman you do that with."

"Do what with?" he found himself asking, his back well and truly up.

"Take what you want and to hell with the consequences. Now, I'm only telling you this because you have to realize that when you go to work on a woman, you're pretty much irresistible. You know this, Jack, so get that sulky look off your face."

He shook his head over his assistant's uncanny abilities: he had been looking and feeling like a spoiled schoolboy.

"I just want you to think about tomorrow with Claire, that's all. Don't forget how she's going to feel when you're not there whispering sweet nothings in her ear anymore," Linda concluded.

"What about how I'm going to feel? Does anyone ever consider that?" He threw the words back at her.

"Well, if you'd ever let anyone close enough to find out, I'm sure they would," Linda said primly before ending the call.

He stared at his handset before slipping it back into his pocket.

Great, now he was copping lectures from his assistant-cum-second-mother. It seemed the whole office viewed him as some sort of female-targeted Terminator, his only mission being to seek out women and destroy their emotional lives.

And it wasn't as though he had any designs on Claire, anyway. If you didn't count the near miss in the boardroom last night.

He simply was going to pop down to the shore, see if he

could catch some of her race. If he bumped into her, he'd wish her luck. End of story, end of drama.

He could just imagine Linda's face if he'd told her his plans: big-time disapproval.

He shook his head. Hell, he was going to watch a stupid race for a few minutes, that was all. Claire was as safe as houses, and his secretary and the rest of the world could just keep their pants on.

THE SHORE WAS packed with bodies, and he had to shoulder his way through the crowd to gain a spot with a decent vantage point. He'd come just in time to catch the bulk of the male tri-athletes wading out of the water and racing toward their individual stations to towel off and shove on their running shoes.

He was contemplating what a crazy, rigorous, exhausting sport this was when an added roar from the crowd alerted him to the fact that the first of the female competitors had finished the swim leg and were landing on the beach. Two women he didn't recognize surged out of the water and leaped over the last shallow waves and onto the sand. Then he saw Claire, her face intent as she followed in their wake.

His spontaneous whoop of encouragement took even himself by surprise, as did the flash of pride he felt. She looked amazing, her tanned body taut and strong as she raced up the beach toward her station. Even at this distance he could see the water dripping down her body, and he watched intently as she carefully dried her feet before tying her track shoes on. She looked up once, scanning the crowd. He waved, wanting to let her know he was there, then felt a twinge of disappointment when she didn't spot him.

Then she was off, her body falling into what was obviously a familiar rhythm as she hit the running leg of the race. He craned his neck and body to watch her for as long as he could.

The rest of the crowd pushed around him. He realized he was grinning like an idiot, and he sobered for a moment. Maybe Linda was right, maybe he should just go back to work.

But somehow he found himself working his way through the crowd, trying to locate someone official-looking who could tell him where the race would end.

CLAIRE KEPT her head down and her mind on nothing but breathing and the fact that the bike leg was just minutes off. She'd managed to maintain her position in the field, and she was confident she could hold her own on the bike. She couldn't stop herself from glancing at the faces alongside the route as she ran, always searching for her father. It was ridiculous to expect to spot him, and just as ridiculous to feel disappointed that she couldn't find him. She'd hoped to see him before the race, had kept an eye out even as she set up her station and limbered up for the swim, but he hadn't come to find her.

The feel of concrete beneath her feet gave way to grass as she ran between the barriers and funneled down toward her station. She pulled her bike away from its stand, then stuffed her feet into her locking pedals. She glanced just once along the rows of faces lined up behind the fences before she took off. Impossible to know if Harry was there or not….

The secret to the bike leg for her was to always take the hills hard. A lot of other competitors conserved their energy on the hills, but she knew she had the stamina to grab a lead there and hold it. She might not be tall like some of the other women competitors, but she had strength and determination on her side, and if she could grab herself an advantage on the hills, she'd go for it. For a moment, she allowed herself to imagine winning. She wanted it so badly, but she found it disturbing that when she pictured herself racing across the finish line, it was her father she imagined coming forward to congratulate her, not some faceless official.

JACK STOOD on his tiptoes to try and get a better view, apologizing yet again for jostling the backpack of the young blonde

standing on his left. She gave him a smile, then looked away flir-
tatiously, and he recognized that she was giving him all the right
signals. He also recognized that he couldn't be less interested.
She was attractive—all right, very attractive—in her brightly
colored bikini top and short-shorts, but for the life of him he
couldn't scrape up anything bar a sort of general approval of her
appearance. She was hot, but he was not. Not for her, anyway.
Now if it were Claire standing next to him…

This disturbing thought was swept to one side as he spotted
the lead cyclist coming around the corner. He'd already memorized Claire's number—twenty-three—and he saw with disappointment that it wasn't her. But the second cyclist wasn't far
behind, and he saw Claire's lime-green cycle helmet with a thrill
of excitement.

Hell, she could win this thing! He found himself yelling out
her name as she bent low over the handlebars of her bike, his own
legs unconsciously tensing, his own breath coming faster as he
willed her forward.

"Come on, come on! You can do it, baby!" he hollered, punching the air with his fist.

They were in the home stretch now, and Claire was nipping
at the other woman's heels, each powerful stroke of her thighs
pulling her closer and closer to the lead.

God, he wanted her to win. He felt all her anxiety and desire
and drive, and he wanted her to have this moment.

"Come on!" he yelled, vaguely aware that the blonde was covering her ears now.

Only half a bike length between them now. Both women were
out of their saddles, leaning hard over their handlebars as they
sprinted toward the finish line. He could see the look of an-
guished effort on Claire's face, and he held his breath.

Could she do it?

With a surge of power, Claire shot into the lead, racing over
the finish line a full bike length ahead of the other competitor.

He whooped with joy, standing on several people's toes behind him, smiling and apologizing even as he began elbowing his way to the finishing line.

It took him about ten minutes to get there, but he was still smiling like a crazy man, reliving the moment again and again. She'd won! What an effort! She was amazing, really amazing.

He could see Claire stretching out her calves as one of the officials spoke to her. She looked oddly flat as she nodded, obviously responding to the man's questions, her eyes constantly scanning the crowd.

He gave little thought to anything except congratulating her, but a potbellied man laid a hand on his chest as he moved to duck under the barrier separating the crowd from the finishing area.

"Sorry, buddy, officials and support crew only through here," he said.

He frowned, unprepared to accept this when Claire was just a few steps away. He wanted to see her.

"I'm support crew. I'm with number twenty-three, Claire Marsden," he said.

Mr. Potbelly looked him up and down, obviously skeptical. Jack adopted his best man-to-man tone.

"Look, I'm actually her boyfriend, and she's not expecting me to be in town—I got held up at a conference," he lied.

Mr. Potbelly seemed to have a core of pure schmaltz because he bought it and Jack found himself being eased through a gap in the barriers and patted on the shoulder.

Claire's back was to him, and without thinking he stepped forward and scooped her up in his arms, spinning her around with a whoop.

"You were fantastic! That was completely amazing!" he told her, looking down into her surprised face.

The surprise didn't last for long, however. A moment of brief, gratifying illumination as she recognized him, and then she stiffened and pushed away from him.

"Jack. What are you doing here?" she asked, and he noticed that her eyes slid off him almost instantly, returning to their constant scanning of the crowd.

Suddenly he was hit by a bolt from the blue—she was expecting someone else.

He felt as if he'd been poleaxed. Why hadn't he thought of that before? Why had he always assumed that Claire was single? He felt like the arrogant fool she was always accusing him of being. Why had he just assumed that she was his for the taking—if he chose to take her?

"I was just…kind of in the area," he heard himself say.

Wow, really snappy. And *soooo* convincing. He tried again:

"I actually wanted to apologize. For yesterday. With Beck. I figure that was kind of my fault…." he finished lamely.

He had her full attention now.

"You're sorry about what happened?" she asked, and he felt as though a lot hung in the balance.

"Of course I am," he said.

Her gaze was oddly intent, and he found himself wishing for the first time in his life that he could read another person's mind. What was she thinking?

"Ms. Marsden?"

They both turned to face the race official approaching behind them.

"This was delivered to our office earlier. I'm afraid we didn't get a chance to get it to you before the race," he said.

Claire accepted the folded note with a faint smile and an assurance that all was okay. Jack watched her face closely as she flipped the note open and read it quickly.

He almost missed the faint tightening of her mouth, the quick swallow in her throat. She blinked quickly a few times, and then she smiled brightly at him.

"Well, thanks for coming down. I really have to get to the showers. I guess…I guess I'll see you at work next week," she said, nothing in her demeanor indicating that something important had just happened.

But he knew it had. He could feel the hurt in her, and he found himself in the unusual position of wanting to help.

"Claire—" He tried to speak, but she was already moving away.

The truth was, he had no idea what to say. Normally, he was the one trying to ease his way out of these kinds of conversations, and he was far more skilled at avoiding talking about feelings and whatnot than he was at inviting confidences.

So he let her walk away and just stood there feeling like a big dummy.

13

HOPE SPRINGS ETERNAL. It was a phrase that might have been coined to describe Claire's relationship with her absentee father. When was she going to learn that she didn't need him, and that what he thought, or felt, didn't matter?

Claire closed her eyes and lifted her face so that the spray from the shower hit her full-on, enduring the sting from the little needles of water because it felt better than giving in to the urge to cry.

"Yo, Claire, congratulations!" one of the other competitors yelled out to her as she passed the communal shower. Claire forced a smile and responded to the rest of the lighthearted ribbing.

She'd qualified for the Hawaii Pro Series now, and she could feel the envy of some of the other women as she toweled off and they discussed the field of likely competitors.

Truth was, at this moment, she wondered if she'd miss it if she never competed again.

She was aware that a dark cloud of disappointment had settled over her with the delivery of her father's belated note of apology, and she knew she was hardly reacting the way she should be. She'd trained so hard for this win. She'd run her best time, and equaled her best bike leg to date. She should be popping champagne and screaming the rafters down with joy. Instead, she was busy manufacturing a party she was attending with friends as an excuse to avoid celebrating with the other competitors.

Yet another disappointment awaited her when she opened her backpack—she'd been so distracted this morning that she'd failed to pack a full change of clothing for after the race, and she sat staring at the lone T-shirt and bra in her kit bag.

"Damn it," she said under her breath, about to reach for her damp swimming bottoms. She'd have to wear the T-shirt home with the towel around her waist....

"What's up, Claire?"

It was Sally, one of the women who she trained with occasionally.

"Just me being stupid. Forgot to pack a change of clothes." She shrugged.

Sally's face cleared.

"Easily fixed. Here, have this," Sally offered, tossing a black bundle toward her. "Give it back to me next week at the gym."

Claire smiled her gratitude, and even managed to keep the smile on her lips as she unrolled the bundle and revealed a halter-neck black cheesecloth sundress, all low back and short-looking flouncy skirt. It was a no-bra kind of a dress, the kind she never, ever wore.

"It'll look great on you, with your dark hair," Sally enthused.

Claire shrugged—she was only going home, after all. She tugged the dress on over her head and let her towel drop. Thankfully it fell to just above her knees, and made her feel less decadent when she decided to forgo the torture of rolling on her wet swimsuit bottoms. Who would ever know, after all? Of course, if she got caught over one of those subway vents à la Ms. Monroe... Or if she got hit by a car... Claire shook off her anxieties, almost laughing at herself. Given that she'd sat through part of an executive meeting sans underpants just yesterday, she could survive a trip home no problems.

"Sall, you're a lifesaver," she thanked her friend, shoving the rest of her gear into her backpack and padding out into the beach club. She had to make her way through a crowd of folk intent on congratulating her and inviting her to various parties as she headed outside to where her bike was waiting, but she managed to keep smiling as she made her by now well-rehearsed excuse about "another party."

She'd just shaken off the last of her well-wishers when she spotted Jack lounging by her bike. Her step faltered. What was he still doing here? Suddenly she was acutely conscious of the air circulating unhindered around her nethers, and she felt her knees clench together as if they could somehow hold that flimsy, flirty skirt down if a chance wind happened along. The thought of just such a wind had her looking around nervously as she crossed the distance between them.

"Jack."

"Claire."

His response mocked her, but his eyes were serious.

"Did you forget something?" she asked, genuinely confused.

"Yeah. I forgot to ask what was wrong. Back there, when you got that note, something happened. So…here I am."

He said it as though he'd memorized it or rehearsed it a few times. She stared at him, baffled.

"Jack, are you feeling okay?" she asked.

He looked determined.

"I'm fine. But you're not. Let's talk about it."

She couldn't help herself. He sounded so earnest and looked so tortured that the smile was curving her lips before she could stop it.

"What's so funny?"

She shook her head, trying to control her unruly mouth.

"Nothing. You just sounded very…Oprah. Or like one of those self-help books. 'I'm okay, you're okay.' You know."

He looked exasperated. "Give me a break here, this is new territory for me."

She narrowed her eyes at him, wondering. What exactly was going on? And then she realized. He felt sorry for her! Steel stiffened her spine and she found herself talking coolly. "Well, you don't need to worry yourself over me. I'm just fine, thanks."

She concentrated on unlocking her bike and adding her repair kit and water bottles to her backpack.

"Could have fooled me."

"I wish I *had* fooled you," she shot back, and she looked up to find a triumphant smile on his face. She rolled her eyes, aware that she'd responded to his baiting like a laboratory rat at the feeder bar.

"Look. I appreciate the gesture. Let's just leave it at that, okay?"

She shrugged her pack onto one shoulder and began wheeling her bike toward the parking lot, hoping he would take the not-so-subtle hint and let her go. Of course, she should have known better. She glanced at him out of the corner of her eye as he kept pace with her. The man had the hide of a rhino.

"So, you're in the finals now?" he ventured after they'd been dodging through people for a few minutes.

"Yep." She wasn't going to encourage him. For starters, she was somewhat lacking in the underwear department, and when Jack Brook was around, she figured she needed all the protection she could get from her own baser instincts. Last time she'd been pantyless with this man, she'd lost all self-respect and self-control.

"Pretty cool. Big party tonight? Guess you triathlete guys must all hang together?"

"There are a few parties on," she replied evasively, aware that she wasn't the best liar in the world where Jack was concerned.

But, as usual, he managed to hone in on her weakness.

"And you're going to one?" he pushed.

She resisted the urge to sigh out her frustration.

"I have other plans," she prevaricated.

They'd reached her car now, and she started to bend down to fix her pedals for the drive home, remembering in the nick of time that she should probably crouch—very carefully—rather than tempt fate. Knees clenched together, she did just that, concentrating on pinning her pedals into a stationary position.

"Do those other plans involve anyone else? Like a boyfriend, for example?"

She looked up at him, confused again about why he was here. "I'm not seeing anyone at the moment," she admitted grudgingly.

He looked smug. The bastard.

"So you're just going home to mope?" Jack asked shrewdly.

She shot to her feet.

"Do I look like a moper?" she asked him defiantly, hands on hips.

She was aware of his gaze flickering up and down her body, and she fought the desire to cross her arms over her braless chest.

"Frankly—yes. You look like you just want to go home and crawl under a rock," he said brutally.

She gasped, staring at him openmouthed for a moment. How did he know? How on earth could he know that was exactly how she felt?

"Takes one to know one," he answered her unspoken question.

"Well, then, from one moper to another, how about a little respect?" she suggested. "How about you let me get on with it."

Jack looked as though he might be considering her suggestion, but then he shook his head.

"Can't do that. Look where my moping got me." He reached out and touched the faded bruise that still marked her cheek. "Or, more correctly, look where it got us. So, no moping."

"Fine. I promise to go home and dance a jig and giggle myself silly. Happy?" she demanded, beginning to feel well and truly cornered.

"Or…you could let me take you out to celebrate. Hell, you just won the state final. One of the guys at the beach club said you almost equaled the record for the running leg. I say that deserves a little champagne, an expensive dinner and a lot of attention."

It was so close to what she'd imagined doing with her father that she had to duck her head to hide the ridiculous tears in her eyes. A strong hand grasped her chin and tipped her face up. She found herself staring into Jack's very blue eyes.

"You don't want to talk, fine. I'm the master of not talking, remember? But at least let me treat you to a nice meal."

She stalled for time, finding his eyes very compelling, aware that her body was clamoring once more for his touch and that that was a very bad and dangerous thing.

"Not a fancy restaurant. Just something nearby," she negotiated.

"Your choice, absolutely."

"And then you let me go home, no questions asked."

He shrugged, oozing confidence now. "Sure. If that's what you want."

His tone suggested she might feel otherwise, and she shot him a wary look. What was really going on here? Was Jack laying a line on her? He stared back at her, apparently guileless.

"I need to take my bike home," she added, hoping that all of her conditions would wear out his good intentions.

"Fine. I'll follow you home."

No such luck.

14

CLAIRE KEPT one eye on his red monstrosity in her rearview mirror all the way back to her apartment. It lurked behind her, stalking her through every turn and traffic light. Just like its owner. Why on earth had she agreed to have dinner with Jack?

It was an unanswerable question, but all of her speculation made her nervous and she could barely meet his eyes when she approached him in front of her place.

"I'll just duck in and change. I'll be down in a tick," she said lightly, already turning toward the entrance.

His hand on her arm stopped her.

"Don't. You look fine—great—like that," he said.

She smiled weakly, her mind fixated on the contents of her underwear drawer.

"But I'm not dressed for—" she began to say, but strong hands were on her shoulders, turning her toward his car.

"Relax. We'll go to this place I know near the river—lots of patio space and a great view. You'll fit right in."

It was on the tip of her tongue to ask if all the other patrons would be sans underwear, too, but instead she just ducked her head and slid into the all-encompassing embrace of his leather upholstered seats.

"I know the owner of this place," Jack enthused as he started the engine. Its low, subterranean hum reverberated throughout the car.

She was aware of his gaze flickering across to her before he pulled out from the curb, and she made a futile attempt to tug the dress hem closer to her knees. Pointless. Sally was a party girl, and this was a party dress.

"They just started up about six months ago, so I try to go there as often as possible. Figure if I'm giving my money to anyone, it might as well be to friends."

He grinned across at her, and she found herself smiling back.

That was a nice thing to do, helping friends out with their fledgling business.

She sat up straighter, giving herself a mental slap about the head. She had to be on her guard tonight. She already knew that she was attracted to Jack. The last thing she wanted was for him to realize that. She could just imagine his amusement if he knew that his pity-assignment was lusting after him this very minute. No, she had to be on the alert. Keep her guard up. One glass of wine, no dessert, straight home. Absolutely.

"MORE CHAMPAGNE?" Jack asked, and Claire found herself nodding blithely, watching the straw-colored fluid rise up toward the top of her tall glass.

A warm haze had settled over her, the result of fantastic food, Jack's witty conversation and two—no, three, counting this one—glasses of champagne. Real French champagne, too, full of yeasty bubbles that tickled her nose.

"This is so nice," she said, raising her glass to her lips.

"Come on, you said you were going to eat half of this," Jack prompted, and she stared at the spoonful of sticky date pudding he was holding under her nose.

"I don't—" she started to stay, but he leaned forward and the spoon with its delicious mouthful was on her lips. Unthinking, she opened her mouth to accept his offering, and she caught a glint of something in his eyes.

Triumph? It confused her, and she snatched up her own spoon when Jack indicated he was ready with another mouthful for her.

"So…the Pro Series. How long have you got to train?" he asked idly, chasing the melting ice cream across the plate with his spoon now.

She answered without thinking.

"Might not go. Who knows?"

He looked startled, and she had to think back over the past few minutes to remember what she'd said.

"Really? You'd just call it quits?"

She shrugged, searching for a way to end this conversational tangent but knowing he was tenacious when he thought she was lying.

"Maybe I got what I wanted out of it," she said, concentrating on scooping up another mouthful of pudding.

He made a grunting noise of disbelief, and she glared at him. Reaching for her champagne glass, she took a big swig before speaking again.

After all, why not? Why not reveal all her petty inadequacies to this man? He'd already seen her passed out from fear, so it couldn't get much worse.

"Maybe I just realized I've been doing it for all the wrong reasons."

She could feel his attention focusing fully on her, and it made her tremble with awareness. What must it be like to have all of that blue-eyed intentness beside you in bed, no interruptions, no hesitations? To have him thinking of nothing but you and him together?

She shoved her champagne glass away from her. Boy, was she a two-glass screamer or what.

"What are the wrong reasons, Claire?" he asked.

She reminded herself that she'd started this. "That note earlier. It was from Harry. I mean, my dad. He phoned yesterday, left a message that he was going to be here for the finals. We had a…discussion, I guess you could call it, a few weeks ago. I told him I wasn't going to be the only one doing any work to stay in contact from now on."

"But he didn't turn up?" Jack prompted.

"No. And the whole race, I was looking for him in the crowd, wondering where he was. I had it all worked out beforehand, too. I was going to win and show him that I was a success, that he'd missed out by not being around. But you know what? When he didn't turn up, I realized it was really all about wanting him to be proud of me, not about me sticking it to him. I have told myself over and over again that it doesn't matter what he thinks or does, but here I am. Ridiculous, huh?"

She couldn't look up. It sounded so small and sad saying it out loud.

"Everyone wants their parents to be proud of them. It must be tough having a father who's not involved. I can't even imagine it."

"But I thought I'd beaten this. When I hadn't heard from him after my little outburst, I thought that was it. That we'd both just do our own things, that any pretence was over and done with. And then he goes and does this, and I jump at the chance to prove I'm worthy of the great explorer. 'Hey, Dad, look at me! Just because I can't climb a mountain doesn't mean I'm useless.' All these years of training—just so I can prove I'm good enough for him, force him to be proud of me."

"What was his excuse?"

"Oh, some sponsorship opportunity or something. It doesn't matter. Harry is a closed book. I should never have tried to open him. He's been seized shut ever since my mom died."

She shook herself suddenly and sat up straighter.

"Well, that's enough navel gazing from me. Next you'll have me confessing I never had a date for the school dance," she joked, aware that she'd just revealed a great deal about herself.

Jack half smiled, but she had a feeling he wasn't ready to let her off the hook yet. She was right.

"You think you won only because you thought your dad was there, don't you?" he asked.

That made her look up, straight into his eyes. How did he know this stuff?

"It's obvious, isn't it? All this training. Pretty much everything I do at Beck and Wise—it's all because I want him to sit up and take notice of me."

There, it was out. She reached for her champagne glass, but Jack was there ahead of her and he slid it out of her reach. She glared at him, but he just shook his head.

"Let's go crazy and have a discussion where both of us are in our right minds," he said, his smile self-deprecating.

"Maybe I don't want to be," she mumbled, acutely aware of how exposed she was feeling right now.

"Reckless talk," he said lightly.

"Sure. I mean, why not? All my life I've done the right thing, toed the line, took what was offered. I've flossed and eaten oat bran and stayed within the speed limit. And where has it got me? When we were in the elevator, you said I was uptight. At the time, I wanted to mess you up, bad. But you're right. I am uptight. I'm so worried about what other people think—what my dad will think—that I don't do anything unless I'm sure it's safe."

She stopped, aware that she had just spewed her innermost thoughts onto the table in front of a man who probably was wishing a trap door would appear at his feet and save him. Then she realized that she was doing what she always did—worrying about what other people thought, allowing herself to be paralyzed by it.

"Are we remembering the same elevator? The one where we jumped each other like crazy people? Doesn't sound like someone who's uptight or plays it safe to me," Jack said.

Claire blushed, mortified that he'd brought up their encounter in the elevator just when she thought they'd both agreed to pretend it had never happened.

"That was different," she mumbled, eyeing her champagne flute with longing. If she had to be embarrassed, she could at least be drunk.

"You're the sort of person who's always going to strive to achieve, no matter what anyone else thinks or wants," Jack continued. "It's in your nature. That's why you're about to start up a brand-new magazine. That's why people respect you. That's why you won today."

She shook her head, intent on exposing all her dark places tonight, for good or bad. He'd said it earlier: reckless talk. She *was* feeling reckless. She'd won today, but she felt like a loser and she didn't like it at all. She hated her life, hated what she'd become in trying to please her father.

She leaned across the table confidentially.

"You want to know how uptight I am? Even now, I'm sitting here regretting having said a word to you about any of this. Worse, I'm sitting here worried about the fact that I'm not wearing any underwear, terrified of every breath of breeze that comes our way. And I'm scared spitless of what would happen if I told you that I wished Morgan had never interrupted us last night. How pathetic is that?"

She raised an eyebrow at him, waiting for him to laugh or mumble an excuse about having to go home and wash the cat or take a violin lesson. But he just stared at her for a moment, his expression unreadable. Then she noticed a muscle in his jaw flexing, and she realized his eyes had darkened to almost navy.

"No underwear, huh?" he asked, his voice husky.

Jack Brook was turned on by the fact that she, Claire Marsden, wasn't wearing any panties.

"Forgot to pack a change of clothes," she said vaguely, absolutely fascinated by the intent look in his eyes.

"Right. You forgot," he repeated.

Suddenly she felt powerful. This man wanted her. He wanted her right now. And she wanted him. And they could do something about that, because they were both grown-ups with no strings attached. Lots of skeletons in the closet, of course, and monkeys on their backs, but no strings. If she could just find the courage to ignore a lifetime of coloring within the lines…

"Take me home."

Her invitation hung between them. Jack licked his lips, took a deep breath, then nodded.

The instant he said yes, all of her newfound courage disappeared down some invisible sinkhole at her feet. Oh, boy, what had she just done?

You want this, she reminded herself. *You've been fantasizing about this for the past two weeks.* Then why was she feeling as if she'd just put her head in the lion's mouth?

She almost jumped when Jack's hand slid around her hip and onto the small of her back as he guided her toward his car. Could he sense the turmoil within her? Was that why he was being so…circumspect? Because she'd kind of expected him to kiss her once they were alone in the parking lot. At the very least. She'd just offered him an incredibly blatant invitation. Shouldn't he be all fired up by now?

She snuck a look at him as he opened the car door for her. What was he thinking? She slid into the car, trying very hard to keep a neutral expression on her face.

JACK CIRCLED around to his side of the car, aware that his heart was beating a little too fast in his chest. Could he make it all the way to her place before he jumped her? It was going to be a close-run thing, but he dearly wanted to ensure complete and utter privacy before he got Claire naked, because he planned to keep her that way for a long time.

She intrigued him. She excited him. And she touched him. While he had supportive parents who erred more on the side of too much attention than not enough, he understood what it was like to yearn for something unattainable. And it must be so much worse when the person you want to connect with should have every reason in the world for wanting exactly the same thing, but didn't.

And just because Claire understood that there were all kinds of fathers in the world didn't make it any easier to accept the facts. Did a person ever fully resign herself to something like that?

And was he a predatory rat for taking her up on her invitation when she was obviously feeling vulnerable tonight? Shouldn't he just drop her off at her place and keep driving? Was he that much of a gentleman?

He glanced across at her, noticing that she was playing with the hem of her skirt. And, inevitably, his thoughts turned to what was beneath that skirt. Those smooth, toned thighs of hers…and no underwear. He'd tasted her once, briefly—too briefly. He wanted more, a whole lot more. He shifted to ease the sudden tightening in his jeans.

So, no, he wasn't that much of a gentleman.

But he would give her the opportunity to back out, if that was what she wanted. That was the best he could offer, because he wanted her so bad that he was half-inclined to simply pull over and make love to her in his car. Only the thought that there wasn't nearly enough room to do everything he wanted kept his hands on the wheel and his foot on the gas. He knew that once he started touching her, nothing short of a biblical event was going to stop him from drinking his fill of her.

But if they got to her place and she wanted to back out, then he'd let her go, he told himself virtuously. This time. Maybe.

15

CLAIRE TWISTED the hem of her skirt around and around, longing for some sign from Jack that he wanted her as much as she wanted him.

Then she remembered exactly what she'd said back at the restaurant: *take me home.*

She closed her eyes briefly. She was such a doofus.

What on earth did *take me home* mean, when you got right down to it? She'd meant "Take me home and make love to me till I forget my own name." But what had he heard? "Please return me to my place of residence now that I've revealed I am lacking in the panty department"? Or, "I'm so desperate and sad and pathetic, please would you consider throwing a bit of casual sex my way to alleviate my pain"?

Writhing internally over her patent lack of skills in the pickup department, she turned her head to stare out the window and saw they were passing the car dealership near her apartment. As the red Mustang slid by her window, she stiffened—they were almost home. Even as she was thinking the thought the car slowed down, then stopped altogether.

She tried to swallow the enormous lump of nervousness lodged in her throat as he exited the car and walked around to open her door. She attempted to smile up at him, but suspected she just looked constipated.

She managed to climb out of the car without revealing more

than she already had, and they stood for a moment, poised on the edge of a decision.

Is he coming up? Or is he trying to find a way to break it to me gently?

She flickered a look at him, but it was difficult to see his expression properly in the dark. Maybe she should be glad he wasn't making any moves, maybe she should just write this off as a bad experience and slink to her bed alone.

But he was standing there, tall and strong and sexy, and she wanted him. She didn't really know how to make it more obvious that she wanted him. The problem was, if he hadn't understood what she said back at the restaurant, she didn't think she had it in her to throw herself at his feet again.

Perhaps if she just…kind of headed upstairs? Then, if he followed her, she'd know he was coming up. Good plan, very good plan. She turned slowly toward the entrance to her building, every sense attuned to him, and felt him following her.

Okay. Right. So he was coming up. He was coming upstairs, to her place. To make love. Or, more accurately, to have sex. A thrill of relief that she wasn't as hopeless at this blatant-sexual-invitation-thing as she'd thought, closely followed by a wave of anticipation, made her knees go weak.

The automatic doors to the lobby opened as they approached, and she headed toward the stairwell, then stopped.

"Um, I usually take the stairs rather than the elevator. It's only on the second floor, but if you prefer…?" She hesitated.

Jack shrugged, gestured toward the stairs.

"Stairs are fine."

She nodded, let out some of the breath she'd been holding and moved across to the first flight of stairs. She was acutely aware of him behind her, and of Sally's stupid flirty dress brushing against the back of her thighs with each step she took.

She was also acutely aware of the fact that he'd yet to make a move on her. It all felt very…businesslike. Was that the way these things were done? Maybe he was just very private?

He waited until they were almost at the top of the first flight of stairs before he spoke.

"Claire?"

She froze with one foot on the stair tread ahead, one below, and glanced over her shoulder at him.

"You know your problem? Sometimes you think too much."

Jack's voice was gentle, low. She managed a real smile, somewhat reassured by the sexy look in his eyes.

Maybe this was going to be all right.

When his hand brushed against her hip as she continued up the stairs, she realized "all right" might be a gross underestimation. Instantly it felt as though every inch of her skin was hypersensitized. When his hand smoothed over her hip all the way to where the dress skimmed her bare thighs, she felt her heart kick up a gear.

And when his hand began stroking her thigh ever so lightly as she continued up the next flight of stairs, she thought she was going to turn into a boneless, quivering mess and slither down to the lobby between his legs.

His touch was light, delicate, searching, and she slowed down, barely moving now, biting her bottom lip to stop herself from groaning out loud as his hand smoothed farther up her thigh, sliding under the dress now and swooping up to just touch the lowest curve of her butt before sweeping down again.

A small animal sound escaped her despite her precautionary measures, and Jack's hand slid up again, venturing closer to her butt this time, then smoothing forward to reach around and just brush against her lower belly. She shivered, aware of the dull ache of desire that was beginning to throb between her legs.

"You like that?" he said huskily, and she noticed that she'd stopped climbing the stairs altogether now, and that he was standing right behind her, his breath tickling her ear. He was so tall that the fact he was standing a step down put them on an even footing.

She opened her mouth to respond, but any thoughts she had were swept away when Jack's hand slid up for another pass, this time reaching around across her hip and smoothing down over her stomach until he was dipping between her legs with firm, knowing fingers.

She gasped, wanting everything, all of it. A collage of ideas and shapes and sensations danced across her closed eyelids, and she wanted them all. Suddenly, she needed to feel Jack inside her, and she turned abruptly to face him, pushing his unresisting body against the wall.

"I want you right now," she whispered, a little surprised by her own audacity.

Jack smiled, a wicked wolf's smile, and she stood on tiptoes and kissed him, wanting to taste his wickedness, wanting to borrow some of his confidence and sexiness. He pulled her close, deepening the kiss, his tongue dancing with hers as one hand swept up under her dress to smooth over her butt again, while the other slid up her torso to take possession of her breast. It felt heavy with need, and when he ducked his head to tongue her nipples through the halter top, she had to lean against the wall to stay upright.

The sound of her gasps of desire echoed around them in the stairwell, and then they heard the scrape of a shoe on cement. Someone else was coming.

It was enough to bring them marginally to their senses, and Jack lifted his head slowly and nibbled at her ear for a moment before reluctantly relinquishing her breasts.

"I want you on a bed. Or at least something that's not concrete," he said, and she nodded dumbly.

She thrilled to the fact that he kept his hand possessively on her hip all the way up to the hallway outside her apartment. Then he took the key from her shaking hand and opened the door, pushing her ahead of him into her living room.

A moment of stillness passed as they stood there facing each other, alone at last, only the sound of their heavy breathing breaking the silence. After all this time of sniping at each other, it came down to this.

"Take it off," he said finally, indicating her dress.

She hesitated a moment, but there was no denying the demand in his eyes. She loosened the tie around her neck and released the halter top. His eyes seemed to flare as her breasts were revealed, and that feeling of power came back to her. Slowly, she reached for the zipper at the base of her spine to undo the skirt of the dress, aware that Jack's eyes followed every swaying movement of her breasts.

The dress slid down her thighs and he crossed the distance between them in a flash.

"Where's the bedroom?" he asked breathlessly, but she could only pant. He just shook his head then, and the next thing she knew she was on the carpet and he was on top of her, his mouth ducking to lick and suck at her breasts, his hands smoothing over her hips and thighs.

She wanted him to touch her *there* so much, but he seemed intent on teasing her, his fingers sweeping tantalizingly close to where all her heat awaited him, and then moving away again. She whimpered with the need for his touch, arching up under him.

"Now!" she demanded, and she felt him smiling against her breast.

He nipped her breast playfully, and she arched her back again.

"Jack!" she asked again, but he continued to tease her with his almost-caresses, and finally she'd had enough.

With a surge of strength, she pushed him away and began tearing at the buttons on his shirt. He kept trying to distract her, his hands plucking at her nipples, but she gritted her teeth and ignored his laughing to tear his shirt apart. Then she reached for his waistband.

"Help me get these off!" she ordered him breathlessly, and he obliged her by lifting his hips so she could pull his jeans over his butt and down his legs. He kicked them away as she ate him up hungrily with her eyes.

He was so beautiful. She splayed her fingers through the hair on his chest, but it was impossible to ignore the part of him that was demanding the most attention. Greatly daring, she slid her body against his, reveling in the spread of her breasts against his hairy chest, capturing his mouth for a brief but intense kiss before sliding back down his body. He tried to distract her as she moved lower and lower, her tongue chasing a hot trail down his chest and belly. His knee came up between her thighs, and she pressed herself against him, wanting so much more, but getting great pleasure from the pressure. Then she slid off his knee and continued down farther still, reaching for his erection and shooting him a challenging look before taking him in her mouth.

"Claire!" he cried out, and she loved the lack of control in his voice.

He tasted good, sweet and hard and she could feel his body tensing beneath her hands as she raced her tongue across the velvety head of his penis, her hand firmly stroking his shaft. A strong hand came down to still her movements.

"Quit while you're ahead, lady," he warned her. He broke away to grab a condom from his wallet, put it on, and then he was on her like a wild thing, his mouth almost too demanding on her breasts, his hands at last finding the centre of her, one finger plunging inside her where she was so, so ready for him. He made an approving noise as he found her clitoris and she bucked under his hand, and while she was still gasping her approval, she felt his hardness nudging at her thighs and she spread her legs wide, rising up to meet him.

It was like coming home. She forgot everything—her name, the rasp of the carpet against her back, the fact that her neighbors could probably hear her ecstatic groans and pleadings. Jack's face was intense and hard above hers, his eyes boring into hers as he thrust time and time again inside her. So deep. So hard and sure and perfect. She felt a pressure growing inside her, at first faint but then increasingly strong and she felt her face contort with the wanting. She closed her eyes, but Jack's voice whispered in her ear.

"Look at me. I want to see you," he said, and she opened her eyes just as she lost her grip on the world and became nothing but pulsating feeling and release.

He seemed to feed off her, and she felt his body tense and shudder as he surged into her one last time.

And then they were once again two bodies instead of one, their chests heaving against each other, eyes rueful as they regretted how quickly it had all gone. Jack kissed her face, slid a tongue along her neck, nibbled her earlobe. She sighed, smoothed her hands down his back, grasped his rounded, muscular butt.

"Give me a few moments, and we'll see if we can break another record," Jack whispered in her ear.

She laughed, then made a little regretful sound as he withdrew from her.

"Shower?" he suggested, one hand trailing down her body, stopping to explore dips and peaks along the way.

"Mmm," she agreed, allowing him to pull her to her feet.

She led the way into her bathroom, loving it when he slapped her behind gently, then cupped it with his big hands as he followed her into the shower.

"I worship this butt," he said, nuzzling her neck from behind.

"Really?" she blurted, surprised.

Jack turned her round, kissed her.

"You have the sexiest, most desirable little body. Don't tell me you don't know that?" he asked.

She shrugged, concentrating on turning on the water and getting the temperature right.

"Claire." He sounded so serious she stopped what she was doing and turned to him.

"Believe this now. I have wanted you since the moment I realized what those boxy suits of yours have been hiding. Okay?"

He was absolutely convincing, and she allowed herself to believe him, even if it was just for tonight.

"Okay."

He didn't look convinced.

"Repeat after me. 'I am very sexy,'" he instructed lightly, reaching for the soap.

"Jack!" she protested, but he had worked up a lather in his hands now and he reached for her breasts.

"Come on. 'I am very sexy.'"

She squirmed beneath his expert touch. "All right, all right. You're very sexy," she laughed.

Jack seemed inclined to force the issue, but other parts of him had recovered quite nicely and she took the matter firmly in hand, so to speak.

"Don't mess with me when I'm holding the remote control," she mock-warned him.

The rest of the shower passed in a haze of murmurs and groans and impatient noises. At last Jack shut off the water, his face hard with desire, and hauled her out of the shower and threw her, still wet, onto the bed.

He climbed on beside her, stalking toward her like a very large, very hungry jungle cat.

"This time, we go slow," he promised her.

He was true to his word. Sliding his body along hers, he pulled her close and kissed and caressed her until she was breathless. It was all so good—his hands, his mouth, the way he fit against her. She felt overwhelmed by desire. It was all too much, she felt out of control and Jack seemed to sense it. Soothing, he toyed almost absently with her breasts, circling her nipples gently with teasing fingers, pressing the occasional kiss into her cleavage. Just as she was beginning to relax into his touch, he picked things up, dancing his fingers across her nipples, then plucking at them more firmly, and finally drawing each straining tip into his mouth one at a time.

Liquid heat throbbed powerfully between her thighs. Once again she ached with need for him, and she reached for his erection with greedy hands. Jack tensed as she slicked her hand up and down his hard shaft and lifted her hips toward him, straining.

"All in good time, baby," he teased, brushing her hand away.

Claire liked the way he took control, the way he seemed to know so surely what she wanted.

But two could play at that game.

As Jack lifted his head from one breast and made to move to the other, she rolled out from under him and shoved him down on the bed. Before he could stop her, she was astride him, the swollen head of his penis pressing against her slick lips, but not quite penetrating her. She slid her hands along his arms until she held his wrists down on either side of his head. He could shake her off with barely a flex of his muscles, but they both indulged the fiction that she held him captive.

"Now I'm in charge," she threatened mockingly, gyrating suggestively against him.

Jack's eyes were navy dark as he watched her, his teeth just showing through his slightly parted lips. Greatly daring, she rubbed herself against him and felt the giveaway tension in his body. Watching him closely, she tilted her hips and guided his hardness into her. His eyes were almost closed now, but she could just see the glint of his eyes as she paused briefly before plunging onto him, taking him deep inside.

He filled her completely and utterly, and she threw back her head and reveled in the ride. Excitement built within her as Jack's hands caressed her breasts more and more firmly, and then suddenly, out of nowhere, she was throbbing around him again, gasping his name. In the aftermath, Jack moved like lightning, flipping her back onto the bed so that he was again on top. In charge once more, he continued the ride, reaching a hand between their bodies and searching for her clitoris. She cried out as he found it, squirming beneath him, sure that she was too sensitive, too stimulated. But Jack knew better, and in seconds she felt the excitement beginning to build again. He leaned over her now, shifting higher so that every thrust provided the maximum stimulation. And before she knew it she was lost, but he was with her this time, shuddering into her, holding her close.

They broke apart at last, panting. She could feel her heart pounding, and she closed her eyes. Had she ever felt this fulfilled, this amazing?

A foot nudged her calf, and she opened her eyes to find Jack watching her. He smiled saucily.

"Don't even think about going to sleep," he warned, and to her astonishment she felt an answering tightness in her body.

She had a feeling it was going to be a long, hot, breathless night.

JACK WOKE before her, and he simply watched her, resisting the urge to tuck an errant curl behind her ear. Her mouth was open a little, and every now and then she screwed up her eyes and made unintelligible noises in her sleep. She'd be mortified if she knew. He found himself smiling, enjoying the small moment.

Then he frowned, realizing something felt different.

He rolled onto his back and blinked up at the ceiling. Maybe it was because he'd stayed the whole night. That was probably it. Because normally he wasn't keen on doing that. There was all that morning-after awkwardness. But for some reason, he'd stayed last night.

His mind tripped over the incredible evening they'd shared. He hadn't seemed to be able to get enough of her, and she'd equaled his passion time and time again. He smiled, remembering how they'd argued like teenagers in the elevator just a few weeks ago. Who'd have thought they would wind up like this?

And then he realized what was different—it wasn't just that he'd stayed the night, it was that he wanted to stay this morning.

He wasn't thinking about getting up and finding his clothes, or concocting a legitimate excuse for hightailing it out of there. He wanted to stay, to talk, to have breakfast. Hopefully to make love again. Whatever. Whatever it was people did when one of them didn't run for the hills the next morning.

He found his heart rate picking up as Claire stirred beside him, her eyelids flickering before she at last opened her eyes and locked gazes with him for the first time in the light of day. And then he registered the look in her eyes, and all his pleasant imaginings withered to nothing. She looked panicked, shocked.

Unwelcoming.

Damn.

He could feel her body stiffen next to his and he froze, unsure what to do. A minute ago he'd been trying to decide if they'd breakfast here or go find somewhere down by the bay. But now she looked as though she was ready to throw a sheet out the window and try to shimmy her way down if that was what it was going to take to escape him.

It seemed he may have miscalculated somewhat. Perhaps she needed a little time to relax and get used to things? He tried a smile, but she stared at him as if he were some oversize cockroach she'd found on the sheets.

"Hi," he said, for lack of anything else.

"Hi."

She'd got more of a grip on herself, he could see. Or more accurately, he couldn't see, because she'd disappeared behind an impenetrable mask of politeness.

"Would you—would you like breakfast?" she asked, and he watched her wriggle away from him to the edge of the bed, being very careful all the while to keep the sheet clutched to her chest.

So it was going to be like this.

He fought back a bitter laugh. All these years he'd been the one to long for a quick escape the morning after. And the one time he wanted to stay, he was being herded toward the door. Perhaps she was worried about what happened next? He honestly hadn't given it much thought, but maybe she wanted to talk about it. Women, in his experience, could never get enough talk.

"Claire—" he began to say, but she cut him off.

"I know, I understand, believe me, it's exactly what I was thinking. We have to work together, and it's awkward, but, hey, it's got to be out of our systems now, right?"

She'd spotted a silky dressing gown on the bedroom floor, and he watched as she stretched out one leg, clenched her toes into the silky fabric, and dragged it toward herself, all the while ensuring the sheet continued to cover all her vital areas. He was so fascinated by it all that he answered honestly.

"Well, in a word—no," he said, and she snapped her head around to stare at him.

"No?" she repeated, her eyes wide.

He fought the urge to lean forward and kiss her. She was just so…kissable.

"No. I don't honestly think I've gotten it out of my system," he elaborated.

She stared at him for a moment, then shook her head decisively. Standing abruptly, she forsook the safety of her modesty sheet and shrugged into the dressing gown. He was treated to a tantalizing glimpse of curvy hip and swelling breast before she pulled the wrap tight around herself and cinched it with a tie-belt.

He found himself facing Professional Claire, the competent, on-the-ball, matter-of-fact woman who strode the halls of Beck and Wise every Monday to Friday.

"Look, Jack, I'm going to be straight with you. I'm not really up for one of your flings. I mean, I know we've sort of had one, a mini one, anyway, but I'm not up for any more than this," she said, sounding very brisk and businesslike.

He could feel himself getting a little annoyed at all the assumptions she was making. Feeling at a disadvantage lying on the bed, he stood and approached her. Her eyes dropped rather gratifyingly below his waistline, but she looked away very quickly.

"What if I don't want a fling, mini or otherwise? What if I want more than that?"

Where had that come from? He'd even surprised himself with that one. Surely he didn't want a…well, a *relationship* with Claire? The idea seemed very strange and alien, but it didn't stop him from feeling deeply offended when she attempted to smother the smile that leaped to her lips. He frowned.

"Are you laughing at me?"

She shook her head, her lips pressed together primly now. But he'd seen it.

"You did, you just laughed at me!" he accused.

Claire at last looked him in the eye, and he saw that any trace of laughter was gone from her face now.

"Jack. Come on, listen to yourself. This is you, consummate playboy, and me, uptight chick from the office. We have nothing in common except for some physical…curiosity, which we fully explored last night."

Jack opened his mouth to tell her that she was wrong, then shut it again, the words unspoken. He didn't know what to say. Worse, he didn't know what to do except to get dressed and go. He didn't even know what his own feelings were, so how could he question hers when she was basically drawing a line under what had happened between them?

"I guess I should go, then," he suggested dully.

She nodded, stooping to detangle the sheets.

"That's probably the most sensible thing."

Jack padded into the living room, blinking at the sight of his clothes strewn all over the floor. There was only one button intact on his shirt—she'd ripped the rest off—and he found his jeans rucked up in the corner near the television. He stood staring at them for a moment, almost driven to turn around and try to talk to her, sort things out. Because it felt wrong to end things this way. He didn't know what else there was to explore, but he felt as though this was incomplete, wrong. But then he remembered the look that had crept into her eyes the moment she'd seen him this morning. That was not the look of a woman who wanted to "explore" things.

CLAIRE FELT as though she was holding her breath as she waited for Jack to finish dressing in the living room. She scooted over to her chest of drawers and grabbed a pair of panties, pulling them on hastily beneath her robe, feeling somehow safer with a bit of satin and cotton between her and Jack's all-knowing gaze. After all, it was the lack of panties that had got her into this situation in the first place.

She could hear the clink of his belt buckle, and she guessed he was probably mostly decent by now. God, she wanted him gone. She needed him gone before she broke down and begged him to stay. Even for just a few more hours. Or—her heart leaped—another night. Whatever he was willing to give her.

Which was why he had to go, of course. She relived the bolt of fear that had ripped through her when she opened her eyes and found him staring at her. She knew from past relationships that she sometimes talked in her sleep, and she had a sudden moment of panic as she imagined what she might have said.

What if she'd said something about him, about her feelings for him?

Oh, anything but that!

Jack would run a mile if she so much as hinted at feeling anything deeper than lust for him. She was so sure of it, so sure that he would reject her, that she quivered at the very thought of it. He had the power to destroy her, she knew, and she didn't have the strength to face him down.

"Claire."

She turned to find him standing in her bedroom door, his shirt held shut with just one dangling button. She blushed, remembering that she'd popped the buttons last night, tearing his clothes off him.

"I'm going now."

She nodded, staring at his back for a moment as he turned toward the front door. She forced herself to follow him out, to smile in a friendly-but-not-too-friendly way at him as he opened the exterior door and then turned to look at her one last time.

"Claire, I really… Look, maybe this is a bad time…"

He seemed lost for words, his face uncertain. For the first time, she doubted her rock-solid instincts where he was concerned. Was it possible that he…?

He seemed to make a decision, his shoulders squaring and his gaze becoming clearer as he looked down at her. She bit her tongue, resisting the urge to throw herself at his feet. He was probably just feeling guilty, trying to find a way to say goodbye nicely.

"I'm going to call you tonight, okay? When you've had time to settle down a little. Get some sleep, maybe."

The ghost of a smile came from him. She'd been right—he felt sorry for her!

"If you want to, that's fine, Jack. But it's not necessary, really," she told him coolly.

She felt proud of that coolness. If she could keep this up, she might be able to salvage a little bit of dignity. Jack stared at her for a moment, and then he turned on his heel and was gone. She stared at the closed door for a long time, telling herself she was relieved.

And she was. She was very relieved that Jack hadn't guessed the full extent of her feelings. That would have been the ultimate humiliation, of course. Here he was, throwing lonely Claire a bone, and she'd fallen head over heels in love with him.

She snorted out loud at her own stupidity. Of all the men on the planet, she had to pick Jack Brook to fall in love with. Hell, she'd probably been in love with him subconsciously for years.

All her posturing about his dating and his demeanor, all her contempt for him—a paper-thin veil to hide the truth from herself. She'd fallen in love with Jack. She adored him. She thought he was witty, kind, intelligent, funny. She wanted to make love to him until it was medically advisable to take a break.

Thank God he'd gone.

Feeling strangely empty, she padded into her bathroom and shed her robe. The sight of her shower brought back a rush of hot, sticky memories from last night, and she found herself overwhelmed by emotion as she stepped under the stream of hot water.

She wanted…she just *wanted*. She felt as though she'd spent her lifetime *just wanting* a whole bunch of things that were never going to come her way. And she was sick of it, worn out from it, over it. Slowly she slid down the tiled wall until she was huddled on the shower base, the water pummeling her head from on high.

She loved Jack, and there was no way he was ever going to love her back. She'd invested her most precious asset in a man who was too scared to let love into his life. She'd watched him avoid relationships with so many women over the past two years. He'd said it himself when they were trapped in the elevator—he made sure that women always knew the score where he was concerned. No strings, no hassles. She suspected a lot of his commitment phobia came from what had happened with his brother, from not being able to deal with his loss. But that didn't make much difference at the end of the day. Jack was the one who had to decide to take the risk of loving someone—and it sure as hell wouldn't be her. They'd fought like cat and dog most of the time they'd known each other, and, even if they'd discovered an intense sexual chemistry more recently, she wasn't the kind of woman he'd change his life for. Katherine, now she was the kind of woman men changed their lives for. And even she hadn't lured Jack over from the dark side.

By the time Claire emerged from the shower, her fingers and toes were prunish and she felt well and truly waterlogged. She made herself a bowl of muesli with skim milk and sat in her kitchen eating it like a zombie, her mind mulling over and over the problem of how to reassemble her life and peace of mind.

Work was the big thing. She was stuck with Jack on the stupid Hillcrest project, and there was no way to get out of it. So she was going to have to suck it up. She was going to have to wear her best poker face and laugh at Jack's jokes and try not to claw out his eyes when she heard he was dating someone else from the office.

Suddenly her muesli tasted like small pieces of cardboard, and she pushed the bowl away.

16

JACK WAITED FOR Monday like a man in the desert thirsts for water. He couldn't stop thinking about Claire. In fact, he picked up the phone at least ten times to call her, but each time he put it back again when he realized he had nothing to offer beyond "Hi." What was he going to say to her, after all? "For some reason I can't stop thinking about you, but please don't take that the wrong way as I'm scared to death of commitment"? Yeah, that'd go over real well.

It had been a long time since he'd felt so confused and uncertain, and he found his thoughts turning to Robbie. That was the thing about having a twin—whenever he'd been down, he'd always known that Robbie would understand. Jack had never had to wax poetic or dig deep to explain himself—Robbie had just known. It had been reciprocal, of course. He smiled as he remembered the times he'd found himself drawn to Robbie's place on a Sunday night, a taste for beer in his mouth, only to find his twin with a six-pack waiting and a problem to share.

Robbie would have liked Claire. In fact, Robbie probably would have seen her for what she was the first time he met her, and Jack would have had a fight on his hands to keep her for himself.

Somehow, Jack wound up in his garage, pulling the dust sheets off the Triumph Triple R motorbikes that he and Robbie had bought each other for their last shared birthday. They'd planned to tour Australia on them. But Robbie had gotten sick before they'd had a chance to do more than a few week-long runs up and down the coast.

Now Jack contemplated his bike, sorrow for Robbie and all the dreams that had died with him welling up inside. Tears rolled down his face, but he remembered their first day out on the bikes. Robbie had insisted on wearing an open-faced helmet with old-fashioned motorcycle goggles, despite the fact that Jack had told him over and over that he looked like a mad-ass version of the Red Baron. They'd stopped at a country general store to get drinks, and Robbie had smiled a big, glad-to-be-alive smile at him—revealing the host of small insects that he'd collected in his teeth as they rode. Even now the memory made him laugh, and Jack wiped the last of his tears away with his shirtsleeve.

Decisive, he threw the dust sheet over his own bike. Wheeling Robbie's out into the sun, he checked the gauges and the spark plugs, and flicked the ignition on. The bike hummed to life with barely a hiccup. Grabbing his leathers and his helmet, Jack climbed on.

The ride had cleared his head on many counts, but he was no closer to solving the problem of Claire by Monday morning. Somehow, though, he still found himself bounding out of bed, taking time over his clothes, making sure he flossed as well as brushed. When he drove past her sedate sedan in its usual spot in the car park, he even felt a smile curving his mouth.

And when she stuck her head into his office first thing, he found himself studying every detail of her appearance, from her curly-topped head to her high-heeled feet. His imagination efficiently whisked away her neat suit and shirt and he enjoyed a full Technicolor image of her naked and willing, panting for him like she had been last Friday night. He dragged his chair closer to his desk to ensure the inevitable side effect of thinking about Claire naked was well hidden beneath several layers of timber and paperwork, and tried to concentrate on what she was saying.

"…called to Sydney for an emergency meeting, so Hillcrest has asked to bring the sign-off meeting forward to this afternoon. He'll be on his way to the airport, so he's offered to swing by here again. How's your schedule looking around two?"

Jack wrenched his fascinated gaze from her full-lipped mouth and tried to rémember that English was his first language.

"Fine. Great. Whatever."

She gave him a look that clearly questioned his sanity. As it was a concern he also shared, he tried to focus his attention on something other than the need to kiss her.

"Right. I've booked the meeting room on my floor. I'll see you down there at two, then."

He snapped out of his self-induced stupor as he realized she was about to leave. And that he didn't want that.

"Claire!"

She turned toward him, her face carefully blank and professional.

He stared at her, trying to think of something to say, something that would mean she would stay in his office and he could keep looking at her and smelling her and being with her.

"Um…how was your weekend?" he finally offered.

She flushed, then focused on the wall behind his head as she delivered a little speech that she'd obviously put quite a bit of thought into.

"Look, Jack, I know that things are bound to be awkward after Friday night…but we're both professionals and grown-ups. It happened, let's move on. I'm sure you agree."

No, he didn't. He wasn't sure why he didn't agree, but he didn't. And she was heading for the door again. And this time he couldn't think of a single thing to say to stop her.

He just sat and blinked and breathed for a while after she'd gone. What the hell was going on? Why was his heart still pounding out of control, and why was he battling the desire to either throw Claire Marsden to the ground and lick her until she screamed the building down, or cradle her in his arms and assure her that everything in the world had purpose and meaning?

IT TOOK FIVE MINUTES closeted in a cubicle in the ladies' room before she felt able to face the office again. God, she loved him.

Seeing him again, sitting opposite her, within reach—it was a new form of torture.

How was she going to get through this? The future seemed to stretch out ahead of her, bleak and comfortless.

She dragged herself back to her desk. She couldn't focus on work, so she spent an hour playing a numbing game of solitaire on her computer, just so she'd look busy if anyone passed by. Tom kept shooting her concerned looks, and he eventually ventured into her office.

"Are you okay?" he asked hesitantly.

She blinked up at him. *No, Tom, I'm not okay,* she wanted to say. *I've fallen for a man who is afraid of love, and, even if he wasn't, would never pick me to love anyway. I'm boring and square and not sexy enough. I annoy him, I know I do. The only reason he spent the night with me was because he felt sorry for me. And, Tom, here's the worst bit—I can't stop thinking about him. I honestly don't know how I'm going to get through our meeting this afternoon without throwing myself at his feet or just plain throwing up.*

"I'm fine, Tom. But thanks for asking."

He nodded and retreated to his desk, but she could see he wasn't happy. That made two of them.

JACK ENTERED the meeting room on Claire's floor with a certain degree of trepidation. She was alone in there, waiting for the Hillcrest people to arrive. And, sure enough, his heart went into overdrive the moment he saw her. Before he could give it much more thought, Hillcrest and his cronies arrived.

It wasn't until the meeting was well under way that it hit him. Claire was handling the cranky old baboon with consummate skill, and he was so closely attuned to her she had only to glance his way and Jack knew exactly what she wanted him to do and say. But, really, apart from the occasional reference to giraffes and rhinos, precious little was expected of him because Claire was so damned good. She knew her stuff, and she was funny, and she was flexible, and she knew when to be a bit cheeky and when to give in. She was amazing. Really, truly amazing.

And then he had his revelation. He was watching Claire talk to Hank, her lips curving into a smile and then a laugh as she responded to something the old guy said. It felt as if something tight and controlled had snapped in Jack's chest and then he felt a warm, unfolding sensation as he stared at her.

He loved her. He loved Claire Marsden. It was like being hit by a tsunami, and he actually reached for the table to steady himself.

Everything slotted into place, and the world froze in its orbit as he examined this new knowledge from every angle. *He loved her.*

Cautiously, he tested the bounds of this new discovery. How would he feel about Claire moving into his house, for example? He remembered all the discarded clothes on her bedroom floor. She was messy—they'd have to deal with that. But she could have her own room for her clothes, like a big walk-in closet. His smile widened into a grin as he realized he actually liked the idea of waking up beside her every day, that he didn't mind if she left her stuff everywhere, as long as he got to laugh with her and hold her and make love to her every day for the rest of his life.

Man, did he have it bad, or what? All these years of being the artful dodger when it came to affairs of the heart, and the one woman who'd always steered clear of him had him in the palm of her hand without even trying.

Vaguely he became aware of Hillcrest saying something: the old guy's lips were moving, but Jack had no idea what was coming out. He must have responded appropriately, however, because Hillcrest smiled and clapped him heartily on the back and shuffled toward the door.

Jack couldn't take his eyes off Claire.

His mom was going to be over the moon. He imagined introducing Claire to his family, and felt a warm glow of pride in his belly. She was so clever and brave and funny. Prickly, of course, and there'd always be arguments. But then there'd always be the mind-blowing sex to make up with, too.

They were good for each other. The way he saw it, they completed each other—she'd made him realize he had to open up and let himself care again, and he'd helped her to relax and live a little. Remembering the hurt in her eyes as she discussed her father's no-show, he made a fierce commitment to himself: he'd make it his life's mission to ensure she never felt unimportant or overlooked again.

He felt as if a load had been lifted from his shoulders and he turned to Claire once the Hillcrest people were gone, ready to spill his guts and offer himself up to her.

"Claire," he said, and she paused in the act of shuffling her paperwork together.

He loved the little frown line that appeared between her eyebrows as she tried to work out what he wanted. He loved the fact that she looked at her watch, her mind obviously elsewhere. It was so *Claire.*

He crossed to the door and closed it to ensure privacy, then turned to face her.

"We need to talk," he said firmly, feeling his way forward into the darkness of this brand-new territory.

She was facing him, her face carefully polite, but he could tell by the set of her shoulders that she was tense, cautious.

He couldn't just come right out with it, could he? No, that would scare her off. He had to be subtle, build up to it. Explain himself.

"I love you."

Of course, straight to the point was also an effective strategy.

He held his breath, his eyes intent on her face as she registered what he'd said. He noted the way her eyes dilated briefly, the way her mouth formed a tiny little shocked O, and the slight flush that washed up her neck and face.

"What did you just say?"

He moved toward her, but Claire put her hand out like a cop stopping traffic.

Okay. Give her time. Let her adjust.

"I love you. I have fallen in love with you," he enunciated carefully.

She still looked shocked. Maybe even scared.

"I don't understand," she stammered.

She'd dropped her papers onto the table now, and was wrapping her arms protectively around her torso.

"What's to understand? I think you're amazing. I know now that all that snapping and sniping between us was just because of *this*," he said, gesturing back and forth between them to indicate their connection. "*This* is very strong, and I'm sick of fighting it, I don't know about you."

"Jack, you don't mean it," she said in a small, distant voice.

He blinked. She didn't sound overjoyed. She didn't sound even slightly joyed.

"Claire—"

"No, Jack. Wait."

Suddenly she was scrambling to collect all her paperwork, scooping it toward herself in a frenzy. She stood with papers bristling out in every direction and confronted him.

"This was all a mistake. We should never have done the sex thing. It messed everything up. I want you to understand that I totally appreciate what you're trying to do right now, but it's not necessary. Okay. So let's just leave it."

She was making no sense, and he didn't believe a word of it, anyway. There was no way she could feel nothing after the night they'd shared together.

"Claire, just stay and talk for a minute," he said, stepping to block her path to the door.

But she was determined, and she dodged to one side and ducked around him.

"It was a mistake, Jack, believe me. You don't love me. You'll realize that and you'll be glad in a few days. And don't worry, it'll be like this conversation never happened. I promise."

He considered stopping her as she flung the door open and shot out into the corridor, but she was determined, and a sudden leaden feeling had stolen into his limbs.

Maybe he'd gotten it all wrong. Was it possible that all the magic he'd been feeling had been one-sided? He forced himself to be brutal as he examined what he knew of relationships. And he remembered a handful of women who'd been demonstrably head over heels with him with very little encouragement at all. Women who'd declared their love at the drop of a hat, while he'd felt only a vague fondness or attraction for them.

He felt sick. Somewhere, deep inside, he recognized that this was the ultimate irony: the guy who always runs from commitment falling in love at last, but with a woman who doesn't love him back.

He laughed, but it came out as more of a groan.

He loved Claire Marsden and she didn't want a bit of him.

CLAIRE SCURRIED to her office and shut the door and drew the venetian blinds down and sat in the semidark staring at nothing. Her heart was pounding, and she felt there was definite potential to lose her lunch.

One sentence kept circling round and around in her head. *I love you.*

Jack Brook had said he loved her. And for a glorious moment she'd seen this vision of the future, a golden, hazy, perfect vision filled with love and happiness and togetherness. And then reality had snapped back into focus.

Jack Brook did not love her. He felt sorry for her, at best. Maybe she *had* talked in her sleep. Maybe he had figured out how much this had all meant to her. Maybe he even realized that the reason she was looking all puffy and just plain wrong today was because she'd been tortured by visions of him every time she tried to get some sleep over the weekend. So, being a nice, kind guy, he'd decided to do the right thing. It was the only explanation she could come up with.

She sat frozen in her chair, alternating between the desire to charge down to Jack's office and make him prove what he'd just said, and the powerful need to hide beneath her desk and pretend none of it had happened.

A rap at the door started her out of her reverie, and she turned wary eyes to the door, dreading to see Jack as it opened. How could she resist the invitation implicit in his declaration again? She wanted so much to believe him, but she was too scared of what would happen if her love proved to be stronger than his. She couldn't survive being the one who was left caring again. Not after a lifetime of it.

"You *are* in! Tom wasn't sure if you were here or not."

It was Katherine. The other woman hesitated on the threshold, obviously sensing something was wrong.

"I was just…" Claire made a helpless gesture, not sure what to say.

Katherine gave her a searching look, then strode into the room and shut the door behind her. She flicked the light switch on and Claire blinked in the sudden glare.

"This is about Jack, isn't it?" Katherine asked boldly.

Claire could only nod, miserable.

"I did warn you. I know he's damned irresistible, but there's just something holding him back—"

"He said he loved me."

Katherine looked stunned. "He did?"

"Yes."

Katherine's face began to transform, a smile creeping across it as she digested Claire's news. "But that's terrific. Amazing!"

Claire stared at her friend. "Are you mad? Jack Brook doesn't really love me. It's not possible."

Katherine looked confused. "But you just said that he told you he did."

"Yes. But he doesn't know what he's saying. He feels sorry for me. Or he's confused."

Katherine was staring at her strangely. "Claire, Jack wouldn't say something if he didn't mean it. And he certainly wouldn't say something like that because he felt sorry for someone. Trust me, I've been there, done that. Not once did Jack ever say anything just to make me feel good."

"You don't understand. It's because Jack knows how I feel. We— He— Well, we shared a pretty intense time on Friday night and I had a bit of a crisis and I'm sure he just feels sort of…responsible for me. That's all."

"Right. He said all this to you, did he?" Katherine demanded, skeptical.

"Not as such. But I know that's what it is."

Katherine just stood there for a moment studying her, and Claire fought the urge to twitch.

"So, how do you know he thinks all this stuff, then, if he didn't say it? You psychic or something?"

Claire stared at Katherine, startled. "Of course not."

Katherine made a harrumphing noise as though she'd just decided something. "You know what I think? You're afraid."

Claire stared at her, affronted.

"I hardly think—" she began to say, but Katherine was nodding knowingly, her expression grim.

"Afraid. Scared rigid, if I have any guess. Aren't you two just the pair, then?"

There was judgment in Katherine's tone, and Claire sat up a little straighter.

"You don't know what you're talking about," she said icily.

"Really? Seeing as I know you and Jack pretty well, I think I'm informed enough to have an opinion on the subject."

"Well, you don't know how I feel. Or how Jack feels, for that matter," Claire said stubbornly.

Katherine sighed heavily. "Claire, if Jack had told me he loved me, I would have jumped at the offer and hung on for dear life. What more do you want from the guy?"

Claire narrowed her eyes at her friend, hating the way Katherine was pushing her.

"You know what, I think you're the one who's in love with Jack. You're always asking me about him, giving advice."

"I was trying to be your friend, Claire. Sometimes outsiders can see things more clearly."

"I know exactly what you mean," Claire said pointedly.

Katherine stared at her. "I hope you don't regret what you're doing. Guys like Jack come along once in a lifetime."

And with that she left, and Claire sank lower in her seat and hung her head in her hands. Why had she been so awful to Katherine?

Because her friend had challenged her, that was why.

You're afraid.

It was ridiculous, of course. Katherine didn't understand. The phone rang, and she leaped on it like it was a lifeline. She didn't have time to sit around contemplating her navel. She had a magazine to launch.

She tried very hard to push Katherine's words and the hurt look on her face out of her mind for the rest of the afternoon, but for the first time in Claire's life, work failed her. She kept remembering the expression on Jack's face when he'd said he loved her, and hope would spring to life in her chest and she'd think *maybe.* Then reality would intrude and she'd stomp all over her stupid, forlorn hope with hobnailed boots of pragmatism. Of course Jack didn't really love her. He couldn't.

Finally her circling thoughts and the churning in her belly got too much for her and she grabbed her bag and headed home early. What she needed was a run—a really hard, punishing run that would wipe all other thought from her mind.

She entered her apartment, slapped on her running gear and was out the door, hitting the pavement as though the hounds of hell were following her.

With each footfall, she pushed Katherine's words away.

"I am not afraid, I am not afraid," she whispered under her breath as she climbed a hill.

But with each mile it became more and more obvious that there was no denying the hard lump of emotion that had been sitting rock-heavy in her stomach from the moment she realized she loved Jack Brook.

Fear. Pure and simple.

Katherine was right—she *was* afraid.

The moment Claire admitted her cowardice, she started justifying it to herself with an avalanche of logic and rationalization. Even if Jack Brook really did love her—and it was a big if—she couldn't risk exposing herself to him. He was tall and perfect and handsome and clever, and she was just Claire. He could have his pick of women—exciting, dynamic, sexy women.

And he'd picked her.

It was such a revolutionary thought that it stopped her in her tracks. Out of all the women he'd dated over the years—including peerless, bombshell Katherine—*he'd picked Claire.*

Hope took advantage of the lull in her defenses to leap to the fore. What if he really did love her? What if he loved her the way she loved him and she'd just pushed him away because she was too scared to even try? What kind of a person did that make her?

She couldn't help remembering the image she'd had of herself when she'd been stuck in the elevator with Jack—a workaholic who buried her lack of life under a training schedule. A dry, humorless shrew who didn't know how to have fun.

It wasn't true. The past few weeks had proven that to her, if nothing else. But if she walked away from Jack's declaration, wasn't she going to become that woman, that beige-suited, hospital-cornered woman who never took risks?

"No!"

She said it so loudly that the man walking his dog nearby turned and stared. She stared back, for the first time registering where her desperate run had led her. She was standing outside the car dealership near her apartment, right in front of the shiny red Mustang convertible that she'd convinced herself she didn't want.

She didn't allow herself to think. Thinking was what stopped her from doing so many things, she realized. This was about taking action, doing what felt right.

"Hey, you," she called out to the car salesman who was buffing a bumper near the back of the lot. "How much for the Mustang?"

He trotted over, welcoming smile in place.

"It's a lovely car, just two owners, both women. Superb leather trim, with—"

She didn't have time for any of this, and she silenced him with an impatient shake of her head.

"How much? That's all I need to know."

"Ten thousand. But don't you want to hear about the—"

No, she didn't. She didn't want to waste any time, because somewhere in the back of her mind she knew she was about to behave recklessly, and that if she paid too much attention to the fact, nothing would happen and this small window of brave, audacious daring might close over and never appear again.

"I'll take it. I just have to go home and get my checkbook," she said, cutting across his sales patter.

He looked bewildered. "Don't you want to haggle?"

"No," she said.

"Not even a little bit?".

"No. This is what I want."

It felt so refreshing to say those words out loud. *This is what I want.* Not what she thought someone else might want her to want. Not what she thought might project a certain image. Not what her father, or Morgan, or even Jack might think was right.

She insisted that he put a sold sign on it before she left him to jog home and get her checkbook. Her blood was fizzing with expectation. She had a sexy car. She wasn't a stick in the mud. She was exciting and adventurous. The sort of woman that Jack Brook was attracted to. The sort of woman that Jack Brook...loved?

It was so hard, making that last leap of faith. As she brushed her teeth and sprayed on perfume and picked out her sexiest, most exciting summer dress, she skirted around the edges of admitting to herself what she had to do next. Like buying the car, if she examined it too closely she was afraid she'd be paralyzed by old fears. So she told herself she was just sprucing herself up for her new car, so that when she drove it off the lot she'd feel the part. But she knew where she was going, what she was going to do.

She was going to see Jack, and she was going to tell him that she loved him.

In a state of suspended panic that occasionally crossed over into exhilaration, she drove her sensible sedan to the car lot and signed over a large chunk of her savings. The salesman was effervescent with goodwill, throwing in a set of car mats and a key ring. Then she drove out of the lot with the radio on, the top down and her heart in her mouth.

She almost turned around several times on the way to Jack's place. She was too good at protecting herself for that part of herself to give up without a fight. She started by making excuses for why Jack wouldn't be home. Then she told herself that buying the car, becoming a convertible-type-of-girl, was more than enough for one day. Baby steps, that's what were required. Perhaps, in a year or two, she could make her way to Jack's place to serve up her soul on a silver platter.

But the memory of what it had felt like to make love to Jack kept her going. The excitement, the belonging, the sheer magic of it. It had to be right. If she didn't take a chance on this, she'd regret it for the rest of her life.

Perhaps if she hadn't been so preoccupied with taming her own terror, she would have registered the familiar car parked in front of Jack's house as she pulled up. But she didn't. She was too busy forcing one leg after the other up the walk, her courage tightly held in both hands as she took a deep breath and rang the doorbell.

There was a long silence, and then Jack opened the front door, dressed in nothing but a towel, his skin still glistening from the shower. She stared at him, struck once again by how damn perfect and beautiful and sexy he was. She loved the faint curl in his dark hair. She loved the little crinkly lines at the corners of his eyes. And the way his mouth always looked as though he was about to laugh. The depth and breadth of his chest. The strength of his thighs. The way he—

She realized that she was staring at him, and she cleared her throat. "Jack, I have something I need to tell you," she said boldly.

"Okay."

He looked wary, and a bit hopeful. Her courage surged. This was going to work out, it really was.

"I just wanted to say, I'm sorry about this afternoon. I'm an idiot. Actually, I'm more of a coward. Or at least I was," she began, warming up to things.

Jack was smiling now, and she found herself smiling back. It really was going to be okay.

Then she heard the voice—the very feminine voice—calling from the back of the house.

"Jack, I thought you said it was going to be a quick shower."

And then she saw Katherine padding up Jack's hallway, barefoot and in shorts, a half-empty beer glass in her hand.

"Claire!" she said, sounding startled.

But Claire was too busy controlling her gag reflex to respond. All the time she'd been standing on Jack's doorstep, preparing to pour her heart out to him, he'd had another woman warming up out back. Not just any woman—Katherine, her so-called friend, the woman she'd accused of having an unrequited crush on Jack just hours ago.

So much for him loving her.

It felt like a slap in the face. It felt as if she'd closed her eyes and leaped, expecting to land safely in someone's arms, only to find that she'd stepped into a chasm. If only she hadn't allowed herself to hope. For years she'd survived without love, but she'd let herself hope, and now this....

She felt frozen to the spot as she desperately called on all those years of not looking disappointed when she hurt like hell inside. As long as he didn't know what she'd come here for, she might just escape with a little bit of dignity intact. Suddenly that seemed very important. As long as Jack didn't know how close she'd come to making a fool of herself, perhaps her pain wouldn't be quite so all-encompassing.

But it was too late. She felt her face crumpling, felt her world crashing down around her.

This was why she never stuck her neck out. This was why she played it safe.

"Claire, let me explain," Katherine said, heading toward her.

"I have to go," Claire managed to choke out as she backed away from the door.

Jack stepped forward, trying to catch her arm.

"Claire, wait!"

Any hope of retaining a shred of pride evaporated as the tears hit. She turned toward her car, already blubbering messy, undignified tears, aware that inside she hurt. She hurt so much she wanted to sink to the ground and howl.

She wrenched the car door open and stabbed the keys into the ignition. Where had all these tears come from? Did she even have this much fluid in her body?

She had to get out of here.

"Claire, will you please just stop and listen?"

He'd stopped to pull on a pair of shorts, but Jack was beside the car now, hovering over her. She panicked, pumping the accelerator madly and turning the key, but the starter motor just whined at her, leaving the engine dead. Furious, blinded by tears, she pumped the accelerator again and twisted the key viciously. Again, nothing. When she moved to try a third time, Jack's large hand reached down to tug the key from her death grip.

"You've flooded it. It's not like your little automatic," he said calmly. "Now, will you please listen to me?"

She glanced up at him through the veil of her tears, registering his concerned face. She felt like such an idiot. She was going to have to quit her job. She'd been fooling herself when she thought she could bear to work with Jack, knowing he was with someone else.

"Just leave me alone, I just want to be alone," she said when Jack tried to open the car door. She hit the lock, and wound the window up. Since the roof was down, it was a fairly pointless exercise, but she was so upset she was beyond caring.

Jack reached over the window, and suddenly the car door was unlocked and swinging open, and she was being dragged out into his arms.

"Put me down!" she sobbed, but he just held her tighter.

"Not until you listen to me, goddamn you," Jack said.

It felt so good to be in his arms, yet knowing that she couldn't have him, that he wasn't hers after all, only made things worse. But he wouldn't let go of her, so in the end she just gave up and rested her head on his shoulder and cried. His hands soothed her back, and he whispered reassurances in her ear. After a few minutes of steady sobbing she was reduced to snuffling against his damp shoulder, dread building inside her with every passing second. He knew, now. He had to know. He knew she loved him, and now her rejection would be complete.

"Now, just listen for a second," he said, obviously judging her to be in a somewhat calmer state. "Katherine came around to talk to me because I asked her to. I know you two are friends, and I needed some advice. Because I'd just told you I loved you, and you blew me off."

His words managed to somehow seep past the mist of tears and pain fogging her brain. Katherine was here for *advice?* Not wild, animal sex? Claire considered this for a few seconds, decided she might be prepared to believe it. Which meant…which meant…

"Claire, I love you. Why can't you believe that?"

She needed to see him. She pulled back from his shoulder, wiping a hand across her face to try and clear away some of the tears. His blue eyes were deeply sincere, his hands gentle as he cradled her face.

"Really? You're sure? Because I don't think I could handle it if you got to know me and you realized…"

She found herself trailing off. She stared into Jack's eyes as the domino pieces of the past flipped over into each other in her mind.

What had she been about to say? That once Jack really knew her he wouldn't—couldn't—love her?

She blinked at him.

"My father—" she began to say, and then she put her hand over her mouth to stop the words from pouring out.

She couldn't stop herself from thinking as easily, however. As Jack waited patiently, she followed her thought through to its conclusion.

How could Jack love her when her own father wouldn't even give her the time of day? And Harry was honor-bound to love her—it was supposed to be genetic, he was her father. If he couldn't dredge up a shred of feeling, what hope was there that the golden Jack Brook could truly love her in the same, all-encompassing way she loved him?

It was as though something large and monstrous had suddenly stepped out of the shadows and assumed life-size proportions. Like confessing to Jack her fear that she'd only won because she'd "done it for Daddy," it was hard acknowledging this last and final truth. She felt rejected by her father, and she lived her life in fear of being rejected by anyone else.

She stared up at Jack, not even knowing where to begin.

But he did.

"I am not your father, Claire. I love you, and nothing is going to change that. I love your laugh, I love your tears, I love the way you think, the way you get that little wrinkle between your brows when you're confused. I love making love to you, holding you in my arms, touching you. I love your passion and your commitment and your sense of what's fair. I love it that you're honest, even if it means admitting that you're wrong sometimes…."

He kissed her gently.

"Oh, Jack," she managed to whisper, moved to tears again, but good tears this time. She threw herself into his arms, squeezing him as hard as she could, proving to herself that he was real. He squeezed her back, and they stood holding each other, loving each other, for a long time.

"Um, is there something you'd like to say to me?" he asked super-casually.

She pulled back from their embrace to stare at him quizzically. He gave her a sad puppy-dog look, obviously expecting something.

"What?"

And then she realized she still hadn't told him she loved him! Here she was, blubbering all over his front lawn, exposing her most painful fears, and she still hadn't told the man how she felt.

She felt blinded by her love as she beamed up at him. Where to begin? She reached up and cupped his precious face in her hands.

"You are the most wonderful, amazing, clever, sexy man. And I love you. I love you so much that it scares me."

Jack leaned down to kiss her, and she felt the familiar excitement beginning to sweep her up. She moved closer, pressed herself against him. He murmured his appreciation, trailing a hand down her back to find her butt and pull her closer still.

The sound of an engine starting broke the moment, and they looked up to see Katherine's car pulling out from the curb. Katherine shook her head at them ruefully and smiled, then made a phone gesture with her hand and mouthed "Call me" to Claire before driving away.

"I'd forgotten all about her," she admitted guiltily. "I was horrible. I was so jealous, I said some awful things."

Jack started nuzzling her neck again. "Sorry, who are we talking about?"

Claire let her head fall back as he nibbled his way around her earlobe.

"Katherine."

"Oh, Katherine. She's fine. She's just been telling me to keep persevering. She said that anyone who reacted the way you did this afternoon had to be in love."

Claire still owed Katherine some serious chocolate and champagne therapy, but Jack's kisses were becoming more and more insistent and for a while the rest of the world faded into oblivion.

"By the way, what's with the car?" Jack murmured a few minutes later as she sagged in his arms, limp and overcome by lust.

"Car? What car?"

She looked hazily over his shoulder, registering the red Mustang with a frown.

"Oh, right. That's mine," she explained as she drew his head back down for another kiss.

A few minutes later, Jack spoke again.

"So you just went out and bought a new car?"

It was hard to concentrate when she had six feet two inches of sexy, loving man pressed up against her, but she made an effort.

"Yes. That's exactly what I did."

He sounded really surprised, which got her thinking. And suddenly it hit her what she'd done. Had she been on drugs an hour ago? Stunned, she looked up at him.

"I didn't even take it for a test drive. I have no idea how many miles it has. I have no idea if it even has an engine!"

He started laughing, then he bent down and scooped her up into his arms.

"That sounds more like the Claire Marsden I know and love," he said as he carried her into his house, then into his bedroom. The sight of his large, welcoming bed went a long way to alleviating her buyer's remorse.

"What am I going to do?" she asked vaguely as he dropped her on the bed and started tearing her clothes off.

"We'll work it out," he promised.

And looking up at him leaning over her with love and lust in his eyes, she realized they always would.

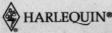